The Governess Diaries

The Hellion Club, Book Seven

by Chasity Bowlin

© Copyright 2023 by Chasity Bowlin
Text by Chasity Bowlin
Cover by Dar Albert

Dragonblade Publishing, Inc. is an imprint of Kathryn Le Veque Novels, Inc.
P.O. Box 23
Moreno Valley, CA 92556
ceo@dragonbladepublishing.com

Produced in the United States of America

First Edition February 2023
Print Edition

Reproduction of any kind except where it pertains to short quotes in relation to advertising or promotion is strictly prohibited.

All Rights Reserved.

The characters and events portrayed in this book are fictitious. Any similarity to real persons, living or dead, is purely coincidental and not intended by the author.

ARE YOU SIGNED UP FOR DRAGONBLADE'S BLOG?

You'll get the latest news and information on exclusive giveaways, exclusive excerpts, coming releases, sales, free books, cover reveals and more.

Check out our complete list of authors, too!

No spam, no junk. That's a promise!

Sign Up Here

www.dragonbladepublishing.com

Dearest Reader;

Thank you for your support of a small press. At Dragonblade Publishing, we strive to bring you the highest quality Historical Romance from some of the best authors in the business. Without your support, there is no 'us', so we sincerely hope you adore these stories and find some new favorite authors along the way.

Happy Reading!

CEO, Dragonblade Publishing

Additional Dragonblade books by
Author Chasity Bowlin

The Hellion Club Series
A Rogue to Remember (Book 1)
Barefoot in Hyde Park (Book 2)
What Happens in Piccadilly (Book 3)
Sleepless in Southampton (Book 4)
When an Earl Loves a Governess (Book 5)
The Duke's Magnificent Obsession (Book 6)
The Governess Diaries (Book 7)
Making Spirits Bright (Novella)
All I Want for Christmas (Novella)
The Boys of Summer (Novella)

The Lost Lords Series
The Lost Lord of Castle Black (Book 1)
The Vanishing of Lord Vale (Book 2)
The Missing Marquess of Althorn (Book 3)
The Resurrection of Lady Ramsleigh (Book 4)
The Mystery of Miss Mason (Book 5)
The Awakening of Lord Ambrose (Book 6)
Hyacinth (Book 7)
A Midnight Clear (A Novella)

The Lyon's Den Series
Fall of the Lyon
Tamed by the Lyon
Lady Luck and the Lyon

Pirates of Britannia Series
The Pirate's Bluestocking

Also from Chasity Bowlin
Into the Night

Part One
Separate Ways

Chapter One

September 15th, 1810
Highview Manor, Buckinghamshire

THE HOUSE WAS unnaturally quiet. There were no bustling footsteps of servants moving to and fro. There were no hushed whispers or random giggles from gossiping maids. The entirety of Highview Manor was in a hush—trapped in that space between knowing something awful was about to occur and having it actually happen. A moment frozen in time, hovering on the cusp of catastrophe.

The door slammed on the main floor, the harsh crack echoing through the house like a shot. The master, the 11th Duke of Clarenden, had returned from his morning ride, and the confrontation that had been brewing for almost two decades was set to begin.

"Oh, dear heavens," the housekeeper muttered under her breath. "It's going to be frightful. I know it."

"Hush, Mrs. Stephens," the butler admonished quietly. "It will be what it will be. We cannot interfere, nor are we entitled to have an opinion on what passes between our betters. We will keep this house as we have always done. Go to the kitchen and make sure that the cook and those gossiping scullery maids have begun dinner preparations as they are supposed to. If not, they will all have their ears pressed to a door as they eavesdrop on things that are none of their concern. Naught will get done."

Mrs. Stephens drew in a deep fortifying breath. She didn't have Mr. Milton's ability to turn off her emotions. She'd wept countless tears over the past twenty years for the poor, wretched creature whose life had ended long before she'd drawn her last breath. Now her heart ached for the boy left behind. For he was still very much a boy. At only nineteen years of age, he could hardly be called a man, after all. He'd never known anything from his father but coldness. She suspected that coldness had been a kind of mercy afforded on behalf of her poor mistress. No doubt the poor soul had bargained mightily for her son's welfare. *And may he never know the cost she paid for his place in that house.* With her gone now, there was naught to staunch the flow of the duke's anger and bitterness. And that poor, precious boy would bear the brunt of it.

"I'm not like you, Mr. Milton. I love that boy. I ought to—I raised him, didn't I? My poor mistress could not care for him, so I did it in her stead even when his father would not," she stated sharply. And she had done so. She'd tended scraped knees and hurt feelings time and again because no one else would. Any governess hired by the boy's father that showed even the slightest bit of warmth toward him was summarily dismissed. But in the confines of the kitchen, when no one else was there to see, she'd been able to be kind to him, to show him a bit of affection and to make him feel, even for a moment or two, that he was loved. "He deserves to know the truth."

"That, Mrs. Stephens, is the sort of talk that will get one dismissed, if not worse," the butler warned, but there was no censure in his tone, only concern. "We are, all of us, in a more precarious position now. Tread lightly, as we all must."

With that warning in her mind, she gave a curt nod and turned on her heel to retreat to the cavernous kitchens and storerooms that were the hub of the servants' domain. Milton would tell her what she needed to know—he would keep her apprised of all that occurred and what was to become of the duke's heir. Not his son. Never that. Just his heir. Her heels clicked on the marble floors as she walked away.

⁂

IN THE STUDY, Lord Nicholas Montford, spare to the Duke of Clarenden, waited for his father. He'd been waiting for the better part of the morning. His elder brother, the heir apparent, Sutton, Lord Highcliff, had already returned to London immediately after the funeral service for their mother. It wasn't unusual for his brother to depart in a fit of pique. In fact, that was typically how Sutton left Highview. He'd storm in and storm out with equal fury.

As for himself and his father, they'd spoken not a word to one another since his mother's funeral service the day before. But it wasn't an uncommon thing to go days without speaking. In truth, it was the only way for them to avoid arguing. They had ever been at odds. It was one of the many reasons he found every excuse possible to be out of doors, to be cavorting through the vast parklands of Highview Manor along with Effie. His friendship with her, growing over the past year, had been his salvation. But now it was more than friendship, at least for him. So much more.

Effie resided at a small neighboring estate, Strathmore Hall, that belonged to her father. It was not the estate where he resided with his new wife and the daughter they shared. He remained at the family seat with them. But upon his marriage, Effie's life had changed dramatically. The illegitimate daughter of a duke, she had been as gently reared as any young lady amongst the *ton*. But she would never be accepted by them. *Not unless she married exceptionally well to someone far better than a penniless younger son.* And so they had banished her to a small country estate to live in isolation, far from all of them.

He was not an excellent candidate for the role of husband to her, given her already precarious station and his limited prospects. He wasn't the heir to the dukedom, after all, but he was still legally the son of a duke. But Effie didn't care about that. He knew she didn't. It wasn't her way to be consumed with money and position. Of course, they were both young—too young, many would say. At nineteen, if he attempted to marry, his father would simply have it annulled. And Effie was only seventeen. They would have to wait a few more years, and then no one would be able to stop them. Of course, he'd first have to find the courage to ask her. Their friendship was precious to him. It was a constant source of comfort and joy to him. It was his only joy, in fact. But daily, his more intimate feelings for her became more and more challenging. He wanted her—not with the lustful impetuousness of a boy, but with the constancy of a man well in love.

The door opened and his father entered. Immediately, tension snaked through him, making his spine rigid and his muscles ache. He could be anything. Cold and dismissive; volatile and violent; scathing and contemptuous—he might be any one of a hundred things, but none of them would be positive. Had he ever had a pleasant exchange with his father? No. No, he had not. Not that anyone had. Even his elder brother, Sutton, was constantly tormented by his father's ridicule and insults. Neither of them had been spared the old sot's contempt.

"At least you are prompt," the duke muttered sourly. "I'll give you that."

"You wished to see me, Your Grace. I am at your disposal."

"Disposal . . . it has a certain ring to it, don't you think? Frankly I'm sick of the sight of you. I have been for some time," his father said, shifting his not insignificant girth behind the desk. "I tolerated your presence for the sake of your mother's reputation—and on the off chance that your presence might offer her some comfort during her last days."

Her son. That was how he always referred to him. Never as his own son, only hers. "Father—."

"Do not! You may never call me that again," the duke hissed out a breath between clenched teeth, his body vibrating with fury. "I tolerated it while she lived because to do less would have been to court public shame! But she is gone now, and I need not support the lie any longer. You are not my son. I will not disavow you publicly as to do so would bare the secret shame your mother brought on this house years ago. I was her husband, but not your father."

It wasn't a surprise. Nicholas had long suspected as much. In truth, it was almost a relief as it meant he'd likely never bear any similarity in character or appearance to the man before him. He had no expectations, after all, that the duke would support him or that, upon the duke's death, Sutton would provide for him. He fully expected to have to make his own way in the world. "As you wish, Your Grace."

"It will be as I wish . . . at long last. But before I impart the foul truth to you, I will let you know this! You will leave my house today and never darken my door again while I draw breath."

Nicholas said nothing to that. Rather, he simply let the man he had known as his father continue to spew his vitriol.

"I've secured a commission for you. You will join the army, at the lowest rank that would not be an embarrassment to this family's honor. And if God is good, you will die in battle and spare me the shame of seeing you return to British soil," the duke finished.

"I've no interest in joining the army. I have plans of my own," Nicholas replied, not bothering to add sir or your grace. The man deserved no respect.

The duke laughed, a low and mean sound. "Oh, I know about your plans . . . you and the bastard whelp of Treymore's whore. Don't think I haven't seen you sniffing after her. She's fine for a dalliance, but she'll never bear the Montford name. I told your brother the same when he came sniveling home after she rejected his suit. I was tempted to allow it just to see the misery it would create for you, but I'll not have our blood tainted by hers. What that trollop possesses to make men think they must marry her to have her is beyond me!"

"You will not speak of her that way!" Nicholas snapped. But his heart was thundering in his chest. Sutton had asked Effie to be his wife. When? Why had she not spoken of it to him? Could she have feelings for his brother? Nothing his father had said to him caused as much pain as that thought. The very idea of her belonging to another, especially to Sutton, filled him with rage and agony.

"That trollop, regardless of who fathered her, is not worth the trouble she has caused. Both of you sniffing after her like dogs to a bitch in heat!" The duke opened the decanter of brandy on his desk and splashed a liberal amount into a glass which he then greedily drank.

"Shut your mouth!" Nicholas shouted at him. "Do not say another word."

"I'll not let the family's honor be sullied that way, by letting anyone who bears my name marry the misbegotten whelp of a whore—"

"Do not speak of her that way!" Nicholas thundered.

The duke smiled coldly. "I can see the monster in you. You're like the man who sired you—he was a monster too. A fiend who became obsessed with my wife, who followed her around and dogged her every step just as you do with that harlot!"

Nicholas shook his head, a bitter laugh escaping him. There was no need to even feign civility anymore. "There is only one monster here and it is you."

The duke smiled, a grim expression revealing his yellowed, crooked teeth. "Is that so? Your mother wasn't the sort for dalliances. She kept her vows, Nicholas. She never willingly lay with another man. Your sire was a soldier who forced himself on her. He raped her. Brutalized her and left her with you growing in her belly—an eternal reminder of the pain she suffered."

He wanted it not to be true. But the duke's glee in the telling was proof enough. He wouldn't have enjoyed the lie as much. "Who was he?"

"A dead man now. I put a blade in his heart before you drew your first breath. I could forgive you for being born. I could forgive you for not being my son. I can't forgive you for being his son . . . for being the bastard of the man who took her from me."

It was nothing he hadn't heard before. His mother had been an invalid throughout his life. She'd barely been in touch with reality, often mistaking him for someone else. She would weep whenever she saw him. Eventually, he'd stopped entering her rooms, stopped visiting at all because it only caused her pain. Now he understood why. "You didn't love her. You're incapable of love. And I do not require your forgiveness."

The duke's gaze hardened, his eyes glittering with menace. "That little bitch of Treymore's does require my mercy, however. If you think to marry her, or if your brother goes near her again . . . if either of you think to further sully our name, I will put her lifeless body in the dirt, Nicholas."

Nicholas shot to his feet, the chair tipping backward to crash against the marble floor. "You will never touch her!"

"I will do as I good and damned well please! And if you test me, boy, I will do my absolute worst."

Nicholas couldn't contain his fury. He reached forward, sweeping everything off the top of the duke's desk and sending it crashing to the floor. Ink spilled on the carpet, mingling with the brandy that trickled slowly from the overturned decanter. "I may not have the means yet to best you, but the Duke of Treymore is a powerful man in his own right. If you go after his daughter—"

"He will do nothing because he doesn't care about her either! He's too busy with his new wife and his legitimate offspring. No, whelp, she's defenseless but for you, and at the moment, you are the very source of danger for her," the duke insisted gleefully. "As long as you stay far away from her, I will leave her in peace. But defy me on this and I will see you both destroyed."

"It should have been you and not her. You should be rotting in an early grave." And if he weren't a coward, he would send him there.

"I'll get there soon enough," the duke said, tapping his fingers on the desk. "Think long and hard about one fact, Nicholas—can you stop me? We both know the answer to that. I have the wealth and the power to hire a thousand men to hunt her to the ends of the earth."

It was true. It was true and he would have no compunction about doing so. "I should kill you myself—"

"But you will not. You lack the courage." The duke smiled with satisfaction, settling back into his chair with his hands crossed over his protruding abdomen. "And even if you thought of running away with her, where would you go? How would you live? You haven't a tuppence to your name unless I give it to you!"

"You said yourself that I have a commission in the army—"

"Which can be taken away . . . and that would leave you penniless once more. And I doubt Treymore would look kindly on any fortune hunter sniffing around even his bastard," the duke insisted. "There is only one thing left to satisfy me in this life and that is to delay your happiness as long as I can. At least long enough for her to get married off to someone else and leave you moping after her for life."

"What a miserable bastard you are." God, how he hated him. And how the man must hate him to go to such lengths to deny him everything he desired for nothing more than spite.

"You'll be a miserable bastard with me until I shuffle off this mortal coil. When I am dead and gone, you may do as you please, but until that time, know that I hold her life in my hands. You will take your place with the army. You will attempt to distinguish yourself on behalf of your country or die in the effort. But you will do it all far from my sight and never darken these doors again. You will join your regiment in two days' time. Write your trollop and tell her goodbye."

Chapter Two

EFFIE WAITED, SEATED on an overturned stone in the ruins of the old round tower. It was nothing more than rubble—a staircase and one wall emerging from a pile of stones. They met there frequently as it was both convenient and relatively private. If anyone else knew that she had spent so much time alone in his company, she would have been ruined. But Nicholas Montford had never been anything but a gentleman. From the moment of their first meeting, when he'd wanted so badly to be heroic only to discover she had already rescued herself, he'd been all that was thoughtful and kind.

It was that very thoughtfulness, that kindness she had witnessed in him so very frequently, which left her reluctant to confess her secrets to him. And for a young woman who rarely did anything that was improper, she seemed to be harboring an inordinate number of secrets of late.

The first one was likely not a secret. He had but only to have eyes to see it. She was desperately in love with him. She suspected that he had some romantic feeling for her, as well, but whether or not they shared the depth and intensity of her emotion remained a mystery. Her other secret was a far more insidious one and one that she suspected might make him very angry, as he and his brother were at odds. But then it seemed Nicholas was at odds with everyone in his family. The duke could not abide him, though the reasons for his dislike of his son were unknown to her.

Sutton Montford, Lord Highcliff and heir to the Duke of Clarenden, had proposed marriage to her. To say that she had been taken aback by the offer was an understatement. He had never revealed even the slightest inclination of interest. Her suspicions were that it was all a bit of dog in the manger. Nicholas' potential interest was likely what had prompted Sutton's.

Recalling how furious Sutton had been when she refused him, though she had attempted to do so as gently as possible, Effie worried now that perhaps he had said something to Nicholas. Her interactions with Sutton had been, up to that point, relatively pleasant. It had been shocking to see his temper. Indeed, had it not been for her threat to inform Nicholas of his behavior, she wasn't quite certain what he would have done. While she could have defended herself against him handily enough, it would have been very awkward to face him afterward. But she felt it was a narrow escape regardless.

Perhaps Sutton had told Nicholas about the proposal, or perhaps he'd told him something else altogether. He might have made it seem as though she had encouraged his advances when the very opposite was true. Any time she had been in Sutton's presence, she had felt his gaze on her, felt his attentions shifting into something that she was very uncomfortable with. But she had not yet told Nicholas of her feelings for him. And if he didn't know that she was in love with him, he might well believe any version of events that Sutton might give. Glancing at the sky, which was beginning to darken with clouds, she couldn't help but wonder if that was why Nicholas was late in meeting her.

No sooner had that thought entered her mind than she heard the thunder of hoofbeats. She rose, her hands clenched at her sides, as he came over the hill. His black coat was swirling about him, and his expression was terribly dark. It was obvious that he'd had another terrible row with his father. They always weighed so heavily on him.

"I'd nearly given up on you," she said as he dismounted.

"I cannot stay." His words were brusque, his tone sharp. His shoulders were tense and his spine unnaturally stiff.

"Nicholas, have I made you angry in some way?" She hated to ask the question, fearful of what his answer might be, but she had to know.

He turned then. "No, Effie. I am not angry with you. But I cannot stay here. The duke has given me marching orders—quite literally. I am to join up with a regiment in two days. I must leave at once if I am to make it in time."

Effie's heart sank. Fear gripped her as she considered what that might mean, what might be at stake. "You're leaving? But . . . will you have to go to Portugal, Nicholas? Will you be going to war?"

He looked away, refusing to make eye contact with her as he answered cavalierly, "I strongly suspect that I will. I expect the duke will have made certain of it. He doesn't mean for me to return, Effie. And live or die, I likely will not return either way. There is nothing for me here."

That wounded her to the core. It wasn't like him to be so cold, and for him to do so on his departure—had he been toying with her all along? "I'm here. Does that count for nothing? I thought—well, we are friends, are we not?"

"No, Effie. We aren't friends. We cannot be friends. Not now. I must leave and you must move on with your life."

"Move on with my life?" Hurt and anger warred within her. At the moment, anger was winning. She wanted to throttle him. "Nicholas, I demand an explanation."

His expression hardened and his hand shot out, grasping her arm roughly. "Then explain to me why my brother asked you to be his wife."

"You're hurting me," she said.

Immediately, his hold gentled. But his expression remained just as fierce. "Tell me, Effie. Why did Sutton think to make you such an offer?"

"I couldn't say. I can only tell you that I refused him," she answered honestly. "I have no interest in Sutton. I've never had any interest in Sutton."

"I would caution you not to change your mind about that. He doesn't want you. Not really. He only thinks to take what he believes to be mine."

"I'm not yours!" she snapped.

"No," he agreed, his voice tinged with something she could not name. "You are not. And you never will be. Goodbye, Effie."

Effie's pulse was racing. A wave of nausea assailed her as the reality of it all sank in. She wanted to scream, to cry. She wanted to do something. Ultimately, she could do nothing but watch him mount his horse once more and ride away, her heart shattering in her breast.

From the Diary of Euphemia Darrow, September 17th, 1810

He is gone. I knew, upon the death of his mother, that things would change. But he was so cold when we met, so distant. I have never seen him such. In the year I have been exiled here to my father's forgotten estate, Nicholas has been my truest friend—my companion almost daily. But I had hopes for Nicholas. Hopes for both of us. I had thought, wished perhaps, that he might have similar feelings for me to those I have for him. As much as it pains me now to say it, I have been falling in love with him for the entire year that we have spent here, running wild through the countryside.

That is a lie. I have not been falling in love with him. I have been in love with him. Almost, I think, from the moment we met. The most damning part of it is that I think we might have been very happy together. Alas, he has made his choice, and that choice leaves no room for me.

Could he have been angered by recent events? Does he think that I was toying with his emotions while also angling for his brother? Surely not. How could I have been when almost every waking moment was spent in his company or penning notes back and forth to one another to leave at the pasture fence. It breaks my heart to think that the boy I knew was not his true self but that this cold and cruel man I met with today is the reality. Have I been that much of a fool? Has he done naught but toy with me from the beginning? And if so, to what end? Surely, no man capable of such lies and deceit would also be such a gentleman—always solicitous, always concerned, and never taking liberties, even when I would have gladly let him do so.

I was stunned when his older brother, Sutton Montford, Lord Highcliff, proposed to me. I'd never shared more than a few words with him prior. I had the strangest feeling that he was only asking for my hand because he wanted to take something that belonged to his brother and Nicholas' words tonight confirmed that.

But I do not belong to Nicholas. I belong to no one but myself. Not even my father has ownership of me anymore, as he has discarded me entirely. I have been given free rein to do as I please in my banishment, not because others feel I am entitled to such independence but because they simply cannot be bothered to govern my life. Though I confess it doesn't feel like freedom. It feels like abandonment. But I will not shed any tears over it. Not now. Not when I have shed so many already.

For now, I will pray that Nicholas remains safe, that he returns home from the war whole and healthy. And perhaps things will be better between us then. Perhaps he will have forgiven me for whatever it is that he seems to think I have done and return to being the boy I thought I knew. And perhaps I will have forgiven him for making me feel small. Insignificant. Disposable.

Part Two
With or Without You

From the Diary of Miss Euphemia Darrow, November 15th, 1816

I attended the opera tonight with my father. We see one another rarely these days, but as my stepmother and their daughters were at a house party outside of London, he was free to acknowledge me once more. I hate the bitterness I feel toward him. But I cannot help it. Understanding his situation, his need to maintain a peaceful home and to preserve the reputations of his legitimate daughters by keeping them separate from someone tainted by illegitimacy, I know he could never allow his bastard child to reside in the same home with them. Still, it pains me, and resentment festers. But that was not the only pain I suffered tonight, and it was not nearly as sharp as what occurred during the intermission.

Nicholas. I saw him there. I cannot explain it in any way except to say that he is not the boy I once knew. He is a man now, but not a kind one, I think. What he has seen in the war, what he suffered while he was a prisoner of the French, it has all changed him beyond measure. This man is different. There are layers to him that I cannot begin to guess at. He dresses garishly, gestures wildly, minces when he walks, and flirts shamelessly. Despite all of that, an air of danger clings to him. It is almost as if he is playing a part—wearing a mask to cover up the darkness that I now sense inside him.

And yet, for a moment our eyes met, and the mask fell away. I saw something in him that told me a truth that is undeniable. He cares for me still. There was regret in his gaze. Longing. Whether it is for the friendship we once shared or the future that I once believed might be ours, I cannot say. Despite everything, I hurt for him. I hurt for the pain he endured during his captivity. I hurt for the years he will now spend in India as he leaves again shortly.

But he is not just a soldier, not just some calvary officer who plays at being in command. Now that Sutton is gone—dead by his own hand, intentionally or not—Nicholas is now the heir to the dukedom. And still he plays this very dangerous game, risking his life when he does not have to. Why?

I know some of the truth now. Not all. But some. As my father banished me to the country at seventeen, his father banished him to the service of the King. And that service is destroying him day by day—robbing him of who he was and who he should be. I know, because it has been entrusted to me by servants in strictest confidence, that the duke specifically asked that Nicholas be given the most dangerous of missions. By what threat or coercion he engineered this, I cannot say. Nicholas could never be compelled to share that with me. And I lack the courage to ask, even if opportunity presented itself.

Chapter Three

September 1828
Bath

THEY WERE AT his home in Bath. They'd arrived in the latter part of the afternoon, after little sleep and many bruising hours in the saddle. Effie had received a meal and a hot bath and had promptly fallen asleep. Now, waking up in *his* bed, Effie realized it was well into the middle of the night. Despite the hot bath upon their arrival, her muscles still ached terribly.

Their journey to Bath had been precipitated by the wicked plots of others—namely Sophie Upchurch's miscreant of a father and one Dr. Blake, who had been systematically poisoning Sophie's charge, the daughter of the Duke of Thornhill. But the villains, if not routed, had at least been uncovered, and the pair of them—she and Highcliff—had traveled on to Bath to tie up the loose ends.

Easing from the bed, Effie stretched, a pained gasp escaping her. It was one thing to be an accomplished equestrienne. It was quite another to take on the kind of endurance riding that had been required of them over the last two days.

"I wouldn't overdo it, if I were you."

Another gasp escaped her, this one in fear, as she whirled toward the sound of that voice. He'd been so silent, sitting in that darkened corner, that she hadn't realized she wasn't alone. But then again, it was his chamber. Where else would he have been?

"I didn't realize you were here, Nicholas," she said breathlessly.

"I returned a short time ago. I tried very hard not to wake you."

It should have made her uncomfortable—the notion that he'd been lurking in the darkness, watching her sleep. But it didn't. Nothing between herself and Nicholas had ever happened in the usual way. Theirs had always been a relationship that followed very different rules. Like with so many other slightly odd things, she simply let it go.

"Where did you go?" she asked.

He shifted in the darkness, stretching his long legs out before him and crossing his booted feet. "I sought out Dr. Warner. He will be accompanying us back to Southampton in a few days. I also paid a visit to the woman whom Dr. Blake, or whatever he was calling himself, was indebted to—Miss Ruby. Though I must say "Madame Ruby" would be a far better moniker for one so long in the tooth and hardened by life. Regardless, that matter has been settled and she will trouble Miss Upchurch and her viscount no more."

Effie blinked in surprise. He had been busy. "How industrious you are! I've managed to do nothing but sleep."

"I did for a while," he said. "I was tempted to join you but knew that sleeping would be the last thing achieved if I were to climb into that bed with you. So I dozed here in the chair, instead."

There was a note in his voice, something that hinted at darker and more terrible things. His nightmares, she thought. "And the dreams came," she surmised. "I know they plague you terribly."

"Memories, Effie. Not dreams. Memories that I can keep at bay in the light of day. But in the dark of night, they are inescapable."

Effie, heedless of the fact that she wore only a borrowed nightrail, moved toward him. "I know they did awful things to you," she said. "I worried so much for you when you were taken prisoner. Everyone else thought you were just galivanting about the continent—a fool who'd run off to join the army on nothing more than a lark. But I knew the truth. I knew that he made you do it and that, at his behest, they gave you the most dangerous and challenging missions. He wanted you to fail." *He wanted you to die.* "And I knew when you didn't come home that something awful had happened. I prayed for you daily."

"I thought of you." The admission was a mere whisper in the darkened room, his voice pitched low and deep. "You accused me of cowardice—of not being willing to admit my feelings, but I've never denied them, Effie. Rather, I always understood the futility of them. But I would have you know that during the darkest and most desperate hours of my life, I thought of you. And that, Effie, is how I endured it all. I could endure anything for the promise of you."

Those words shook her to her core. They hinted at a truth neither of them could face. She knew what she felt for him. Love. Consuming. Obsessive. Inescapable. She'd spent her entire life loving him, it seemed. And in her heart, she believed that he loved her in return. His words in that darkened room certainly seemed to indicate that was so. But he was a complicated man with a complicated history—and obligations to his country that did not allow for the sort of domesticated life she had often dreamed of having with him. He'd told her earlier in that carriage that there would be no happy ending for them. She'd long ago given up any thought of such a thing. But did that mean they could not seize what happiness they could find? They had the night, after all. *They had the here and now even if there was no future for them.*

"You said before that we would finish what we started . . . that you had plans for me," she stated far more boldly than someone of her relative inexperience ought.

He didn't move. That deceptively relaxed posture with crossed ankles and hands lightly clasped before him—it never altered. But the degree of tension that emanated from him became a palpable thing, filling the room and the space that remained between them. "Are you certain?" he queried, offering one last chance for retreat.

"Never more so. You, of all people, should know that I do nothing by half measures. My mind was made up and my course determined before I uttered a single word," she stated.

His answering laugh was soft, but when he spoke, there was no humor in his voice. It was dark. Sensual. Filled with the promise of all the things to come. "I do know that about you. I wish I could give you more, Effie. I wish that I could give you everything... but this is all we will ever have."

"I know. And it's more than I'd hoped for," she said. That was a lie, of course. Hope, for so many years, had been all she'd had. She simply hadn't allowed herself to expect it. And another damning lie fell from her lips: "Whatever we have here, it is enough."

He rose then, getting up from the chair and closing the distance between them. It happened so quickly that it startled her and, as his hands closed around her upper arms, pulling her against him, she gave a soft squeak of alarm.

"It isn't enough, Effie. But it is the most we can have. And I'm too selfish not to seize it."

There was no time to respond. In the next instant his mouth was on hers, his lips taking hers with a gentle intensity that made her knees weak even as her blood heated. He hadn't kissed her so frequently that she'd become accustomed to it. In truth, she could count on one hand the number of times their encounters had become intimate in any way. But it could have been hundreds and she'd never become inured to the need that he could evoke in her with a single touch.

Effie wasn't aware of her arms lifting to encircle his neck or pressing her body against him in a blatant invitation. She was aware of only one thing—she never wanted that kiss to end.

HIGHCLIFF HAD TRIED to stay away. He'd tried to resist the temptation of her, but after so many years of wanting her—of going through the litany of reasons why he couldn't have her—his will to do so had simply been worn down. But it wasn't just about will. He was a selfish bastard. Deep down where it mattered, where it counted, he was the sort to always take what he wanted. Hadn't he been told that often enough in his life? That all he knew how to do was take and destroy—that he was good for nothing else.

Pushing those thoughts aside, trying to deafen himself to the hateful words which seemed to always reverberate in his mind in that painfully familiar voice, he focused on her instead. The feel of her body against his, the sweetness of her mouth, the music in her soft sighs and gasps of surprise—those were all that mattered in that moment. Effie wasn't ignorant. Not in the least. But knowing and experiencing were not the same thing. Selfish as he was, he still wanted to make it good for her—to make it perfect for her—to make himself worthy of her, even if only for a moment.

Without asking for permission or offering any sort of warning, he swept her up into his arms. It was the second time that day he'd gotten to hold her close, to cradle her against him. The first had been when they dismounted before the house and she'd nearly collapsed from exhaustion. If he'd been a better man, knowing all that she had endured over their journey would have stilled him, would have halted his actions. But he wasn't a better man. And having had a taste of her, he'd never be satisfied with less. As he walked with her to the bed, he reflected that he could well become addicted to her nearness if he wasn't careful.

When he reached the bed, he didn't lay her down upon it. Instead, he turned and sank onto the mattress himself, settling her on his lap as he did so, her thighs splayed over him. It allowed him to kiss her without her having to crane her neck. It also gave him greater access to her lush figure. His hands were already exploring, mapping the curves and contours of her form beneath the thin linen of her nightdress. Every sense was greedy for her. Sight and scent, touch and taste... and hearing every sigh and gasp that escaped her.

The goal was seduction. He wanted her desperate with need—and that meant keeping his own needs in check, at least for the interim. But after two decades of desire and self-denial, that would require herculean effort.

A gentle tug and the ties of her nightdress slipped free, the fabric parting and then sliding slowly over her shoulders. Her bare skin gleamed in the moonlight and he was a man lost. In that moment, she was everything to him—life, death, even the breath in his body.

Tearing his lips from hers, he pressed a kiss to the tender skin beneath her ear. His teeth scraped along the sensitive column of her neck, down until he could lick the hollow of her throat, drag his lips over the gentle arch of her collarbone. Lower, over the swell of her breast, and lower still to the taut peak that tasted so sweet on his tongue. She arched forward, pressing against him. He could feel the heat of her, his arousal pressed firmly against her—seeking and needful.

"Effie," he whispered against her skin. "I've needed you for so long."

"I've needed you, Nicholas," she replied breathlessly. "Always."

Those words were a balm to his soul, but they were fuel to the fire that raged in his blood. With one quick move, he rolled her onto the bed, leaving her lying on her back—naked and spread out before him as he removed his boots and then his shirt. The breeches he left on for the moment. He needed some restraint after all.

When he climbed back onto the bed, he didn't simply come down on top of her. Instead, he settled back on his haunches and allowed his gaze to roam over her. The moonlight seeping through the curtains painted her body in a shimmering, silver glow. He wished for more. He wanted to see her in the bright light of day, to know every freckle, every dip and curve, to know the color of her perfect nipples and exact shade of the soft curls that shielded her sex. He wanted everything in perfect relief so that when he revisited in his mind, time and again, that memory would be crisp and perfect.

"You've no idea how beautiful you are," he said. "I've dreamed of you this way. So many times, I cannot count them all."

"Then show me," she urged him. "I may be hindered by a lack of experience, but that doesn't mean I lack certainty when it comes to knowing what I want."

"And what do you want, Effie?"

Her gaze locked with his and she uttered the sweetest words he'd ever heard. "Only you."

"You have me." With that, he slid his hand up her thighs, gripped them lightly and paused for just a second. Then he leaned in and pressed his mouth to her, drinking in her essence even as she cried out in both shock and pleasure.

Chapter Four

EFFIE COULDN'T THINK. She couldn't speak. She wanted to beg him to stop and alternately to beg him to continue. But all she could do was sob out her need and pleasure as his questing mouth moved over her. She'd never known such pleasure was possible. It was so intense that it was almost frightening, and yet she could do nothing but give herself up to it and to him.

The release rocked through her suddenly, ebbing and cresting like waves. She trembled with the force of it. But he was not done with her. One release simply flowed into another as he continued to manipulate her tender flesh with his mouth and with his hands. He parted her flesh, sliding his fingers deep inside her, working them in and out even as she shuddered with pleasure.

She peaked the second time, her body drawing taut and arcing up off the bed. Then he was surging up, his breeches finally gone, levering himself between her thighs. The hot press of his flesh against hers, the sensation of fullness—of rightness—as he entered her was more than she could have ever imagined. It wasn't pleasure, but it was perfection. It was fulfillment. For the first time in her life, she felt complete. There were no parts of her missing.

Thought fled. In the wake of such a primal expression of need, of him moving inside her to drive them both to that glorious peak once more, there was no room for thinking. It was all about sensation, about feeling, and savoring all of it.

Her fingers tangled in the bedclothes, an anchor for her as the world simply fell away. One of his hands closed over hers. His mouth found hers, lips clashing as their bodies came together in the darkness.

Nothing existed beyond the two of them in those moments. And as the pleasure built, the anticipation of release hovered around them. It was instinct that had Effie locking her legs around him, clinging to him as her release crashed through her again, searing her to her very soul.

He surged into her once more as she trembled beneath him, then he withdrew completely. She could feel his body shivering against her, the heat of his seed on her inner thigh. Because even at the end, he'd been protecting her.

"We're ruined now," he murmured softly. "Marked by this for the rest of our days."

She didn't disagree.

HIGHCLIFF STAYED IN the bed beside her, listening to the sound of her breathing and savoring her nearness. It wouldn't last long. The dawn was coming and with it, reality would intrude. Their brief and passionate interlude would come to an end, and life as they knew it would return to normal. At least outwardly. For himself, he'd never be the same again. Having even a taste of Effie had been simultaneously too much and never enough. The feel of her beneath him, of her body closing around him, welcoming him—it would haunt him for life.

While he hadn't lived like a monk, every woman he'd ever been with had been only a poor substitute for the woman who currently lay beside him. They'd been an effort to chase the ghost of her from his mind. And like everything else he had attempted it had been a miserable failure. He'd accepted it now—that she would consume him and obsesses him for every day that he lived and possibly beyond.

But his father still lived, lingering in a state of poor health for a number of years that defied reason. It was nothing but spite, to his mind. And so long as that fact was true, Effie would never be safe from him. But it wasn't only that. He couldn't ask her to give up the life she had created—the school and the children that were so very important to her. And he brought with him an element of risk that she could not possibly understand.

When he'd been shipped off to the Continent during the Napoleonic War, she'd forged ahead and made a life for herself that was complete without him. Upon his return, when he'd discovered what she'd done for herself in his absence, he'd accepted then that she would likely never be his. Even when his father did finally give up the ghost, she'd have obligations that she could not walk away from. And with the enemies he'd amassed during his life, none of them would ever be safe. Loving Effie—and he did, more than anything—meant being willing to give her the freedom to do as she pleased.

A shaft of light speared through the curtains and Effie stirred. She rolled over, curling into him, her thigh draped over his and her face pressed to his chest. It was a perfect moment. He hovered between the overwhelming urge to have her once more and to simply savor the comforting weight of her against him.

"Good morning," she murmured sleepily.

"Good morning," he replied. "Are you hungry? I can probably manage to persuade one of my two servants to provide some sort of meal for us."

"Why do you keep so few servants?" she asked, blinking up at him in the light. "I've often wondered."

"Servants gossip. The more of them you have, the more vulnerable you are to others knowing what you're doing and why. In my line of work, it's imperative that my comings and goings are not overly noted by others," he explained. "Each of my servants is handpicked by me. And they are incredibly loyal, if somewhat unconventional."

"No one is more unconventional—or loyal—than Mrs. Wheaton. I think I can appreciate your reasons very much," she observed. "She would fight the Devil himself for me, I think."

"And win," he concurred. "She is your fiercest protector."

"Next to you. You protect me, as well," she observed. "And my girls. You've certainly moved heaven and earth to help them."

He sighed. "They do find trouble, Effie. Like magnets to steel."

"They do not call us the Hellion Club for nothing," she mused. "Women who refuse to quietly go along and do the bidding of everyone around them often find trouble, Nicholas."

"You've never done anything quietly," he said, rolling over so that he pinned her beneath him. "In fact, I'd like to test that theory. Can you be quiet, Effie?" He cupped her breast with his hand, his thumb teasing the hardened peak of her nipple.

"Do you want me to be?" she challenged.

"No," he confessed. "I want you to scream with pleasure. I want you to shout the rafters down around us."

"Make me."

And so he did.

From the Diary of Miss Euphemia Darrow, March 28th, 1820

I saw my sisters today, though they would certainly balk at being called such. I entered a shop on Bond Street to purchase new gloves for myself and a few hair ribbons for the girls. There I came face to face with my stepmother and my father's other children. I have never been in a place so quiet. No one dared even breathe. I haven't seen them in years. Indeed, had it not been for my stepmother's presence, I would hardly have known them. They have grown so tall and now look so very much like my father.

And they looked through me. All of them. I did not exit. I refused to be cowed. It did not matter, of course. I was invisible to them. My father has never seen that part of it. He's never seen it when they treat me with such coldness. I think, perhaps, that he does not wish to see it. If he is blind to it, then he need not address it. He need not do battle with his wife and his legitimate offspring on behalf of his bastard. His embarrassment.

When I returned home, there was another child on my doorstep. Another poor, hollow-eyed waif who has been told time and again that she has no worth, no place. Her name is Louisa, and despite the agony that her life must have been, she smiled so sweetly at me that it nearly broke my heart. My father's inattention and my stepmother's coldness are not so bad in comparison. In truth, I have very little to complain about. I have never been cold or hungry. There have been very few times in my life when I faced danger at all. And these girls have faced it daily while living under the harshest of circumstances.

All these girls—they have been looked through and been invisible to others just as I was today. The pain of illegitimacy is something I am all too familiar with. I know it very well. I know what it means to be born into a world that you have no place in. I was raised to be a lady, to take my place in society. I was taught from birth that I was the daughter of a duke and, as such, deserving of certain things. I resent my mother for that—for giving me expectations where I should have had none.

Society has no place for me. These girls who have come to me, they will have a place. Perhaps they will not be ladies. Perhaps they will only ever be in service to those who would look down upon them for the circumstances of their birth. But, if it is the last thing I do in this life, each and every one of them will know their worth. They will know their value and they will know that they deserve to be loved and to be valued. Not everyone will discard them. And they will have choices. They need not be scullery maids or vessels for men's pleasure. Their bodies and their lives are their own to do with as they please.

Chapter Five

It was late afternoon. Effie had dressed in borrowed clothes, allegedly left at Highcliff's residence by his cousin, Bess Carlisle. She was a famous actress, and the somewhat outlandish garb would certainly fit with someone who was slightly scandalous. But it was just as possible that the clothing had belonged to a female of another sort altogether, but she was happier not to think of that.

Her morning shopping expedition along Milsom Street had been a success, however. She had an assortment of hairpins to restore some semblance of order to her tresses, which were currently contained in a simple braid tucked beneath her bonnet. The purchase of several chemisettes had also been necessary as the possibly-Miss-Carlisle's wardrobe was far more daring than anything Effie would normally choose for herself.

In her assortment of parcels, Effie also had a new journal. It seemed that after the events of the previous night a new one was warranted. Happy endings, or endings of any sort aside, her thoughts and feelings would be different going forward and they deserved to be recorded in a book of their own.

It had been a habit that her mother had instilled in her when she was a child. Effie often wondered if her mother's insistence upon recording every aspect of her own life in a journal had been prompted by some premonition of her very limited time. She still kept those diaries. In her loneliest and most desperate hours, she would read them and find comfort in her mother's words.

Shaking her head at her own maudlin turn of thought, Effie determined to think of brighter and cheerier things. *And Highcliff.* She was very determined to think of Nicholas.

The pealing of a bell drew Effie's gaze toward the imposing fence that surrounded the workhouse there. But it wasn't that hateful and terrible place which held her attention. She stared at those iron gates as her heart skipped a beat. Standing near the fence, staring out at the street beyond, was a familiar face. Younger, softer, but still achingly familiar. It was his face. Highcliff's, but on a young girl of no more than twelve.

No. No. No. No.

The word was a litany in her mind as she prayed for it not to be. He knew how to prevent conception. After all, he'd taken such precautions with her. And yet, a child from out of nowhere stood only feet from her, appearing for all the world to be his. The resemblance was uncanny. She had his dark hair, his indigo eyes, the same thickly lashed eyes with their distinctive downward tilt at the outer corners. Everything was the same, even to the slight cleft of her chin and a dark freckle near the corner of her mouth.

Effie closed the distance to the fence, pulled there against her will. She didn't want to know, and yet, she had no choice but to ask. Tremulously, she murmured, "What is your name, child?"

The little girl looked up at her. "Why you want to know?"

The faint cockney accent was not what she'd expected. This was a child from the London streets. What was she doing in a workhouse in Somerset? "Because I'd like to help you." *Because I think I know who your father is, and it is breaking my heart.*

"Alexandra... most just call me 'girl' though. Don't bother learnin' me name, now do they?"

That broke through the wall of Effie's own pain. It allowed her, in that moment, to see the child and not the origin, not the complete loss of hope she represented. "Well, Alexandra, I think the first thing we need to do is get you out of the workhouse."

The little girl shook her head. "Don't want to work for no abbess. Watched my mother do that and it's a bad end. Beaten up, riddled with pox. No."

"I'm not abbess. I am, well, what most people would call a reformer. I operate a school for young ladies like yourself. I teach about deportment, etiquette, reading, writing, science and mathematics. You will learn to dance and play a musical instrument and learn to speak several languages. When you graduate from my school, you will be able to work as a governess or companion. You will be able to support yourself in a respectable manner," Effie explained. "My purpose in life has been to prepare girls for a life without forcing them to be dependent on men, who by their nature are undependable."

"That costs money. An' if I 'ad money, I wouldn't be 'ere."

"I have money of my own," Effie said. "My father is very wealthy, and he has been very generous with me . . . at least with funds. Would you like to be one of my students, Alexandra?"

Effie was having the conversation calmly. Rationally. As if her heart hadn't been ripped from her chest, breaking with every damning word from the child's mouth. Was she Highcliff's child? Could she be anything else? Had he abandoned her to a life of degradation in some lowly brothel? It pained her to think that of him even more than it pained her to think of him with another woman.

"I might," the little girl replied. "Won't have to do nothing bad, will I? I'm a good girl. Don't care what they say, 'ere."

"I believe that you are a good girl, and I will never ask you to do anything bad. I will only ever try to protect you and help you. But I must ask, Alexandra, do you know who your father is?"

The child shook her head. "Never met 'im. My mother told me 'e was 'ansome though. She said I looked like 'im."

It was like a knife to her heart. He could have committed murder.

Treason. A dozen other ghastly crimes would have been easily forgiven. But to father a child and leave that child to the vagaries of fate—that was an unpardonable sin in her eyes. One perfect night. He'd been so very right when he'd told her that was all they would ever have. Because she would never look at him the same way again.

"Let me go speak to the gentleman in charge of this establishment, Alexandra, and we will get you out of here," Effie offered.

"I don't why you're doing it . . . but if I can get out of 'ere, it don't much matter. I 'ate it 'ere."

"I know you do. Give me a few moments and I will have you free."

HIGHCLIFF ENTERED THE house to find it empty. Effie was gone. He knew she'd planned to go shopping but thought she would have returned by then.

"Has my guest not returned?" he asked the butler.

"She did, my lord, and begged me to inform you that she has taken a room at the Saracen's Head. She means to depart for Southampton from there on the morrow." The man paused ever so slightly. "She and the young person who accompanied her were here for only a short time."

"Young person?"

"Yes," the butler said. "She had a young girl with her, sir."

Highcliff nodded. It would make sense that, if Effie had procured another charge, she would not want to stay under his roof with the child. But it bothered him that she left without seeing him first.

"I'll find her at the Saracen's Head, then. Thank you."

The butler shuffled off, the elderly man moving at a very slow pace, as Highcliff turned once more and headed out the door. It was a short walk to the Saracen's Head, just over a quarter of a mile. By the time he reached Broad Street, he was moving quickly. He had the overwhelming feeling that something was wrong, even if he didn't know what it was precisely.

As he stepped inside, he heard Effie's voice from a small, private dining room just off the main tap room. Immediately, he moved in that direction. "Here you are," he said.

She looked up, her expression remarkably cool. "Indeed. Here I am. Here we all are."

Highcliff's gaze shifted slightly, taking in the child. She was a pretty, young girl, although she was dressed in little better than rags. "And who is this?"

"This is Alexandra," Effie stated. Her tone was positively chilling.

Highcliff shifted his attention back to Effie, taking in her rigid posture and her clenched jaw. She was clearly angry about something. "It appears that you have something you wish to say to me in private."

She nodded. "Indeed, I do. Alexandra, wait here for me. You may help yourself to the sandwiches and the tea. You may eat as many as you like but you must eat them slowly. Each of those small sandwiches consists of at least four bites. And each bite must be chewed thoroughly. All right?"

The little girl nodded but her hand shot out immediately and snagged two of the small sandwiches as Effie rose from the table. They stepped out into the taproom and around the corner into a narrow corridor.

"Have I made you angry, Effie?" he asked curiously. "I thought initially that you had left because you had procured another charge and wanted to observe proprieties. But this seems to be much more."

"You don't even see it, do you?"

"See what?"

Effie shook her head, her lips pressed into a thin, firm line. "Alexandra is the very image of you, Highcliff. The very image. It isn't just that she resembles you—she looks exactly as you looked when you were a boy. Everything is the same."

"You surely do not think that I would have fathered a child out of wedlock, Effie! You and I both know my feelings on such a matter. I have done everything possible in my life to prevent such consequences!"

"I do know that, but I also know that all the precautions in the world are not a guarantee," she snapped. "Twelve years ago. You had come home from the war, battered and broken by what they had done to you, and you were preparing to return to the front again, despite everyone's wishes to the contrary. You were—you were not yourself, were you? You were drinking heavily and—her mother was a prostitute, and I know for a fact that you frequented certain establishments in that time."

He had been frequenting those establishments but not as a client. Brothels and gaming hells were the places where men spoke most freely. For a man like himself, a man who dealt in information, frequenting such places was a necessity. But he *had* been drinking heavily at that time, trying to conquer the nightmares that plagued him about his captivity. Those attempts had resulted in gaps in his memory. "You know what I do, Effie, and you know why I was in those places!"

"Can you swear that you were never with any women in those places? Can you swear it?" she demanded.

He couldn't. Not because he had, but because there were many nights when he had drunk so much he could not remember it clearly. "Effie, if I had fathered a child—."

"There is no if. She is your child. There is no other explanation for the resemblance . . . unless the man who actually fathered you is still alive. Is he?"

"No," he said. He'd never told Effie the ugly truth about the circumstances of his birth, but he had never hidden from her that he was not the duke's son. All he had for certain was the duke's word, though it was never to be completely trusted. "To my knowledge, the man is dead, but I have no proof."

"Then, until you can point me in a different direction, until you can offer me some alternative explanation for why the child is your mirror image, I will be sending you the bill for Alexandra's education. You may finally assume the appropriate responsibility for her," she stated with a cold snap to her words. "And there is nothing left to be said between us. I could have forgiven you anything else, but I do not think I can forgive you this."

"Effie—" he began, but she was right. There was nothing for him to say. He couldn't deny it, nor could he confirm it. All he could say was that he didn't think it was true.

"Of all the things, Nicholas, of all the things you could have done—to abandon a child, to leave her to the brutality of this merciless world with no one to protect her and a mother who couldn't even protect herself—there is nothing so damning as that."

He knew that. Just as he knew why Effie felt about it the way she did. Her pain at her father's rejection of her, of his casting her out when she needed him the most, had marked her for life in ways that no one but those she chose to let in could see. For a time, he'd been one of them. "I will find out the truth about her," he said. "And if she is my child, I will care for her. You have to believe that."

"You will provide for her, you mean," she corrected. "Caring for her implies some depth of feeling, a connection. And you are twelve years and at least one workhouse too late for that, Lord Highcliff."

She whirled away from him, heading back to the private dining room and the child that he had no knowledge of.

<hr>

IN THE PRIVATE dining room, Alexandra chewed her sandwich slowly. It wasn't because she'd been told to do so, but because she'd learned that it was impossible to listen to the conversation between the pretty lady and the gentleman if she was chomping on her food. She'd learned long ago that it was very important to always listen to adults, especially when they were having conversations that they didn't want overheard. It was her ability to listen, her ability to gauge the intentions of others, that had kept her safe thus far. She'd never have put it in those words, though—mostly because she knew very few of them.

Alexandra trusted the lady. Even though there were things that she wasn't being told, she believed she was safe with her. The gentleman was still an unknown risk for her. It was clear that the lady, Miss Darrow, had been hurt by him. Likely because he'd lied. All men lied, at least that was what her mother had told her before she'd shipped her off to live with a cousin who'd then shipped her off to the workhouse. So much for her better life in the country. What did she know about the country? London was her home, the place where she felt safe. Well, at least there she understood the risks.

The door opened and the woman entered the private dining room once more. She was obviously sad. There were tears in her eyes, but she smiled politely in spite of that.

"You've shown remarkable restraint with your sandwiches, Alexandra. I think, under the circumstances, that should be rewarded. I'll ask the innkeeper for some scones or other sweets for you," Miss Darrow offered.

"Who was 'e?"

"Who?"

"That man what was 'ere." It was a test. She wanted to see exactly how honest Miss Darrow would be with her.

After a moment's hesitation, Miss Darrow replied, "I believe he is your father. And as such, I will be tasking him with taking responsibility for your welfare and providing for you as he should have all along. You are the daughter of a gentleman, Alexandra, and you should be cared for in the manner befitting your status."

"Not likely," Alexandra scoffed. "Men like 'im don't ever provide for their bastards. My mother told me that."

"What is your mother's name?"

"She's called Pearl. That's not 'er name though. Just what they call 'er at the 'ouse where she worked. They all 'ave names like that. Ruby. Pearl. Opal. Name themselves after jewels at the house she's in now." she stated. "Never called 'er anything but Mama before that. She never told me what 'er real name was."

Miss Darrow's expression shifted into one of sadness. One of pity. "You don't know your mother's name?"

"No. Don't matter though," she denied quickly. "She weren't much of a mother."

"Well," Miss Darrow said, "let's get those scones for you, shall we?"

Part Three
When It's Love

Chapter Six

Four Months Later

HIGHCLIFF LEANED AGAINST the brick wall of the building. It was dirty and grimy, covered in all manner of filth and refuse. But it provided cover and that was vital at the moment. They were looking for him. He'd been doing his damnedest to hunt down any information he could about Alexandra's mother. And in so doing, he'd climbed from the frying pan directly into the fire. Haunting the hells and bawdy houses, he'd encountered old enemies. Resurrected enemies, even.

He had made his way in from Southwark Bridge. If he could get to St. Paul's, the rector there would aid him home. But he would have to hurry. The streets were bustling, filling with people. That would give him a temporary reprieve from those in immediate pursuit as they preferred to have no witnesses to their brand of handiwork, but it would expose him too much. The last thing he needed was for the world to know how gravely injured he was. It would only make him more of a target.

Pressing his hand to his side, he felt the stickiness of his own blood as it oozed between his fingers. There was no question that he had lost too much already. The dizziness made it nigh impossible to walk. Still, he managed. Putting one foot in front of the other and leaning against the filthy bricks, he kept his eye on the skyline—watching the dome as it gleamed in the early morning light.

One foot in front of the other, one step after another. It's how he'd been getting by for the past four months. *Since Effie had cut him from her life.* He didn't blame her for it. The truth was, he might well be guilty of all she accused him of. But still he ached for her. Not simply physically, though nothing had compared to the joy of finally being with her after so many years of denial. He missed her company. He missed her easy smile. He missed sneaking into her office late at night to play chess and drink brandy when all of her students were abed.

In recent years, they had rekindled the friendship of their youth, and it, in turn, had rekindled much more. He was as in love with her as he had ever been. But he had to find the truth, for her sake and his, and he had to eliminate any potential threats that might harm her if there was even a chance for them to be together.

He stumbled, righting himself even as pain exploded from the wound on his side. Christ, nothing had ever hurt so badly. Hissing out a curse under his breath, he rounded the corner and saw salvation. The church was just across the way.

Staggering across the street, dodging carts and piles of refuse, he let out a pained gasp as he pressed his back to the stone walls of Christopher Wren's masterpiece. Inching his way around the corner, the sight that greeted him was one that he had not anticipated. She was there. Unless he was already dead and the Devil was playing tricks with him, Effie stood only a few yards away.

"Good heavens!" she exclaimed.

It was hardly an appropriate epithet given that he was likely headed in a very different direction, but it was also very much Effie. He tried to smile at her, but only a grimace emerged as his legs finally gave way beneath him. The last of his strength had simply evaporated and he slumped against the side of the church once more, sinking down to the pavement.

It was a flurry of activity then. People bustled about him. Wide eyed children peered around the skirts of the gathered ladies, their faces agog at the sight of him. It might have been amusing under any other circumstances. But he only had eyes for her. For Effie. He saw the dawning horror on her face, saw the fear cloud her eyes as they swept over him. A glance down and he understood why.

Laid out as he was, the amount of blood lost was glaringly obvious. It was pooling at his side even then. Everything was beginning to grow dim and indistinct. Montgomery was barking orders.

"Pistol or blade?"

Highcliff struggled for a moment to put the pieces together, to determine what was being asked of him. Finally, it clicked into place and he managed, despite the dryness of his mouth and the seeming thickness of his own tongue, to say, "Neither. A warehouse exploded... I can't be certain, but I think this might be part of the door, perhaps the hinge."

"You don't keep enough servants in your house to care for you... and I can't take you to my house because I cannot risk the children. So where are we taking you?"

"To the Darrow School," Effie said.

No. No. It was too dangerous! Highcliff tried to protest, but he couldn't force out another sound. His body had gone mutinous, no longer listening to the commands of his mind.

"You cannot be serious," Montgomery said.

"I can. I am. We have the Hound directly across the way for protection. My reputation and that of my students is unlikely to be affected by his presence. And heaven knows Mrs. Wheaton is capable of keeping anyone at bay," she stated.

"It's the only option," someone else chimed in. "Really. It's for the best."

"You two go enjoy your wedding breakfast," Montgomery instructed. "Miss Darrow and I will ferry the patient home."

Suddenly, Highcliff felt himself being lifted, hauled up by Montgomery and a strong footman. Between the two of them, they half carried and half dragged him to a waiting carriage. They laid him on the floor and Effie was already there. Before the door even closed, she was holding a wadded cloth against his bleeding side. It was agony, not simply from the pressure on the wound, but also seeing the pain and fear etched on her face.

He'd hurt her. In countless ways, countless times—he had hurt her. And he was hurting her still. Perhaps, he thought, it would be better if he simply died. She'd be free of him then, in a way that he would never permit her to be if he lived.

It was the last thought that crossed his mind before darkness took him entirely. One last look at her and then he slipped into the welcoming blackness of unconsciousness, a reprieve from the pain.

***

EFFIE'S HEART STUTTERED in her chest. "Nicholas? Nicholas? Look at me! Please don't . . . no."

"He's just unconscious," the Earl of Montgomery said. "It's for the best. If he can stay that way until we get him settled into a room at the school, it will spare him a great deal of unnecessary pain. Try not to worry so. He's a very strong man. And much too stubborn to die."

Effie didn't know whether to laugh or cry. "You are probably correct on all counts. You must think me very silly for my unnecessary hysterics."

"Not at all. I think you a woman very much in love," Montgomery observed. "But I would caution you, Miss Darrow—Effie. I love Calliope. I love her more than anything. And since she loves you, your wellbeing is terribly important to me. So I must tell you this is a grave injury he has sustained. How long it will take him to recover, or even if he will recover fully, is not something I can say. You must prepare yourself for that."

Effie stared down at his pale face. There were deep hollows beneath his eyes, and she'd never seen him so ashen in her life. Sweat beaded on his skin and his breathing was labored and shallow. He might be unconscious, but he was far closer to death than anyone else knew. She could feel it.

Leaning down to whisper next to his ear, Effie knew that the earl could overhear every word. She simply didn't care. "If you die on me, Nicholas, I promise you that, in this case, the living will haunt the dead. I will give you no peace. If I must seek the services of every self-proclaimed mystic in all of England to follow you into the afterlife and make it a misery for you, I will. You will not slip into the darkness and leave me alone now. I will not have it."

From the Diary of Miss Euphemia Darrow, September 4th, 1823

I saw Nicholas once more today. I knew that he had returned from another one of his journeys. Where he has been off to and what he has done, I cannot say. He appeared to be, for lack of a better description, haunted. There was a darkness in him that I have not seen before. I know he is not what others see him to be. I know that the garish clothing and foppish manners are nothing more than an affectation. Others are fooled. Others think he is nothing more than a dissipated rogue who went off to war as a lark and came home a sot. A rogue who makes free with brandy and other men's wives.

I am forced to question if he has any inkling that I am aware of his subterfuge. Surely, he must know that I would not be so gullible. That I will not have forgotten who he was all those years ago in the face of the mask he now presents to the world. I still cannot pretend to understand why he was so cold to me upon our parting, but the wisdom of years and the soothing passage of time have made one truth very clear to me. That day, whatever his reasons, that was not his true character.

I must ask myself why it matters. He has not sought my opinion. He has not spoken to me, nor has he acknowledged my existence socially. And yet, on the occasions when our paths have crossed, I have felt his gaze on me. I know that he looks at me, that his eye seeks me whenever we are in the same sphere—seldom though that may be. Is it only the fondness he once held for me, our remembered friendship? Or, like me, does he have regrets? Is he equally tormented by thoughts about what might have been? I wish I knew the answer. I wish I could ask him. I wish that I could believe whatever answer he would give me. But I cannot.

Because he is a man living a lie. And there must be a reason for that.

Chapter Seven

THE ROOM WAS dark, deep shadows filling every corner. Only a narrow band of light entered between the curtains. But that wasn't right, he thought. There were no curtains where he was. No windows. Just a dark hole in the ground that he shared with vermin. Or he did until his captors would drag him out into the glaring light and beat him for their own amusement.

Sound filled that dim space. Garbled and indistinct. Words and phrases that meant nothing in conjunction with one another. They would only make sense if put together with the random words and phrases memorized by the others. Others. He couldn't tell anyone who they were. If he did, the lives lost would be beyond compare.

He needed to get away. He needed to get some place safe where even if he did say something, it wouldn't matter because there would be no one to hear. Struggling to get up, to get to his feet, he became aware of something else in the dimness. A soft and soothing touch on his skin, feather light and gentle. It didn't belong in that place.

"Nicholas . . . Nicholas, it's me! It's Effie. You're safe."

It couldn't be. There was no world in which she could be where he was. He'd left her behind long ago and he would never drag her into the hell that his life had become. A trick. Lies. Just another way for them to get inside his head and dig for the things they wanted to know. Then the fury came. How dare they use her to torment!

Roughly, he grabbed the hand that touched him, twisting the wrist viciously.

"Nicholas," she whispered, "you're hurting me."

It was the pain he heard. The anguish in an all too familiar voice. He loosened his grip, but he still couldn't allow himself to believe it. "It isn't you. It's some foul trick of the mind . . . you can't be here!"

"Where is here, Nicholas? Where are we?" The questions were posed softly, gently. They were posed in the way that one might speak to a frightened child or wounded animal.

"That hellhole of a prison in Marseille," he whispered. "But you know that!" It couldn't possibly be real. He couldn't allow himself to believe it.

"This isn't Marseille, Nicholas. You're in London. Mayfair. You've been terribly injured, and we brought you to my school to recover!" With one hand, she dragged the velvet backing of a coverlet over his skin. "How many prisons have velvet coverlets?"

And the fog lifted. For a moment, for one blessed moment, clarity entered. He could see her. Not the girl he'd loved as a callow youth, but the woman who cared for him even as he could see it breaking her heart. "Effie?"

"I'm really here. You are really here," she insisted.

He shook his head as if to clear it. "I dreamed of you so many times while I was there."

She smiled despite the tears that he could see in her eyes. "I dream of you. All the time. I have for all of my life."

He didn't know how much time he had. He could feel the clamoring darkness again, seeping in, stealing him away from her. The past and the present bled into one another in such a way that he couldn't tell what was real and what wasn't. But her touch—it was real. So he did the only thing he could. Like a man starved for her, he grasped her and pulled her to him, kissing her with all that he had. All the aching need and regret for a lifetime wasted, he poured into that kiss. Because he knew it might well be their last.

And then his strength fled once more. He was falling back onto the bed, unable to hold her any longer, unable to hold off the lingering shadows in his mind.

"Nicholas, please! Look at me! Look at me! Stay with me... please, stay with me," she pleaded with him.

That desperation in her voice tugged at him. He wasn't even certain what he was saying to her. He only knew that it was important. She had to know. "It's in my boot."

"What?"

"Effie, look in the damned boot," he whispered harshly. And then his eyes closed. He was lost to the darkness and the torment of his fever once more.

SHE WANTED TO scream. Or cry. Instead, she snatched up the small vase that rested on the bureau beside the bed and threw it with all her might, sending it crashing against the door where it shattered into pieces.

Hurried footsteps sounded in the corridor and then Mrs. Wheaton appeared in the doorway. "What is this? The fever is affecting his brain, miss! 'Tis too dangerous for you in here with him alone... not to mention very improper."

"I don't care. I will stay with him... and no one else. He talks insensibly and the things he says are not things he would want others to know. I will not betray him that way," Effie stated flatly. "Bring me a broom and I will clean up my mess."

"Your mess?"

"Yes, Mrs. Wheaton. I threw the vase. It wasn't Lord Highcliff," she answered stiffly.

Mrs. Wheaton clamped her lips together tightly, even as she blew out a harsh breath from her rather red nose. She reminded Effie of an angry bull in that moment.

"He hurts you every time he darkens this door."

"He does not!"

"He does!" the housekeeper fired back. "He does. He might not mean it. He might not even know it. Lord knows you lock it up right tight! But seeing him, when a man like that will never be yours... it hurts you, my girl. And I can't help but hate him for it."

Effie felt her eyes tearing up then. The woman was the very definition of ill-tempered and bullish, but she was also fiercely loyal and had loved and protected her since she was little more than a child herself. "I hate him for it sometimes, too... but not enough to let him go. Get the broom, Mrs. Wheaton."

The housekeeper nodded and then bustled out, her skirts swishing with the exaggerated sway of her ample hips. Alone with him once more, Effie rose and crossed the room to where his mostly ruined clothing remained in a heap. His boots were buried under the pile, the once highly polished Hessians stained with blood and muck.

It was so well concealed that at first glance she didn't even see it. But inside the left boot, there was a small pocket sewn into the lining. Slipping her finger inside it, she fished out the folded scrap of paper now stiffened with dried blood. It held only two bits of information—a name and a location. "Miss Henrietta Clark. Garraway's Coffee House."

Turning the piece of paper over in her hand, she examined it from every angle. But it wasn't until she held it up to the light that she saw the mark. It was a seal, of sorts, embossed into the paper at an earlier time, but long since worn down so that it was barely visible. The seal was for the City of Bath and the workhouse where Alexandra had been discovered.

He'd found the girl's mother, or at the very least identified her. He'd kept his promise. And it might well cost him his life.

Effie closed her fist around that scrap, holding it as firmly as she would have a lifeline in a raging sea. Her pride—and if she were honest, her past—had brought them to this place. She'd held him accountable, punishing him for things he would never have knowingly done. And now she faced the terrible burden of the truth. He was injured, and possibly dying, because of her. He'd been out doing whatever it was that had seen him hurt so gravely in the course of trying to find the answers that she had demanded of him.

"What have I done?" she murmured to the now silent room.

From the Diary of Miss Euphemia Darrow, July 14th, 1813

I have done something reckless. Something impossibly bold and potentially disastrous. It was an impulse, really. But I could not ignore the suffering of those children. I had no notion when I paid a call on Marianne, the daughter of one of my mother's oldest friends, who now works for a girls' school, that I would meet what can surely be naught but my destiny.

Two young girls, half siblings, and both of them looking so terribly lonely and sad. They were clinging to one another as they stood in the courtyard of the school, heavy buckets filled with stones straining their thin arms. It was a monstrous punishment, and I remarked as much to Marianne and wondered what horrible thing it was that they had done to receive such a consequence. Their only crime, according to Marianne, was that they were the illegitimate daughters of a nobleman who couldn't be bothered to care for them.

Those words scored me to my soul. I looked at those children and saw myself, saw where I might have been and what I might have endured if my father had been a different sort of man. I may not be viewed as a treasured member of his family now, but he has provided for me. He does care for me.

But those poor young girls had no one. No one to defend them. No one to stand between them and the cruelty that the world so often inflicts on those who bear the stain of their parents' sins.

So now here we all are. The three of us tucked away together in a room at a coaching inn, halfway back to London. I liberated those children from that awful school and the viciousness of their cruel headmaster by invoking the only real power I possess—my father's name. I informed the headmaster that if he attempted to stop me, if he attempted to intervene in my removal of those girls from his care, that I would bring the full wrath of the Duke of Treymore down upon him.

It's very likely that my father would not have done as I asked, but the weaselly little man did not know that and now he will not have to. I have in my care now the two illegitimate daughters of William Satterly, without planning or preparation, and I am at a loss as to what I will do with them. Educate them, I suppose. Prepare them for a life where they will, if such a thing is possible, not be dependent upon the whims of a man. If I achieve nothing else, these girls will know independence and, despite their father's lack of care or concern, they will know their worth. Somehow, I will see to that.

Chapter Eight

EFFIE HAD LOST count of the days. It could have been two or three. It might have only been the passing of one. Other than a moment here and there to see to her most pressing needs, she had not left his bedside. It was beginning to take a toll. Her back ached. Her neck ached. And, Heaven help her, her bottom ached abominably from sitting in that hard chair. If she'd had any inkling the dratted thing was so uncomfortable, she would have tossed it out ages ago.

A glance at the bed showed Highcliff to still be pale and wan, his face ashen. Yet he was resting easier, at least for the moment, no longer quite so lost to the fevered imaginings that haunted him so.

The soft knock at the door had Effie calling out for that person to enter. She never bothered to glance at the door, however, assuming that it would be one of her students or perhaps Mrs. Wheaton come to yell at her again. She knew she needed to rest, but there was no rest to be had when she couldn't be certain that he was being cared for properly.

Effie longed to reach out to him, to touch him—to smooth his brow or perhaps feel the warmth of his breath on her hand. Of course, she knew that such a gesture was not for his comfort but for her own. It would only disturb him from his somewhat peaceful sleep.

"Effie, you look terrible."

That voice pulled her from her reverie. She glanced over her shoulder, surprised to see Minerva there. She was a former student, recently graduated and in her second placement, and Effie had thought Minerva had gone off to the country with the family who currently employed her.

Minerva continued, "You have exhausted yourself caring for him, and if you do not rest soon, you will be of no use to anyone. Not yourself and certainly not Lord Highcliff."

Effie shook her head, a slight and barely perceptible motion. But it wasn't enough of an explanation. From Minerva's dubious expression, that was glaringly apparent. She tried to explain, "I'm afraid to leave him. If he awakens—he's had terrible nightmares, Minerva. Some are not just figments of his fevered mind, but terrible memories he would not wish others to know."

"And no one will know the difference between the two but you and Lord Highcliff himself," Minerva replied.

Effie blinked in surprise. That was certainly true. Perhaps, if she'd had more than a few stolen moments of sleep, she might have thought of it. As it was, she'd had only one concern—to keep him safe at any cost. "Oh. I hadn't—well, that had not crossed my mind."

"Of course, it hadn't. You've worn yourself ragged. Get up. Go to one of the few empty rooms in this monstrous house and go to bed. Sleep before you fall over," Minerva insisted. "If you need me to, I will sit with him in your stead."

Effie took in Minerva's appearance with some concern herself. The young woman had dark shadows beneath her eyes and there was a tension in her that hinted at a heavy and troubled heart. "You are not exactly refreshed yourself. I know why I had a sleepless night. Why did you?"

"Men are the plague of all women," Minerva answered with false flippancy. "But we can discuss it later."

Effie was not fooled by that. "There are no men in Mrs. Entwhistle-Graves' house, unless you count her sons."

Minerva sighed. "I am no longer in Mrs. Entwhistle-Graves' house. She moved us all to the countryside to the estate of her nephew, the Duke of Hargrieve. Then she promptly abandoned us all. So, my situation has changed though my employment has not. Go rest, Effie. I mean it. You are pale, your eyes are shadowed, and you have lost weight you could ill-afford to sacrifice. All for a man who only ever causes you pain."

"You sound like Mrs. Wheaton," Effie replied, though she did rise from her chair. In doing so, she nearly collapsed to the floor. She had to place one hand on the back of the chair and one hand on the nearby bedpost to steady herself. It felt as if the room was spinning around her, everything whirling to and fro.

"Men have some uses after all," Minerva mused. Walking to the door, she called out into the corridor until one of the younger girls came running. "There is a gentleman downstairs. Mrs. Wheaton will know where to find him. We require his assistance here."

"What are you doing?" Effie demanded after sinking back into the chair.

"It is quite obvious that you will not make it to another chamber under your own power. I may have my own issues with the duke, but he is gentleman enough not to let you fall on your face."

After a few moments, the girl returned, the duke in tow. He entered the sick room, took one look at Lord Highcliff and then at Effie. To Minerva, he said, "You required my assistance?"

"Miss Darrow has been looking after Lord Highcliff much to her own detriment. I fear she is too weak now to make it safely to another chamber on her own. Would you be kind enough to carry her?" Minerva asked.

Effie took in the interplay between them. There was a tension that existed between them that hinted at far more than just being employer and employee, and yet they were very distant with one another. Then there was the matter of Minerva actually ordering the man around. It might have been framed as a question, but it was quite clear that it was not a request. Not only that, but the man—a duke, no less—immediately turned toward Effie as if he intended to cart her out of the room at her former charge's request. What had passed between them to create such a strange dynamic?

Immediately, Effie protested, "That is not necessary—"

"Miss Darrow," the duke said gently. "Forgive me for saying this as we are not well acquainted, but it is very apparent that you have cared for Highcliff until you are on the verge of collapse. As a show of my gratitude for your care of an old and dear friend, please allow me to assist you."

"He is your friend?" Effie asked.

"Yes. I owe my very life to him, Miss Darrow. He would not wish you to make yourself so ill to care for him. Please . . . let me help you."

If she'd thought he meant to simply offer his arm, Effie was taken off guard when he simply scooped her into his arms and carted her down the hall. But she was also wise enough to admit that she likely would not have been able to make the journey under her own power.

"That room at the end of the corridor will work . . . it was Minerva's. I haven't moved another student in there yet," she explained.

One of the girls lingering in the corridor, staring at the duke as if she'd never seen a man before, suddenly rushed forward to open the door for them. He nodded at the girl, who beamed at them, and then promptly ran away.

"My home is in an uproar. We have never had so many men here at one time. The girls do not know what to do with themselves," Effie commented.

"How was Highcliff injured?"

Effie shook her head. The truth was, she didn't know the details, though she suspected what the duke was asking about was something different. His question was less about the manner in which it occurred and had far more to do with his concerns about who might be responsible. "There was some sort of explosion. Part of the door's hinge or latch tore into his side. He has broken ribs, though the doctor says his lungs are clear. How the man can say that with any certainty is beyond me. But the fever has raged in him for days. Half the time, he is not even certain where he is or who I am. It's been impossible to learn more."

"When you do learn more," the duke stated, "you will tell me all of it. I have very few friends, Miss Darrow, and I mean to keep Highcliff in their number for some time to come."

Effie nodded her assent. The severity of his tone and the solemnity of his statement tugged at her heart. Highcliff needed friends. They both did. "I will keep you informed."

He lowered her to her feet next to the bed. "Sleep. Rest as long as you can. I will leave Minerva here to watch over Highcliff and leave Meredith in the apparently tender loving care of Mrs. Wheaton. And when he can tell us more, I will help to end any threat against him."

It was uttered resolutely and with complete sincerity. Effie believed that the duke would keep his word. She also believed that Minerva was far more to him than simply his ward's governess. When she wasn't exhausted beyond measure, she would be looking into that. As it was, she had no choice but to lie back on the bed. The room was spinning around her, and her muscles trembled with fatigue from simply holding herself upright. Her eyes had closed before he even shut the door.

From the Diary of Miss Euphemia Darrow, January 10th, 1828

He came tonight. It was well after midnight when he entered the garden. I knew the instant he arrived. I could feel his presence. He accepted the challenge I issued to him in the carriage only days earlier—he'd come for his chess match. We both knew that it had to do with more than simply chess. The game was naught but a pretext.

It had been years since we played. Yet the rhythm of the game was easy and familiar to us both. But there were things that were not familiar. I once said he was not the boy I once knew, and that is very, very true. Yet he does not elect to don his mask before me. He dressed entirely in black, ostensibly to remain unseen, but it suits him. Dark, dangerous, mysterious, and yet familiar. It's more than just his choice of clothing that sets him apart as very different in my presence than in society as a whole. The foppish affectations have been discarded. The sarcasm and ennui that mark him as being thoroughly jaded and thoroughly debauched are absent as well.

We drank brandy. We played chess. We talked of inconsequential things. And we ignored both the past and the future. I feel as if he is now a man who lives only in the present, a man whose past had to be discarded and whose future will ever be uncertain and precarious. And yet, when he departed, I felt a kind of lightness within myself that I haven't known in years. I hope, against all hope, that he felt it too. That perhaps spending those few hours in my company gives him back just a small fraction of what he has sacrificed of himself. He may no longer be the boy he was, but I think I am his only link back to that version of himself. I keep that boy alive in my memory. I keep him alive in my heart.

Chapter Nine

WHEN HER EYES opened in that small, darkened room, Effie was confused at first. The pealing of the clock on the landing had woken her. She was much closer to it in Minerva's old room than in her own. Counting the chimes, she knew that it was well into the wee hours of the morning. Two or three, depending on how many of the chimes she'd slept through.

At first, it was all a muddle. Why she was in that room, why she'd slept in her dress, and why every part of her body ached. But very quickly it all came rushing back. Pushing herself to a sitting position, she scrubbed her hands over her face and wondered how it was possible to sleep for so long and still be utterly exhausted. She'd slept for hours. Highcliff's fever had broken earlier in the evening, and he'd sent her off to bed, insisting that she was hovering on the verge of collapse. He hadn't been wrong.

Pushing back the blanket that someone, likely Mrs. Wheaton, had draped over her, she rose from the bed and stretched. Her back creaked and groaned, her neck as well. She felt as though she were well into her eighties rather than six and thirty. Still trying desperately to work the kinks from her neck, she opened the door and peered out into the corridor. All was quiet.

Creeping down the hall, mindful of the floorboards that were prone to squeaking, she opened the door to her own chamber.

Immediately, she stopped short. Highcliff wasn't alone. He was sitting up in his bed—*her* bed—propped against a mound of pillows. The white bandage around his abdomen was just visible in the open 'v' of the banyan he had donned in light of his current company. Alexandra.

"What are you doing up?" Effie asked, directing her question to both of them. Indeed, it was a question they both needed to answer. Alexandra should long since have been in her own bed, and Highcliff should not be taxing himself by sitting up so.

"I wanted to check on him," Alexandra said. "And I wished to speak with him."

"I see," Effie said. The girl certainly had the right to do so, though her timing could have been better. "And you, Lord Highcliff, are you up to such endeavors?"

"I think I can manage a bit of conversation now. The fever is gone, and my insensible ravings with it. I daresay I will not be dancing a jig anytime soon, however," he answered evenly. But there was a cautiousness about him that set her on edge. He clearly was not comfortable with the situation.

"Well, shall I leave you alone to your conversation or should I remain to act as a mediator?"

"You should stay," Alexandra insisted. "I trust you to tell me the truth. And I trust you to know when he is lying. Him . . . I don't trust him."

"Nor should you," Highcliff said. "You do not know me, after all."

"Be that as it may," Effie interjected firmly. "It is inappropriate to speak to your elder in such a disrespectful manner, Alexandra. You may think and feel as you please, but one, for the sake of propriety, must often moderate one's speech and behavior." It was a gentle correction, a way to teach Alexandra what was and was not appropriate.

"Ain't it inappropriate to get a woman with child and then walk away?" Alexandra demanded pointedly. "I want to know if he's my father. I have a right to know!"

Effie didn't bother to correct Alexandra's grammar. It was clear to her from that slip, especially as the child had been so careful with her speech of late, that Highcliff's presence in their feminine bastion was very distressing to her. Why wouldn't it be? They were all existing in some sort of limbo without any real answers about her parentage. And so much was hanging in the balance based on the answer to that one not-so-simple question.

"I do not know. Not yet," Highcliff answered after a moment. "And that is the truth. I have not been able to track down your mother. She left the last house where she was employed, apparently under the protection of a gentleman whom she did not name to any of her compatriots. Therefore, I cannot ask her. At least not yet. But I have managed to locate a woman—her sister—who was also working in the same house as your mother at the time you were born. But there are . . . complications."

"What sort of complications?" Effie asked, beating Alexandra to that very pertinent point.

"The kind that involve very dangerous people," he replied. "And that is as much as I mean to say about it right now. Until I am able to investigate the matter further and determine whether the events surrounding my injury are truly connected to my search for Alexandra's mother, I want you both to stay out of the matter."

Effie had no intention of agreeing to that, but she also had no intention of arguing the point with him. He could be ridiculously highhanded, as evidenced by him chasing her to Southampton when she'd gone off after Sophie. "There you have it, Alexandra. He's being honest. His left eyebrow always lifts when he tells a lie. He's told us what he knows and what he means to discover."

"Do you believe him?" Alexandra asked, a note of hesitation in her voice.

"Yes, I do," Effie stated. "To be frank, I feel he's too weak and too ill to lie."

Alexandra glanced between them, considered it all for a moment, then gave a curt nod. "I see. I have another question, however."

"Ask it," Highcliff replied.

"If you are my father, and if you'd known about me, would you have let them put me in the workhouse?"

Effie realized that was the only time Alexandra had actually sounded like a child since she'd first met her. It wasn't her words. It was the needfulness that they contained, the desperation to be wanted—to not have been discarded without a thought. It made her heart ache for the child, and, for an instant, it pulled her out of her own misery.

The room grew incredibly quiet. No one even breathed for the longest moment. Then Highcliff simply shook his head. Finally, after the silence had stretched to the point it seemed ready to snap and break, he murmured, "I would never have let you go there."

"But you wouldn't have kept me with you," Alexandra surmised.

"More than likely, no. I would not have. I have too many enemies, Alexandra . . . too many people who would harm those close to me as a way to control me or punish me for the wrongs they think I have done them," he admitted softly.

"Because you're a spy."

"That is one of the reasons," he concurred. "But certainly not the only one."

Alexandra rose from the hard chair then, straightening the wrapper she wore over her nightrail and gave a curt nod. Then she simply turned on her heel and walked away, brushing past Effie where she stood in the doorway. The child had walked out with all the dignity of a duchess.

When the child was gone, Effie let out a ragged breath. "That was certainly not what I expected to walk into the middle of."

"What were you expecting?" he asked sharply.

"To find you dead or raving insensibly again." It was a blunt answer to a blunt question. "I was half convinced that your fever breaking earlier was nothing more than a dream."

"This is no dream, Effie. It is all very, very real. So is the danger that I've put you in."

"You cannot go on this way, Highcliff. No one can play the game you are playing forever. You've been injured before, but never like this. This time—" she stopped abruptly, unable to speak a truth they both already knew. He'd been perilously close to death. Far closer than she was comfortable with.

A heavy sigh escaped him, one laden with a wealth of emotion. "No one does play this game forever, Effie. We tend to live very abbreviated lives. I am the outlier. It's a fact we are both well aware of."

"Then get out of it! It no longer only affects you." The bitterness of their first conversation about Alexandra had faded, but the censure remained. There was a child involved—a child who needed more than simply his financial support. And there were other matters, things she was not yet ready to tell him.

"I'm trying. Whether you believe that or not, I am trying. But there are loose ends that must be tied up—and I am deeply entangled in them at the moment. And that is why I must leave here. As soon as possible."

The man was the most infuriating human to have ever walked the earth. She was utterly convinced of it. "Unless you plan to be carted out like Cleopatra on a barge, you're simply going to have to wait. No doubt if you attempt more than two steps under your own power, you will fall flat on your . . . face."

His lips quirked upward in amusement, even as he leaned his head back against the pillows. It was clear that he was exhausted. The pallor of his skin, the sharpness of his features which had been enhanced by the weight he'd lost with his injury and fever—he looked so much older than his years. He was only thirty-eight. Two years older than she was. And yet, at that very minute, he looked positively ancient. In a moment of clarity, Effie realized she hadn't seen her own reflection in days. She likely looked just as haggard and worn. Events had taken a heavy toll on them both.

"You can say arse," he said. "I've heard you say it before. I'm not one of your pupils to be impressed by your impeccable grasp of etiquette and the finer points of the social game."

"Be that as it may, I've learned my lesson on certain scores, Lord Highcliff. I know the danger of forgetting one's sensibilities—of giving into temptation."

"I didn't lure you into temptation," he snapped. "I tried, at every turn, to cling to what little bit of honor I possess."

"I never said you lured me, Highcliff. We both know, and I am certainly honest enough to admit, that I leapt into temptation of my own free will. I have regretted it with the same intensity with which I welcomed it."

It was said to wound. And from the expression that crossed his face, it was apparent that she'd hit her mark. The urge to offer an apology was there, but pride had her bite her tongue rather than call those words back.

"Regrets were the last thing I wanted you to have." His tone was low, his words uttered so softly that she almost thought she had imagined it. Then he continued, "But given the circumstances, it is easy enough to see why you would. I wish I could offer you assurances that she is not my child—but I cannot. I didn't live like a monk, Effie. I tried to banish you from my mind in a dozen different ways. By courting danger. By falling into barrels of brandy. And with other women. But none of it worked. And I was always, *always*, as cautious as one can be."

"Except for the nights you cannot remember and the fact that, as we said before, there are no guarantees. There is only one foolproof method of preventing conception, and abstinence was not your choice.

Nor was it mine, so I should not cast judgement."

"Yet you do," he said pointedly.

"I do," she agreed. "And perhaps I am simply jealous. I didn't have the luxury of throwing myself into vice to forget your rejection of me, Nicholas. There were no other men. No brandy. No danger. Only isolation and loneliness until I determined that I would not be some tragic figure. Then there was only finding some purpose to my life—my girls have given me that, at least. I found it when you left me before. I will have it still when you leave me again."

"I cannot stay. If you love your girls, and I know that you do, Effie, you must understand that I cannot stay here. Every moment I am under your roof places everyone here in the gravest of danger," he admitted.

A sense of inevitability filled her. He was doomed by his own stubbornness. "When do you plan to leave? I can talk to you until I lose my breath about how weak you are and how foolish it is, but we both know you will not listen. You will do as you please, just as you have always done."

"As soon as I can manage to get myself down the stairs," he answered. "Before the dawn though, regardless."

She was furious. Livid with him. Livid with herself for caring. Livid with the situation—because even as much as she hated it, she knew he told the truth. If he said others would be looking for him, coming for him, then they were not safe with him there. And she had more than him to consider. More than herself. More even than the girls she loved so dearly.

"Then go. Do what you must. But know that I will too." She whirled on her heel and left, ignoring him even as he called her name.

Chapter Ten

It was just after dawn. Sweat poured from him. He could feel it snaking down his spine, dampening the linen of his shirt. His coat and waistcoat were long gone. His breeches were stiff with dried blood. Mrs. Wheaton had apparently refused to launder them. Not surprising given her general view of his sex. His shirt was little better than rags at that point, but it would see him home, at least.

He'd only just reached the foyer. There were several yards still to go to reach the front door and the street beyond. Then he'd have to hail a hack, assuming one was about and would stop to pick up such a sorry, disheveled, and thoroughly disreputable looking man. After all, not everyone roaming the streets of Mayfair could be called a gentleman.

Stepping down off the staircase and onto the marble floor of the entryway, he grasped the banister to steady himself. The newel cap went rolling, the wood banging loudly against the floor even as he bit out a smothered curse. "A seasoned agent of the crown . . . a man who has been dealing in government secrets for nearly two decades. And I can't sneak out of a bloody girls' school without waking the house."

"Likely not without waking the dead, much noise as you're making."

Highcliff turned his head, wincing as the movement pulled at his side. Mrs. Wheaton stood just behind the staircase, loitering in the corridor that led back to the dining room and kitchens. No doubt, given that she had so many mouths to feed, her day started very early. But he had the sneaking suspicion that her presence there had much more to do with watching him than with her daily chores. "Mrs. Wheaton, given your penchant for lurking, perhaps you should take up a position in espionage."

"I don't think so. I haven't the knack for dishonesty that such work requires," the housekeeper said sharply, her northern accent giving the words a distinct bite. "I don't think I need to say this, but it'd be best if you didn't come back. She's not for the likes of you. Never has been. Once—when she was a girl, when she had hope and youth on her side—then maybe. But she's been waiting and hoping for years and been disappointed again and again when you chose everything else in the world over her. So don't come back. Don't hurt her again. You've done enough."

The housekeeper had gutted him more effectively than the goddamn explosion. "I never meant to hurt her."

"I believe that. If I didn't, Lord Highcliff, I'd have killed you myself already. She and Miss Alexandra will get along just fine without you. Send the money as she needs it. Same way you always have. Half the students here are under this roof by the grace of your purse and well we both know it, even if she does not. Then you can just leave her be."

"I'll do what I can," he said. "But until I know they are not in danger because of me, I cannot simply turn my back."

"You're a spy, Lord Highcliff. You have been for two decades. I think you can manage to have them looked after without doing it personally."

He simply stared at her for a long moment. Then he gave a curt nod.

Mrs. Wheaton walked past him and opened the front doors, carefully undoing all the locks and bolts that kept the unwanted elements outside. "I've already summoned a hack for you. They'll see you home."

"Always efficient, aren't you, Mrs. Wheaton?"

She looked at him then, and her gaze wasn't cold. It was warning. "I had a daughter once. Pretty little thing. Always fragile though. Sickly as a child, tenderhearted as a woman. She'd have been Miss Darrow's age had she lived. But she fell in with a bad man. A man who liked cards, and spirits . . . and other women. But he was bad at the cards. Betting more than he had and losing more than they could ever hope to pay. When they came to collect from him, he was already gone. Run off to save his own skin. And so they took from my girl the only thing she had. They left her bloodied and broken, Lord Highcliff, and they all walked away. Men never have to pay for the wrongs they do."

"I am sorry, Mrs. Wheaton," he said. It was sincere and heartfelt. He could see her pain and would not have wished it on anyone.

The housekeeper continued, not acknowledging his expressed condolences. "She couldn't pick up the pieces of herself when it was done. She wasn't strong, my girl. Not like Miss Darrow. And maybe Miss Darrow doesn't need me to protect her the way I failed to protect my Sarah, but I'll do it anyway. Because I'll never see another young woman in my care broken by a worthless man ever again. Good day to you, my lord."

Dismissed and chastened, Highcliff managed to stagger past her and onto the street, where the summoned hack waited to take him home.

※※※※

ACROSS THE STREET, from the window of what, in other houses, would have been a drawing room, the Hound watched the Darrow School. More importantly, he watched the mysterious and apparently multifaceted Lord Highcliff emerge from the school. Clearly wounded and disheveled, the nobleman had looked better. Significantly better.

"Stavers!" he called out.

Immediately, the door opened and the rough looking man, who served as both butler and brute force, entered the room. "Yes, sir?"

"There's something afoot at the Darrow School."

"Begging yer pardon, sir. Those are troublesome women. Always something afoot."

The Hound grinned. "I like those troublesome women, Stavers. They remind me not everyone is like me ... and you. Especially our Miss Darrow. She's the last of the truly good ones, I think."

"Good what, sir?"

"Just good, Stavers. Just good. And now Highcliff's slipping out in the wee hours looking like he's been to hell and back," the Hound observed. "Since I know Miss Darrow has tender feelings for the ass, be certain he makes it home safely. Hate to see something happen to him and her have a guilty conscience over it."

"Yes, sir," the butler answered. Without another word, Stavers disappeared once more. Within seconds, he was outside, hailing a hack of his own and following Highcliff's at a safe distance. Stavers was nothing if not loyal, he thought.

"Now, the real question—what have you gotten yourself into Highcliff... and what danger have you brought to Miss Darrow's door?"

Turning away from the window, the Hound moved back to his desk. It was littered with papers, stacks of them here and there. Heavy, leatherbound ledgers were stacked neatly, each one carefully marked with his own code to indicate what was held within. It wasn't all gambling debts, though a goodly portion of them were. But there were debts of another nature entirely. Favors. Secrets. Lies. All the things he could use to ease his way in the world and to supplement the fortune he had already amassed.

Within the walls of that room, he had everything he needed to shift and manipulate every powerful man in England. And he used it to his advantage whenever he deemed necessary. He was deeming it necessary in that moment. Because he knew something that Miss Darrow and possibly even Lord Highcliff himself did not. It turned out the Duke of Clarenden was perfectly willing to commit a little treason if that was the cost of exacting his own petty revenge. The letter the Hound had acquired—through somewhat larcenous means—was proof of that. Clarenden had provided Highcliff's location to the French, allowing him to be captured. The bastard would do anything necessary to ensure that his wife's illegitimate offspring never inherited the dukedom. And the Hound would do whatever was necessary to ensure that the duke never got what he wanted.

To that end, he wrote a single letter, his instructions veiled, but the recipient would know what needed to be done. With the task complete, he folded it, sealed it with wax, and tapped it against the green baize that covered the writing surface of the desk. It was a moment's indecision, a hesitation as he considered whether or not he was overplaying his hand. But time to play those cards was running out. If he didn't do it now, he might never get to.

"May that wretched old fuck die as unhappily as he lived," the Hound murmured to himself. He then rose from his desk and walked out into the grand entryway that greeted his guests when they came to lose their fortunes. There, he placed the letter on the silver tray for Stavers to have delivered later. It wouldn't go by mail. The post could not be trusted, after all. Anything that was run by the government couldn't be trusted. No, a handpicked emissary would deliver it to its final destination.

Satisfied with his choice, the Hound hummed a naughty, jaunty little tune as he made his way to his kitchen. As a general rule, he didn't cook, but he'd cobble something together for himself. Revenge made him hungry.

Chapter Eleven

Effie tidied her room, remaking her bed. *Reclaiming it.* Highcliff was gone. He'd slipped out sometime in the wee hours of the morning. It shouldn't have bothered her. She'd known he was going, after all. But a dozen scenarios played out in her mind, all of them involving him lying in a gutter somewhere, bleeding to death.

Gathering up the soiled linens, a task that Mrs. Wheaton or one of the girls could have done, she bundled them into a basket and made her way down the back stairs toward the kitchens and laundry. Keeping herself occupied would keep other things from her mind. There were things she'd have to deal with—uncomfortable truths to be faced—and, as always, consequences to be dealt with. As she often told her girls, consequences could be delayed but they could rarely be avoided entirely.

Opening the door, she descended the last set of steps into the kitchens, the basket of linens balanced on her hip. Mrs. Wheaton looked up as she entered. "What in Heaven's name are you about? That's no fit task for the mistress of the house!"

"But it is a fit task for the headmistress of a very busy school. You've been doing the work of three people for entirely too long, Mrs. Wheaton. You may protest as much as you like, but I think it is long past the time when we must take on another pair of hands," Effie insisted.

"Don't need them. They'll only do things the wrong way and I'll have even more work to fix the muddle they make of it all," the housekeeper complained.

"Mrs. Wheaton, really! You cannot do it all and neither can I! So many of the older girls have moved on to placements or homes of their own—and the younger girls are not up to many of the tasks. Nor should they have to be," Effie protested. "It will not hurt to try."

The housekeeper gave a weary sigh. "I'll take care of the hiring of them. They'll tell you some woe begotten tale and be moved into the finest chamber in the house before the day is done."

Effie didn't bother to disagree with her. It would have been a futile task. Placing the basket in the laundry, she started to return to her room but a commotion at the front of the house halted her progress. "Goodness! What could that all be about?" Hurrying away from the kitchens, Effie made her way through the corridor and entryway. But she paused in the opening of the front door, her eyes wide and her mouth slightly agape at the sight which greeted her.

The Duke of Hargrieve and Minerva were in the street, facing off against a young man, whom she could only assume was one of Mrs. Entwhistle-Graves' sons. The youngest child, Meredith, was in his grasp, a knife to her throat. To say the situation appeared volatile was, at the very least, an understatement.

Before Effie could even ascertain what the true danger of the situation was, a hulking figure approached from across the way. It was Stavers, the butler for the Hound. Effie knew their association was somewhat scandalous, but the man who ruled London's underworld had only ever been a gentleman to her. A good number of her pupils had come to her through his charity. In her opinion, it elevated him far beyond many of the so-called gentlemen who would have sneered at him.

Stavers, the fearsome butler, diffused the dangerous situation with a simple maneuver that freed Meredith and disarmed the boy in one fell swoop. The duke then leapt at the boy, taking him to the ground and binding his wrists with a cravat. The situation had been dealt with handily, and yet Effie had the feeling things were far from settled. She could see the tension in Minerva and knew that it had very little to do with the recent dramatics. Something else troubled her former charge, and she had the distinct impression that it had far more to do with the duke himself than with any of his relatives.

And then it was all over and done with. Stavers went back to the service of the Hound, and the duke hauled his captive inside while Minerva and Meredith made their way up the steps. Mrs. Wheaton, who had come up from the kitchens right behind her, was working to disperse the girls and get them out from underfoot. And through all of it, Effie simply stood there feeling as if the chaos of her household was happening to someone else. She felt disconnected from all of it—because her mind was on him. Her thoughts were wherever he was, focused on his safety, his well-being... on the fear that something terrible would happen to him, as it almost had, many, many times.

It took the longest time to get everyone calmed down. The children were all at sixes and sevens over the strange events that had taken place. She settled the girls into their various classrooms on the main floor. And then, as she was going to check on Minerva, she found herself face to face with the duke.

"You must talk to her, Miss Darrow. You must make her see reason," he implored.

"What must she be made to see reason about, Your Grace?" Effie asked. She was growing weary of being told what she must do by everyone.

"Agreeing to be my wife," he said simply. "It isn't that she does not wish to, Miss Darrow. If I thought that was the case, I would not pursue this. But she does. I am certain of it. And yet she is paralyzed by fear. Speak with her. I implore you."

Destined to intervene in the love lives of others while her own withered and died. She wanted to refuse, but it was just pique, just her own envy and resentment at the happiness of others when her own had been denied. After a moment, she simply nodded. "I will speak to her, Your Grace. But she will set her own course."

"Of course, she will," he agreed. "That is all I want for her. For it to be the choice of her heart, Miss Darrow, and not the cage of her fears."

She knew all about being caged by fear. So did Highcliff.

Effie said nothing further. Instead, she turned on her heel and made her way to the stairs. Climbing them heavily, as if she carried the weight of the world on her shoulders, she found Minerva and Meredith in one of the bedrooms on the upper floor. Effie stood in the doorway for a moment, watching as Minerva fussed over the child.

"You need to tend to your own injuries," Effie said softly.

"I will get to them," Minerva answered. "How is Lord Highcliff?"

"Gone," Effie answered. She strove for an unbothered tone, but knew she fell far short of the mark. She could hear the slight quavering of her voice. If she were lucky, it might be blamed on exhaustion rather than the tears she was barely keeping at bay. "His fever broke entirely last night and he insisted that I leave him to rest myself. When I awoke this morning, the room was empty, and he had taken his leave like a thief in the night. Or the morning, as it were." It was a carefully edited version with the omission of their nighttime chat.

Minerva straightened Meredith's clothing, smoothed her hair with a gentle pat, and said, "Go downstairs to the kitchen. Mrs. Wheaton will likely have a nice treat ready for you."

The little girl, clearly wise beyond her years, gave her governess a baleful stare. "You are only telling me that because there are things you want to say that you do not wish me to hear."

"And like all well-behaved children, you will go to the kitchen as you have been bidden," Minerva replied.

Meredith sighed heavily, rolled her eyes, but rose from her perch and made her way to the corridor and beyond to whatever sweet Mrs. Wheaton would ply her with.

When they were alone, Minerva turned back to her. "Has he broken your heart entirely then?"

"Have you broken the duke's?" Effie demanded. She didn't wish to discuss Highcliff. Not anymore. Discussing him changed nothing. It made nothing better or worse. It simply reminded her that she was where she had always been with him. Stuck. Loving him too much to walk away yet not enough to simply be grateful for the pittance of affection he could offer her.

Minerva looked away. "He told you that he proposed, didn't he?"

"He did," Effie replied, stepping deeper into the room. She collected bandages and salves from the assortment of provided supplies and approached Minerva purposefully. It would not be the first time she'd tended Minerva's scrapes and bruises, though the other woman had been much younger then. "He thinks I can sway you. Of course, we both know that of all my girls, none have ever been as stubborn as you. If you do not wish to marry him, nothing I could say would ever sway you."

"You once told me that my stubbornness was a fine quality and would serve me well in life." Minerva seated herself on the bed and allowed Effie to treat the worst of the scrapes.

Effie applied the salve lightly. It would help to keep down bruising and prevent scars. Or so Mrs. Wheaton had always insisted. "And so it could. But obstinance for the sake of it, versus actually considering one's options and making a sound choice to put that stubbornness behind? That's the hallmark of foolishness, as we both well know. So the question is what you want, Minerva. Can you answer that?"

Minerva didn't have to answer the question. Effie could see it clearly on the younger woman's face. Minerva did love the duke. And the duke had made it abundantly clear that he loved Minerva. There were enough unhappy people in the world, enough people who were forced apart by circumstance when they should have been together.

Effie sighed heavily and then continued. "The man I want more than anything else in the world runs from me, Minerva, because he feels he does not—that he cannot—be worthy of me. You run from the man who wants you more than anything in this world for the same reason. But you are good enough for him. You are good enough for anyone. Do not sell yourself short by assuming otherwise ... to do so is to sell me short. To say that all I have done for you, all I have taught you to do for yourself ... that it is not enough."

"You think I should accept him."

Effie knew that Minerva didn't want to make the choice for herself. She was looking to be told what to do, looking to be advised and guided as she would have been when she was a child. But Effie couldn't dictate what the other woman should do in that way. She couldn't tell her whether or not to marry the man so she clearly loved. But she could impart one piece of wisdom that she'd gleaned during the course of her life. "I think, Minerva, that you should accept yourself. You are not your mother's fall from grace. You are not your father's descent into iniquity. You are simply you. And you deserve to love and be loved if that is what your heart desires."

"I love him," Minerva admitted. "I didn't mean to, but I do. He's so very kind. And he's been so alone for so long. I worry that it is only that loneliness and isolation that drew him to me ... that if any woman had crossed his path who was kind to him, he might have felt the same."

Effie clucked her tongue then gently cupped Minerva's face. Every girl who had come through her house, who'd been guided and educated by her, had been special to her. They all had something unique to their character that made them exceptional. Minerva was no different. It saddened her that in all the years Minerva had been with her, she hadn't yet discovered just how extraordinary she was. "Then I have failed you, because I have let you leave my home without ever knowing your worth. Trust in him, Minerva, until you can trust in yourself. Love is too precious to let it go . . . especially for such an ugly illusion."

Her own words echoed back to her as she hugged Minerva. Could she let him go? Whatever she believed him to have done in his past, could she let him go? Of course, she knew that she could not. She would not. Wounded pride and wounded feelings aside, they were so entwined with one another that not even death would ever free her of him.

Chapter Twelve

It had been four days since he'd left the Darrow School. Two days since he'd seen Effie. The first day had been recovery—the second day had been back to work, only reconnaissance, ferreting out information from secondary sources. And now, he was back in the line of fire. To that end, he was tucked into a private parlor at one of the more notorious gaming hells in Mayfair.

Highcliff laughed at the drunken and ribald comments being passed around the Faro table. He didn't wince. Not even when laughing pulled at his stitches and made the wound at his side ache. After all, no one in his present company needed to know that he had been injured. All the men gathered were suspect, after all. Each one had considerable debts. Each one had a record of military service that was less than stellar. Each one had ties, either directly or indirectly, to the late Margaret Hazleton, Lady Marchebanks. That viperous witch had managed to avoid the noose for her part in recently uncovered treasonous plots by consuming a very liberal dose of laudanum.

"You've been out of sight for a while, Highcliff," young Lord Ransom observed. "Where have you been hiding? Or should I ask with whom? No doubt, you've become entangled with some new lady love!"

Imperceptibly, he tensed. Did the man know he'd been recuperating in Effie's home? Or was it simply an offhand comment? "No lady loves. Women are a complication I can ill afford. It was family obligations that have kept me occupied of late."

The younger man nodded. "Called on the carpet by the duke, were you?"

"Something along those lines." It wasn't outside the realm of possibility that his father was responsible for the attempt on his life. It wouldn't be the first time, after all. Still, Highcliff suspected his father had more important things on his mind given that his own health was failing so dramatically.

"Last I heard, the old man was only one sneeze away from the grave," Ransom observed.

Another of the players, Lord Heathcote tossed his cards down. "You've won enough of my money for one evening. I've nothing left to wager, at any rate."

"There's your arrangement with Cleo," Ransom insisted. "That's the most valuable thing in your possession. Half the men of the *ton* have been vying for her favor!"

"The lady's affections are not a prize to be wagered and won. Nor are they mine to give. I've been dismissed, at any rate. Now, I mean to visit Mrs. Ember's Pleasure House and have my every whim indulged by a bevy of beautiful *ladies*."

Mrs. Ember's was a well-known brothel, one that catered to the more exotic pleasures. It was also very exclusive. No one was admitted without being a member or the guest of a member . . . and memberships were very expensive. "I'll be curious to know how you like it," Highcliff offered casually. "I take it you have an invitation?"

"Yes. Colonel Winchell was kind enough to offer his hospitality and sponsorship for the evening," Heathcote replied.

Winchell. That was the key, Highcliff thought. Winchell and Margaret Hazleton had been lovers. He was the primary reason that she had been free in her home to commit suicide rather than locked in a cell. The man had pulled countless strings and called in countless favors to keep the gossip to a minimum. "Do you think he'd be kind enough to extend his hospitality to another guest?"

Heathcote shrugged, but the gesture lacked the casual appearance it should have had. There was a tension in him that made the entire situation seem somewhat off—incongruous. "I do not see why he wouldn't. After all, it's quite the party he's arranged there. A private event. What's one more?"

Highcliff grinned, seemingly at ease. "Excellent." It was a trap, of course. But he was walking into it with his eyes wide open. "I cannot wait to see what Mrs. Ember's has in store."

"We should go then," Heathcote said, abruptly getting up from his chair. "Wouldn't do to be late, would it?"

"Not at all," Highcliff agreed, getting to his feet with deceptive ease. He was weaker than he would have liked, still struggling with the pain from the vicious wound that had nearly ended his life. But there were greater concerns than his discomfort. Despite Lady Marchebanks' plotting being brought to light, shipments of weapons and supplies to both India and Portugal were still going awry and winding up in enemy hands. It put British forces at risk. And if goods were being intercepted, that meant someone was feeding information about those shipments to the traitors. If that information was being leaked, what other secrets were being bartered off?

Apparently, Lady Marchebanks and her cronies had been only a fraction of the real problem. Following the war, Winchell had taken an advisory position with the East India Company—a company that was now losing a vast number of shipments while Winchell himself seemed to only grow richer.

A part of him resented that he couldn't simply walk away . . . to let it be someone else's problem. Highcliff saw the importance of his actions, but he was reaching a point where he wanted someone else to take on the risks. There were matters in his own life that needed to be settled. Matters like Miss Henrietta Clark. He had men watching the coffeehouse, watching for her to return. But thus far, she'd been scarce. He needed answers about Alexandra's parentage—her parentage and his own. It was hurting Effie. Every day it remained a mystery hurt her more.

The last mission, he decided. It was his last mission for Whitehall. He'd said the same thing countless times before and countless times before they had lured him back in. But Ransom had been correct about one thing. The duke was at death's door. He'd been hovering there for some time. His passing could occur at any time and when it did, he would finally be free.

<hr />

EFFIE WAS IN her study. She stared at the ledger in front of her but the columns of figures were simply a blur. There was no more lying to herself about the truth of her very precarious situation. With each passing day, her certainty about the matter only increased.

"Finally occurred to you, did it?"

Effie looked up to see Mrs. Wheaton standing in the doorway. "What has occurred to me?"

"That you're increasing. That your dalliance with Lord Highcliff has had unintended consequences."

"Oh, that," Effie said. "I had reached that conclusion some time ago, Mrs. Wheaton. When did you have that startling realization?"

"When I heard you casting up your accounts this morning after you walked through the dining hall," the housekeeper replied. "It should have occurred to me much sooner, but with all the upheaval it did not."

"How do you know everything in this house, Mrs. Wheaton?"

"I do the laundry, don't I? And you've not had your courses since before you went hying off to wherever it was and came back from with young Alexandra in tow and Highcliff cut from your life . . . or so

I thought."

"He was never cut from my life, Mrs. Wheaton. I have treated him very badly."

"And hasn't he treated you just the same?" The housekeeper's temper was riled now. She stepped fully inside the room and closed the door behind her, more forcefully than was necessary. "You think I don't know how he's hurt you over the years? Every time he ignored you in public, it took a piece of your heart. And then he comes sneaking around... slipping in through the window to play chess. Chess my eye!"

"It wasn't like that. You know what he is, Mrs. Wheaton. You know what he does for our country. Highcliff has sacrificed so much of his life and so much of his own personal happiness for the greater good."

"I don't care for the greater good, Miss Darrow. I care for your good. For your happiness. And here you are, sitting in this room all alone, brooding about his child growing in your belly while he's off galivanting as he pleases!"

"No. I wasn't thinking about that at all. I was thinking more about the fact that I am sitting here idle—doing nothing to aid either Alexandra or Lord Highcliff. And I fear they may both need my help more desperately than I initially realized."

"What can you do? I know he asked you to stay out of it, that he told you how dangerous it was to interfere," the housekeeper warned.

"He did. But I've faced danger before. I'll likely face it again. With the girls that come through here, Mrs. Wheaton, danger is simply our lot in life. Highcliff was correct in his assessment. We do find trouble. Time and again."

"And it's not just you to consider. It might not have come about the way it ought, but you are carrying a child. Not to be cruel, but given your age, 'tis likely the only one you'll ever have. It wouldn't hurt you to be cautious."

"I intend to be cautious, Mrs. Wheaton. In all things, I intend to be cautious."

The housekeeper sighed. "You'll do as you please. Hardheaded, as always. You ought to tell him, at least. I don't know that it would change anything, but he ought to at least have the option of doing the honorable thing."

"I sent a note to him," Effie admitted. "Yesterday morning. I told him that I needed to speak with him—that it was a most urgent matter and could not wait. As he has failed to reply, I feel he's made his position on the matter of our relationship clear."

The housekeeper's lips firmed. "That's not right."

"Right or not, it is what it is," Effie said, in a manner far more cavalier than she truly felt.

"No. I don't mean it like that. I mean, much as it pains me to ever say anything positive about the man—about any man—it isn't like him. He may never marry you, but whenever you've called for him, he's come. I cannot but think there is something afoot. Something foul, Miss Darrow."

It echoed her own thoughts—the fears that she dared not give voice to. Whatever had passed between them, whenever she'd needed him, he had been there. For him to ignore her entirely was out of character. Had he fallen ill again? Had his injury festered once more? Or was it something even more sinister? It was entirely possible that the enemies he'd alluded to might have found him. "Then it's high time I stop sitting idle and interfere as I had planned," Effie stated.

"Where do you plan to start?"

"Garraway's Coffee House," Effie said. "With one Miss Henrietta Clark."

※

HIGHCLIFF GROANED IN the darkness, the coldness and dimness of the earth beneath him seeped through his clothing and chilled his skin. Where was he?

Fragments of memory, bits and pieces of the events that had transpired to bring him to such a low place flitted about the periphery of his memory. The gaming hell, the conversation with the two wastrel lords, and the invitation to the bawdy house. But there were other pieces of it that he could not quite put together. They were always slightly out of reach, like petals on the water. The harder he grabbed at them, the further they floated away.

Voices drifted in and out of his consciousness, some familiar and others not. They discussed him freely, as if he was not there.

"How long will he be out?" one male voice asked in the distance.

"Not long enough. She won't come here until tomorrow and I don't wanna tangle with 'im again. Bad enough getting 'im in 'ere the first time," another man replied.

The conversation grew more muffled. Then moments later, rough hands grabbed him, shoved a cup to his lips and forced a noxious liquid into his mouth. With large hands covering his nose, there was no choice but to swallow it. And then the blackness was closing in again, leaving him in that same darkness he'd been in only moments earlier, but this time, nothing penetrated. No voices. Not even a single shaft of light. It was just him in the dark.

Chapter Thirteen

EFFIE WAS IN a borrowed carriage—nondescript and unremarkable—watching the exterior of Garraway's Coffee House. It was late, but not so late that no one was about. The coffee house, after all, was near the theaters. It catered to a different sort, people who lived a very nocturnal existence.

But it seemed that Effie's patience was finally paying off. A lone woman approached, walking from the direction of one of the smaller theaters toward the coffee house. Her heeled boots clicked on the paving stones. Wrapped in a thick cloak, there was nothing about the woman that was readily identifiable. And it was that—that she was so well obscured—which made Effie suspicious. It wasn't so very cold outside, after all. That manner of dress hinted more at concealment than the need for warmth.

Reaching up, she rapped softly on the roof of the carriage. "I'll be getting out here, driver!"

"Yes, ma'am," the driver replied. It was clear from his tone that he found her actions questionable. It was also clear that he would report the incident back to her father, from whom she had borrowed the carriage.

Once he'd opened the door and lowered the steps for her, he aided Effie down to the pavement. She crossed the muck-covered street quickly, carefully dodging piles of refuse and other filth left by passing horses in order to keep her skirts clean. When she reached the coffee house, she drew in a deep breath before opening the door and stepping inside. So much hinged on what she might learn from this woman.

She saw her immediately as she entered. The heavy cloak had been removed and she sat alone at a table near the back of the establishment. Perhaps the most shocking aspect of the situation was how very respectable the woman appeared. Dressed in a modest gown, with her hair swept back in a neat chignon, a simple silver cross on a length of black ribbon encircled the woman's throat. She might have been taken for any shopkeeper's wife or gainfully employed spinster. Certainly not a woman who had worked in bawdy houses and who now worked in the theaters, dressing the actresses for the stage and for assignations with their lovers. Like Highcliff, the woman wore a disguise, one that required specific knowledge to be seen through.

Without giving the woman an opportunity to refuse her, Effie simply walked over to her table and sat down across from her. "Good evening, Miss Clark."

The woman's eyebrows arched upward, and she appeared quite nonplussed by Effie's boldness. "You appear to have the advantage, madam. You know my name while I do not have the benefit of having yours."

"I am Miss Euphemia Darrow. And I believe that I am currently housing and educating your niece . . . Alexandra."

Immediately, Mrs. Clark's expression shuttered. "I have no niece. Now, if you don't mind, I'd prefer to enjoy my coffee in peace."

"I found her in a workhouse in Bath," Effie continued. "Painfully thin. Discarded there by a cousin, I believe. Her mother had sent her to reside with them in Somerset and they elected to keep the funds sent for her care without feeling overly burdened to provide that care. But I must wonder, Miss Clark, why Alexandra's mother would have felt compelled to send her daughter to a cousin in Somerset when her own sister was right here in London."

"Miss Darrow," Miss Clark whispered in a frightened manner, "You have no notion of what you are involving yourself in. There are reasons for everything that has happened, and that is all I am at liberty to say."

Effie stared at her for a moment. And feeling she had no other choice in the matter, did something she rarely would. She invoked her father's name and position. "I'm afraid I require more than that, Miss Clark. My father is quite a patron of the arts. Many of the theater owners would be loathe to employ someone who had given offense to the Duke of Treymore or any member of his family—even an illegitimate one."

Miss Clark's lips pressed together into a thin, hard line. "So that's the way of it, then? Normally bastard children are not so free to make promises about what their fathers would do for them."

"I am not most people," Effie answered sharply. "My father will grant my request if I make it. We both know that."

"I'm offering you a warning, Miss Darrow. One you should heed. I urge you to walk away from this. Send that child out of the city . . . send her anywhere that is far from London. It is not safe for her here. And it is not safe for anyone who would harbor her. The last man who asked questions about her was nearly blown to bits when a dockside warehouse exploded."

Highcliff. She could only be talking about Highcliff. So it hadn't been his work for the Crown but his investigation into Alexandra's past that had endangered him. Or were the two connected in a way she could not yet see? Either way, she needed answers, and she was determined to get them. "I am tired, Miss. Clark. I am beyond exhausted. I will not spend another hour fumbling in the darkness while everyone else knows the stakes of the game and I am left at a disadvantage! Tell me the truth . . . all of it."

Miss Clark leaned back in her seat, wilting before her like a flower in the heat. It seemed she aged decades in just a moment of time.

"Very well, Miss Darrow. Alexandra's father will see her dead before he allows her existence to prove he was in England—in London, no less—at a time when his military orders would have him elsewhere."

"Why is that worth killing for?"

Miss Clark leaned in, whispering hotly, "Ambitious men are dangerous men, Miss Darrow. It would mean the end of his career and all his aspirations. He is set to take a position in Parliament—to become a very powerful player in the House of Commons."

"Yet this man is a deserter . . . a deserter and, if the stakes of discovery are truly this high, possibly a traitor. To have such a position in government—"

Miss Clark shook her head. "As always, money begets power, and power begets money. And scandal has the ability to snatch it all away . . . a scandal that the child in your care is the key to. She's the proof that could ruin him, and he will never let that happen. No matter the cost."

Effie slapped her hand flat on the table. "No more games, Miss Clark. No more riddles and warnings. Give me his name."

"That would see us both dead. I am not so foolish."

"Miss Clark, I care not what that man's political aims are. My reasons for wanting to know the identity of Alexandra's father are more personal in nature. More depends on this than you can possibly imagine," Effie insisted. "Please. I am imploring you to help me. To help her."

After a long, silent moment—one that seemed to stretch forever—Miss Clark gave another sigh. "Fine. His name is Colonel Silas Winchell. And he is a monster. If my sister were here, you could ask her, but I've no notion where she went, and we are both better for it. I can never betray her to him should he find me. Now, I beg you, leave me be. My work as dresser at the theater isn't the most respectable or the best paying, but it's all I have. I've missed too many nights' work already! I've a man that cares for me . . . poor though he is. He comes to collect me here every night after the shows are done, and he cannot work since he lost his arm in battle."

"About your niece—"

"I do not have one," Miss Clark insisted as she rose from her chair. She was donning her heavy cloak and speaking very rapidly. "My sister is dead to me along with any children she might have, Miss Darrow. That's the only way for us all to get by. Now, please... go. Do not ever come here again."

Effie watched her walk out, puzzled by everything that had been revealed and even more puzzled by the things that remained unknown. If Colonel Silas Winchell was Alexandra's father, what was his relation to Highcliff? And what foul deeds had the man committed that such lengths were required to hide his presence in London when Alexandra would have been conceived?

Ignoring the curious stares of the other patrons, Effie rose and made her way to the exit, emerging onto the sidewalk just as Miss Clark stepped into the street. She was walking toward a gentleman across the way who had one of his coat sleeves pinned back, empty—the injury identifying him as the man Miss Clark had been waiting for to collect her home.

But Miss Clark never reached him. A carriage came rumbling forward, picking up speed with every inch as the coachman, swathed in black, hastened the team. She could see it coming, could see clearly what was about to happen right before her eyes. But even as Effie called out a warning, the carriage struck the other woman, sending her sprawling to the cobbled street. It was a sound Effie would never forget. Nor would she forget the frisson of fear that swept over her like an icy wind as she saw the curtains at the carriage window open slightly and a shadowed face peered out—at her. While the person's face was concealed, she could feel their eyes on her, she could feel the menace in that gaze. The dangerous position she had placed herself in became terrifyingly clear to her.

"Highcliff," she whispered. He'd been correct. She needed to warn him what she'd done—what havoc she had created.

Returning to her carriage, she called out an order to the driver. "Park Lane," she snapped. "And quickly. You know the address." Anyone who knew anything about her at all would know that she needed to get to Highcliff.

"Aye, miss."

With the carriage speeding off toward Highcliff's home, Effie spared a glance out the window. She could see the man still cradling Miss Clark's head in his lap as a crowd gathered round them. From the amount of blood that streaked her dress, it was apparent that Miss Clark was dead or so near it there was no chance of recovery.

"It's my fault," Effie whispered again. "I did this, and now I must repair it as best I can."

Chapter Fourteen

"What do you mean he isn't here?" Effie demanded of the aged butler.

"His lordship has not returned home," the butler stated simply, blocking the door to prevent her entry.

"Then tell me where he has gone."

The butler shook his head. "I cannot say, miss."

"Cannot or will not?"

"Cannot and would not," he replied evenly. "His lordship is very insistent that I never provide information to you about his whereabouts as he believes you would be likely to place yourself in a dangerous position."

"How long has he been gone?"

At that question, the butler's expression shifted into something that revealed the true nature of his feelings for his employer. Effie knew that every servant in Highcliff's employ was someone who loved him fiercely, someone whose loyalty was unimpeachable. But it wasn't just loyalty. It was love. The man loved Highcliff like a son. "He left yesterday, miss. Said he was off to his club and then to visit one of the gaming hells. But he should have been home by now. Would have been if things hadn't gone wrong."

Effie's heart simply stopped. When it began to beat again, the ache in her chest was unlike anything she'd ever known . . . except for when he left her the first time. "Who was he meeting?"

"Lords Ransom and Heathcote," the man said. "I shouldn't tell you these things. If he yet lives, he will kill me for it!"

"If he yet lives, I am his only hope," she replied. "Let us both pray that I am not too late." With that, she turned on her heel and left. It was time to ask for help from a very unlikely source. But first, she had to get Alexandra far from the city, just as Miss Clark had suggested.

<hr />

THE CELLAR WAS dark and dank. The hardpacked earth beneath him was cold and made his bones ache. Or it could have been that his body was still battered and near broken from his prior injury and the fever that had come perilously close to ending him. To have survived that only now to die in a dark, miserable hole would be a poor kind of justice. He laughed at that thought, the motion causing his split lip to bleed again. Details of his abduction were a bit hazy, but he knew he'd put up a fight.

Highcliff forced himself into a sitting position and scooted back against the wall, leaning against the damp stones. His ribs ached. His head ached. The still-healing wound on his abdomen had remained blessedly closed, but that didn't mean infection wasn't running rampant in his body. At least, he thought, he was lucid. Whatever he had been drugged with to start had finally worn off entirely. Naturally, they would have waited for that to begin their torture. Let them do their worst, he thought. He'd withstood torture before. He could again. He'd never betray his country, not for any reason. Nor would he betray Effie and Alexandra.

The door to the cellar opened. Highcliff waited. One step. Two. He counted the footfalls on each stair until he knew, even without the benefit of any light, how many steps it would take to reach that door. The first thing to come into view were flounced skirts. He'd known there was a woman involved. The smell of her perfume had been very distinct and very familiar. It had hit him the moment he stepped into Winchell's carriage—the last thing he could remember clearly. Then the cloth had been shoved over his mouth and he'd slipped into the darkness.

As she cleared the steep and narrow staircase that led down into the cellar, the glow of her lantern became more apparent. Then her face came into view. To say that he was stunned was an understatement. The woman before him looked remarkably fit for a corpse.

"Lady Marchebanks," he said. "Why aren't you moldering in your gave?"

She laughed softly. A tinkling sound that filled the musty air of the cellar. "I will be eventually, I'm sure. But it will not be due to an overabundance of laudanum. No, that was a wonderfully devised scheme that, unfortunately, necessitated the sacrifice of a very loyal servant. She'd been with me for ages. Pity. Good servants are terribly hard to find."

Highcliff struggled to reposition himself. It was a bit of artifice, exaggerating his weakness to make him seem less threatening. It was to his benefit for her to presume he was still terribly hindered by his injury. "And when you attempted to blow up half of the docks the other night? Was that a necessary sacrifice as well?"

She hummed a tune, a waltz, before answering in a childish, sing-song tone. "Necessary. That warehouse was supposed to be full of weapons, after all. We had to do something to disguise the fact that they'd all been stolen. It was quite enjoyable, as well, since it very nearly eliminated you. But I confess I'm pleased it didn't succeed—it would have been too quick. You need to suffer, Highcliff. You need to lose everything you love, just as I have."

"Hardly everything," he said. "The diamonds winking at your throat would beggar most people."

"Since you will never leave this cellar alive, there is no need to keep the truth from you. I did slip most of the jewelry out under Marchebanks' nose," she admitted. "My nephew never knew that I was slowly exchanging them all for paste. You see, I grew very bored with him over the past few years. It was time to move on."

"Lover, nephew—your understanding of familial relationships defies comprehension."

"I was his aunt by marriage only. It isn't nearly so tawdry as you imply," she answered with a blasé tone and a wave of her bejeweled hand. "But he's dead now, so it doesn't matter, does it? And I have had a new love in my life for some time... someone whose values are more in line with my own."

"Someone like Colonel Silas Winchell—traitor, opportunist, thief... murderer," he surmised. It had been the one piece he hadn't quite put together before she'd supposedly committed suicide. Who was their contact within the military? Who set up the buyers for them? "And I think you mean your lack of values, Margaret. I can call you Margaret? After all, I feel that I know you so well."

"You are very, very bright, Lord Highcliff. And so handsome. What a pity that I must make you pay," she smiled coldly. "You've been quite the thorn in my side, Highcliff. You have cost me a great deal of money and no end of trouble."

He lifted his bound hands to rest them on his drawn-up knee. "Not enough trouble, apparently, as you are still here and not swinging at the end of a rope with your name and face plastered all over the broadsides. Or, as the world believes, rotting in unhallowed ground."

She laughed. "No... I'm still here, Highcliff. I'll be here for a very long time. Certainly long after you depart this world. I would kill you myself but there is no profit in it. And I dislike the mess." Her head cocked to one side: weighing, considering, then she shook it very slightly, just enough that her artfully arranged curls bounced becomingly. "No. I've worked out something quite special for you. You see, you are quite right in thinking that our enterprise stretches far beyond

English shores. In fact, we've had a contact in France for decades, now. You've known him for years."

Her gleeful smile was a kind of warning. Whatever she had to say next, he knew it would be dreadful.

"Monsieur Bechard... perhaps the only person in the world who hates you as much as I do!"

Highcliff's heartbeat thundered loudly, the harsh tattoo briefly drowning out the sound of her voice. Yet, when he spoke, his voice was calm and composed, even jovial. "How is the bastard butcher? Still as grotesque as ever? I must say, Lady Marchebanks, for a beautiful woman you do keep very ugly company."

She approached him then, stooping over to look into his eyes. "I can't say how he is. We've never met face to face. Silas knows him though—and has for years. You know, Bechard is the one who actually got Silas into this little scheme?"

That was new information. "No. I did not know that."

She smirked. "Oh, yes. You know I did not start out to involve myself in treasonous plots, but it's been a family tradition for many years. The Marchebanks coffers would have been barren generations ago had they not been so flexible in their allegiance. My late husband was the one who initially knew about Bechard. And Bechard knew about Silas. Initially, we did go after Silas' elder brother, but he was a bit too honorable, too honest, and could have brought the whole thing down around everyone's ears. So he had to be eliminated, I'm afraid, and Silas was only too happy to do so as it would move him up in the chain of command. He is an ambitious man. It secured his position in Bechard's scheme and gave him a tidy bit of profit to set himself up well enough after the war was over."

"He's a traitor and means to take his place in the House of Commons as if he has the right to it," Nicholas snapped. The outrage wasn't feigned, but it was certainly exaggerated for her benefit. If she thought she was getting to him, she would keep talking.

"Yes. He will. Sadly, that will be the end of my own relationship with Silas. After all, I'm done for in London. But there are other places and other men. Tell me, Highcliff, is Bechard as ugly as all that?"

"He's a monster, and that has naught to do with his appearance," Nicholas answered with complete honesty. If she thought her feminine wiles would give her the upper hand with Bechard, then she was sadly mistaken. The man was cold through and through. Cruelty was not a tool he used but a pleasure he indulged.

Her smile widened to one of absolute glee as she, no doubt, imagined the torment he'd devised for him. "He remembers you very well. I heard that he was quite handsome before you ravaged his face with a blade. If you had marked my face in such a way, I likely wouldn't forget it either."

It hadn't been a blade but a broken bottle, and it had been the only weapon available to him. Neither of them had left that battle unscathed. Highcliff bore his own scars from it.

Realizing she'd lost his attention, Margaret boxed his ears, setting them to ringing, even as she spoke calmly. "I've sent word to him. I would say it has even reached him by now. No doubt by the dawn he will be on a ship set for England. When he arrives, I will be well compensated for delivering you to him for slaughter. But I'd have done it for nothing more than the satisfaction of hearing you scream in agony."

"He will kill me," Highcliff acknowledged. "But when he's done, he'll kill you. There is no amount of money that will stop him."

"Oh, Highcliff... has Miss Darrow so blinded you to the charms of other women that you cannot fathom I have much more to barter with than just money?"

"I know he has no compunction about murdering someone he knows even in such an intimate manner. You and any others who have involved themselves in this scheme of yours will be a liability to him that he will mitigate at any cost. If you think you can trust him, then you're a fool."

She reached out, her hand snagging his hair and tugging it back so fiercely that his head slammed into the stones. "Be careful, Highcliff. If I fear him, then I might just see you dead myself before I depart for warmer climates. At least this way, you have a day or so to say your prayers and beg for the Lord's mercy and forgiveness. For myself, I have none to give you. Remember that."

Highcliff watched her walk away, listened to her footfalls on the stairs. When she was at the top of them, she paused, then knocked softly. A moment later, the door opened and she exited. So there was another person standing guard. That was all he needed to know.

In the darkness, he went to work on the bonds that secured his hands. They were sloppy, tied hastily and without skill. It wouldn't take long to break free of them, though whether that would help him to escape his current hellish environment was debatable. But it would at least give him the option to fight back. And he had to. Because Monsieur Bechard knew his greatest weakness. He knew about Effie. And if Highcliff didn't get to her before Bechard did, Effie's blood would be on his hands.

From the Diary of Miss Euphemia Darrow, February 25th, 1814

I have had the strangest encounter. It is no secret that the house just across the street is one that is far from respectable. The gentlemen in various stages of inebriation going to and fro. The women who often appear in the early morning hours, walking home in their evening clothes—women who would never be mistaken for ladies. Everything identifies that house as one of iniquity.

And yet, this very afternoon, an unlikely looking butler who stated he works in that home has deposited a young girl into my care. His employer, a man he referred to only as 'the Hound', has offered to pay for the care and education of the now orphaned child of a rookery prostitute. I demanded from this butler, Mr. Stavers, to know if his employer was the child's father. The man actually laughed at me. Then he informed me that the Hound has a propensity for rescuing strays—dogs, children, servants. If I am willing to take on the child without asking questions about her origins, then the Hound will be a silent "patron", offering scholarships for students in need.

I cannot afford to refuse him. But if such an association were known, any respectability that my relatively new school has obtained would be lost in an instant. I am training these girls to be governesses for the finest families in society—offering them a chance to have not just the respect of others but to retain their own self-respect. That is, sadly, something that very few occupations will ever afford to a woman. It is imperative that the school, and I, remain above reproach.

What a tangled web it is that I now find myself in. But if I accept this offer, then my school will be independent of my father's support. I will not have to go begging with hat in hand for his aid to keep the butcher paid and coal in the bin. I debate with myself even now, as if the decision isn't already made. My father's support is not a certain thing, not if the Duchess of Treymore has any say in the matter.

The Hound and his bare-knuckle butler it is, then.

Chapter Fifteen

EFFIE ENTERED THE room that Alexandra shared with several other girls. She went immediately to the side of the young girl's bed and shook her awake. When Alexandra's eyes opened wide, Effie immediately placed her finger to her lips, shushing her. She leaned in and whispered. "Get your clothes and come with me. There isn't much time."

"Is everything all right?"

"It will be," Effie promised the child. "But do hurry. And try not to wake the others."

Moving as swiftly and silently as possible, Effie left the girls' room and made her way to her own. There, she retrieved money from the box she kept in her dresser. She also took a muff pistol that she kept hidden for protection. Louisa would be accompanying Alexandra to Strathmore House—the very house where Effie had been residing when first she'd met Nicholas. The older girl was very capable with a firearm, and as they were traveling alone, it would at least give Effie the illusion that the girls were safe.

He'd warned her, Effie thought. He'd asked her not to involve herself in the matter and to leave it alone. But she hadn't listened. Now a woman had been murdered before her, and Alexandra could be next. But how could she leave it alone when he was missing? Highcliff himself had disappeared, and even his loyal servant had given him up for dead.

"It's my fault," Effie whispered softly. "It's all my fault." She kept repeating that phrase again and again as she gathered up items of value and use for Louisa and Alexandra, and every time she said it, it felt more true. If she'd listened and stayed out of it, Miss Clark might still be alive.

Logic intervened then in the form of Mrs. Wheaton. The elderly woman entered Effie's room and took one look at the gun before crossing her arms over her ample chest. "There is enough noise in this house right now to wake the dead. What is the meaning of all this?"

Effie ignored the question in favor of practicalities. "Prepare some food to tide over Louisa and Alexandra as they travel to Strathmore. We must focus on getting them to safety."

"What has happened? And do not think to put me off," the housekeeper snapped. "I've known you too long, and I love these girls like my own."

Effie knew that, and it only intensified her feelings of guilt. Reluctantly, she admitted, "I've made a terrible error in judgement. Please do not say 'I told you so.' I've recriminations enough of my own." Effie paused to wipe away an errant and useless tear. "I must send Alexandra away. At least for a time. Her safety must be paramount."

"And what of your safety?" Mrs. Wheaton demanded. "And the child you carry?"

Effie shook her head. "I have it in hand, Mrs. Wheaton. Highcliff is not just ignoring me as I first suspected. He is missing. I've spoken with his butler, and it's been two days since he returned home."

"He's dead then," the housekeeper surmised. "He's dead, and your father will have to find you a husband if you don't mean to bring another bastard into the world."

Effie's head whipped around and she all but hissed in her anger at the elderly woman. "Is that helpful at all?"

Mrs. Wheaton arched one silver brow. "Yes. Because you need to look at the facts, Euphemia. You are no longer a young woman with a fortune. Your fortune has been spent caring for the bastards of others, and now you haven't the wealth or the youth that most men require in a bride. Little though you may know it, most of the funds that are used to support the girls in this house come from either Highcliff or the Hound. It's the only reason I tolerate them. I go to the butcher, and the bill has been paid. I go to the cloth merchant, and there is suddenly a massive credit on our account. How do you think those things happen?"

She wasn't so ignorant as all that. It had occurred to her on more than one occasion that they had anonymous benefactors, but for the sake of her own heart, she had not looked too closely. "Mrs. Wheaton, please! There is much to be done and little time in which to do it!"

"There certainly is! You've taken care of everyone else's children for long enough. 'Tis time you started to look to your own! Aside from the miracle of Highcliff being alive and willing to wed you or the assistance of your father in procuring a suitable husband, you have no other options available to protect your unborn child. Of the two, which is the most likely?"

The bare facts of it, laid out in Mrs. Wheaton's typically forthright manner, brought Effie to her knees. She sank to the worn rug, her hands falling limply at her sides—the money and the pistol hitting the carpet with a dull thump. Silent sobs wracked her, her shoulders shaking from the force of it. Tears streamed down her cheeks, hot and silent.

"I cannot accept that," she finally managed. "He cannot be dead. Not now."

Mrs. Wheaton shook her head. "Wanting it to be untrue will not make it so, my girl. You need to make your peace with it and look to securing your future. If you give birth to a child out of wedlock, the prospects of every girl in this household will be ripped away from them. Unfair as it is, it would mark them even more than their own parentage did, and no one would ever hire them."

The brutality of that particular truth had been pressing on Effie from the moment she had first realized the consequences of her improper behavior. It had weighed heavily on her every minute of every day. "Do you honestly think I do not know that?"

Mrs. Wheaton shook her head sadly, and when she spoke, her voice had gentled. It was almost kind, or as close as the woman ever came to it with anyone over the age of twelve. "I'm not certain what you know. The danger of men is not in the lies they tell us, but in the lies we tell ourselves for them."

With that last bit of parting wisdom, Mrs. Wheaton turned and exited the room. Effie was once more alone with her thoughts, alone with the all-consuming fear that she might have set something in motion that would destroy all of them. But there was no time to contemplate what might be. She had to take all necessary precautions to keep everyone safe, and that meant getting Alexandra far from the city and anyone who might mean her harm.

Effie dried her eyes then picked up the small pistol and the money once more, her hands trembling as she placed them in a reticule. All her effort and energy needed to be focused on mitigating the damage she had done. Getting Alexandra far from the city, getting her to a place where she could be safe and well-guarded—she had to concentrate on that above all else.

Making her way back downstairs to the main floor, she found Louisa waiting in the entryway with a sleepy-eyed Alexandra. Both clutched worn valises that held their clothing and personal items. She passed the reticule to Louisa. "The carriage is waiting outside. It will take you to Strathmore. Mrs. Wheaton is preparing a basket for you so you will have food for the journey. You must not allow anyone to see you. Do not go into any of the inns when you stop along the way. It is imperative that you both remain hidden at all times."

"What's happened?" Alexandra asked. "Why must I leave now?"

"Lord Highcliff told me not to interfere," Effie admitted. It was not the time for her to gloss over the truth. In order to keep them safe, they both needed to know the danger they were in. "He told me to let him handle things and I, foolishly in this instance, did not listen. When I did not hear from him, I elected to take matters into my own hands, and I've only muddled it all terribly. Now, I'm afraid that the man who is actually your father—a man who is apparently quite a villain—is alerted to your existence and will be searching for you. None of this was my intent—somehow, Alexandra, I will put it right. And until I can, I need to know that you are safe and far from trouble."

"My father wants me dead," Alexandra echoed. "I thought he just didn't want me at all. This is so much worse!"

"For now," Effie said. "But it will get better. I promise."

"How?"

Effie elected to be as honest as possible. "I'm going to ask someone for help . . . someone who isn't Highcliff. Because I think your father may have reasons to want him dead also."

"Who?" Alexandra demanded. "Who could possibly help us now?"

The Hound of Whitehall—an enigma of a man who ruled the shadowy recesses of London with an iron fist and frequently dropped rescued orphans and waifs at her door. A man who had a tremendous capacity for both kindness and cruelty.

"I'll look after her," Louisa promised when Effie remained silent, taking Alexandra's hand in hers.

Effie looked at the older girl and offered a grateful smile. Louisa was only seventeen, but she was quite mature. She'd been with Effie since she was a very young child, abandoned on her doorstep like so many. "I know you will, Louisa. You are very brave to do this. You are both very brave. I shall try to be just as brave and get all this sorted out and bring you both home as soon as possible." With that, Effie embraced them both and then ushered them out the front door. No sooner had it locked behind them than she was rushing to the back door and the garden beyond. She'd already sent a note summoning him, after all. It wouldn't do to be late. Not when she so desperately required his aid.

THE SMALL GARDEN behind the Darrow School was dark. Only the palest glimmer of light seeped from between drawn curtains to illuminate the space. As the Hound entered the garden gate, he could see Miss Darrow sitting on the bench, patiently awaiting his arrival. It was an odd thing for him to be summoned to a woman's garden in the wee hours of the morning. It was an odder thing still for him to comply.

When she glanced up, relief washed over her face, evident in the pale moonlight. "Thank you for coming." The words were expelled on a relieved sigh. "I wasn't certain you would."

"I've never received an invitation for a midnight meeting in the garden of a respectable lady. It amused me to see what prompted you to be so bold," the Hound replied softly. With Miss Darrow, he never slipped into the cockney accent he used with others. They had few occasions to meet, but he never wanted to frighten her. Not when she provided such a bastion of safety and gentility in the world. He maintained the illusion of a cultured and urbane gentleman in her presence. She did not need to know just how far from the truth that was. He admired her. In another life, another world, he might well have pursued more than simply friendship with her. In another life, she'd have been just the sort to tempt him to the altar. But in their present incarnations, she was not for him. And he most definitely was not for her. It was a thought accompanied by a pang of regret far greater than he might have anticipated.

"I rarely summon gentlemen to my garden, sir. And many would question your choice of words—I am hardly a lady." There was a great deal of self-censure in her tone and no small amount of embarrassment.

"Miss Darrow, I care not for the opinions of others. In my estimation, you will always be a lady. The circumstances of your birth will not change that, nor the fact that you have elected to make your life one of purpose rather than position."

She ducked her head, clearly unaccustomed to such compliments. "Thank you, sir. You are far kinder to me than I deserve. You may yet change your good opinion of me, however."

"My good opinion will not change, regardless of what I hear tonight. And, alas, we are both well aware that you did not request my presence here for a midnight tryst. Your affections have always been otherwise engaged. Regardless of the time or the location, we both know that this is hardly an assignation," he observed.

"You would not have come if it were," she said with a smile.

He ducked his head in acknowledgement. "I would not. But not for the reason you think. You are a beautiful woman, Miss Darrow, but not the sort a man dallies with. I have far too much respect for you and what you have done here to ever distract you from your calling. These children need you. And I believe, wholeheartedly, that you need them."

"You are kind to say so . . . but in light of what I must tell you, you may change your mind about my suitability for the role I have taken on. I need you to locate someone for me."

"Who?" There was no question that he would do it. Not for everyone, but for her and the children she had given a home to—for it was so much more than simply a school—he would always move heaven and earth to aid them. Likely because he wondered how different his own life might have been had someone like Miss Darrow taken him under her wing.

"Highcliff," she replied. "He was recuperating here after being wounded . . . but I have no notion of where he is now, and it is imperative that I find him."

The Hound laughed softly. "My dear, Miss Darrow, you need only wait. He can never stay away for long."

"Be that as it may, we cannot afford to wait. I've made a grave error in judgement, and it has already cost one woman her life," she admitted brokenly. "But there is far more at stake. My life, my school, my reputation—it all hangs in the balance, and time . . . well, it is of the essence."

There was silence for a moment. It stretched between them in the darkness as the implication of what she had said registered. "Highcliff has left you in danger . . . and in a *complicated* situation?"

"That is certainly one way of looking at it," she replied softly.

"I do not wish to cast aspersions by guessing, Miss Darrow. Speak plainly, if you please, without any fear of judgement from me."

"You are a man of the world, sir. Must I spell it out?"

"Yes," he stated emphatically.

"I am with child. And, before you think too poorly of him, he does not yet know."

The Hound laughed bitterly. "He knows it is possible. Beyond question, he understood the risk was present."

"He did know, but we are facing danger from many sides and in many forms. To protect us, he left my home far sooner than he should have . . . certainly far sooner than his injuries could safely permit. He was at a great disadvantage, and I fear the people who meant him harm knew that."

He grew quiet again, his anger palpable. "How can you defend him when he has placed you in such an untenable position? Miss Darrow, you are too forgiving for your own good. Were I truly a gentleman, I would call him out!"

"Please, you must understand that he is trying so very hard to see everyone safe and I have only managed to make the situation more dire for everyone involved."

"What I see, Miss Darrow, is that he has taken advantage of your tender feelings and seduced you. Now, he has abandoned you to bear his child alone while fending off the enemies he has cultivated in life!"

"No," she denied quickly. "In point of fact, he very specifically forbade me from involving myself in what he advised me was a very dangerous situation. Alas, I did not listen. As for the seduction—I pursued him, sir. Rather shamelessly. But that can all be addressed once we know where he is and that he is safe. I've had to send Alexandra away because I fear I have made a target of her, as well."

"Alexandra?" he asked cautiously. He knew the child's identity, of course. The moment Miss Darrow had returned to London with the girl, he'd known it. And unlike Miss Darrow, he understood exactly why Alexandra's presence in London was a danger to them all. He also understood how the child was connected to Highcliff—the girl was Highcliff's first cousin, their fathers brothers. And Miss Darrow could never know his own true relation to Highcliff. *She could never know that he was the bastard son of the Duke of Clarenden.* If she learned the truth, she would be compelled to do something horrible like try to make things right.

"A child I encountered while in Bath a few months back," Miss Darrow replied hesitantly. "When I returned to London, I brought her with me and have since installed her at the school as a special pupil, if you will. I had reason to believe that she might be Highcliff's child. I have come to realize that is not the case. She is not his child, but there is a familial connection, even if I do not fully understand what it is at this point. There can be no other explanation for why there is such similarity in their appearances."

Miss Darrow had been very busy, indeed. He'd known of the girl's existence for many years, but where she had been taken after her mother had sent her from London had been lost to him. But he couldn't afford to let Miss Darrow know that he had information she was not privy to. Now that he understood precisely who was involved, he could be a bit more forgiving of Highcliff's decision to vanish. Miss Darrow had wandered into a very dangerous situation and while he meant no harm to her, Highcliff (assuming his intentions were honorable), or his young cousin, they were key players in a game he had been playing for a very long time.

"I will make inquires and I will let you know what I discover. In the interim, Miss Darrow, I would advise you to remain as much in your home as possible. I will have more men patrolling the street and watching the house," he offered. "Where have you sent the child?"

"She and Louisa have left only an hour ago to Strathmore."

"I will send men to guard them . . . from a distance, of course."

"Why?"

"I'm sorry?"

"Why?" she repeated. "You have done far more than you are required to. Far more than anyone could expect or hope for. From the very moment you moved into that house across the street, you have looked after us in your way. I have found myself wondering why long before now. Please do not insult my intelligence by dismissing it as simply your desire to be helpful because you think my school serves a valuable service to our community. I've known for some time that you have an ulterior motive. I simply do not have any notion what it is. And, at this time, I'm not certain I can afford to refuse any offer of aid, regardless of the motivation behind it."

His lips quirked upward. Miss Darrow was a delight, truly. "Would an assurance that I mean no harm to you, Alexandra, and your Lord Highcliff suffice until I am at liberty to tell you all?"

She shook her head, rising to her feet once more to pace the length of the garden. "No. Because whether you mean us harm or not, I need to know that if it comes to a choice between your own aims and our welfare, that our welfare will take precedence."

It was a fair question and it only made him respect her more. She was good, yes, but not innocent. "Your suspicions do you credit, Miss

Darrow. You possess a singular intelligence that I find very admirable. And I promise to keep your safety and the safety of those you hold dear at the forefront of my objectives."

"That isn't what I asked," she pointed out.

"It is the best I can offer," he countered. "Do you still want my help?"

With her hands clasped before her, she nodded. "It isn't as if there are other avenues open to me. It will have to do."

"I must tell you, Miss Darrow, it is quite possible that Lord Highcliff—well, if he was as badly injured as you say, it might be too late to aid him."

"You think he's dead. You can say it. I've certainly thought it enough already," Effie admitted, her voice breaking on the word that held such terrible finality. More breezily, as if she weren't on the verge of falling apart entirely, she continued, "Mrs. Wheaton is so certain of it she thinks I should begin looking for other matrimonial candidates."

The Hound nodded, a subtle movement barely perceptible in the darkness. "She isn't wrong."

"I'm well aware of what may occur. No one knows better than I what difficulties an illegitimate birth can create for a person in our society. And I recall very well the pain my mother endured as a result of her position in society . . . as a fallen woman."

"You are not fallen, Miss Darrow. Half the women in the *ton* go to their marriage bed without the benefit of virginity. You, Miss Darrow, are simply caught. It's a very different thing and you should have no shame for it."

"But I do. Because I knew the risks and took them anyway— selfishly because that was what I wanted . . . to be with him in what I thought would be the only way I ever could. I risked my reputation, my livelihood, and the future of every girl who has ever been entrusted to my care."

The Hound sighed heavily. Comforting people was not his forte.

Under any other circumstances, he wouldn't have cared enough to bother trying. But he disliked seeing her hurt. He disliked seeing the ugliness of the world take some of the sparkle and verve from a woman he admired. So, he offered the only solace that he could. "I've seen him, you know. He would come here almost nightly. Sometimes he went inside. Sometimes he lurked in the garden. I think simply to be close to you. What is it, Miss Darrow, that makes him not simply offer for you when he is clearly in a position to do so?"

"The past," she answered sadly. "It's held him in its teeth for far too long. He is a better man than he believes he is."

"I hope, Miss Darrow, for your sake, that you are correct."

And then he did what he always did when he stayed too long in the world of people finer than himself—he vanished. Like a shadow, he slipped out of the garden, blending completely with the night. In so doing, he left her alone with her thoughts and fears that he knew would give her no peace.

Chapter Sixteen

Highcliff estimated that it had been at least twelve hours since Lady Marchebanks had revealed herself to him—live and in the very corporeal flesh. It was easy enough to understand why she'd done it. She was the sort who wanted to gloat, to revel in her pettiness and vindictiveness. It would be much harder for her to enjoy his fall if she believed him to be ignorant of her orchestration of it.

Church bells pealed in the distance. He counted them—it was five in the morning. Twelve hours exactly. He hadn't lost his touch. Despite the fact that his overly ornate and ostentatious pocket watch had been taken, along with the gold buttons from his waistcoat and coat, he hadn't lost the ability to accurately gauge the passage of time—a useful skill, given the nature of most of his previous missions. Before long, it would be daylight. Soon the faint gray light of dawn would begin to shine down on the dirty hovels and elegant mansions that comprised the breadth of the city's populace.

But his mind was focused solely on one particular home—a mansion from the exterior and a girls' school and dormitory inside. Effie's home. The place where they'd enjoyed late night brandies and chess matches. The place where he had kissed her so passionately in her study. The place where he'd remembered all the countless reasons that he had fallen in love with her the first time. The place, he thought, where he'd realized that no matter what passed between them, he would never be free of her.

And then it happened, what he'd been waiting for all night—dawn. In the dark, it had been entirely hidden, but with the first brilliant rays of the sun that penetrated, he could see that there was a lone, grimy window in that cellar. A single streak of light filtered through the glass, revealing its location in a pit that was otherwise entirely black. It would take some doing. The window was very high and very dirty. He'd have to feel his way toward it silently. In a dark and unfamiliar setting that would be difficult, but not impossible. Carefully, using the wall at his back for support, he pushed himself up to standing. *So far so good.*

They'd focused primarily on his face, blacking one eye and splitting his lip. But the drug Heathcote had slipped him had done most of the work for them, sparing him a truly horrendous beating. And apparently, Margaret Hazelton had not informed them of his recent injury—or she did not know of it herself. Regardless of the cause, he had avoided being punched in his already broken ribs and his stitches still held.

Inching his way along the wall, he placed his feet carefully, making certain there were no loose stones, no rubble, no refuse or detritus that would make even the slightest noise and give him away. When at last he reached the window, he shrugged out of his coat just long enough to rip the lining from it, then he put it back on. If he meant to convince them his hands were still bound, letting them see that he could remove his coat would be an error he could ill afford.

When he was done, he used the lining to scrub at the grime on the window. The view was limited but revealed a small and poorly tended garden. Patchy weeds and overgrown hedges marked it as having been left to ruin for some time. Carefully, he released the window latch and attempted to open it, but it wouldn't budge. It was either nailed shut or the wood was swollen from years of the house being neglected. But he recognized the area, he thought. It was a modest neighborhood on the edges of Mayfair. Not quite fashionable, but not completely beyond the pale. In short, he was close enough that he could probably make it home. *If he could get free.*

Cursing softly, he stooped to the ground and picked up dirt from the floor, smearing it over the window he'd just cleaned. No need to give away his one view to the outside. Moving back to the same spot he'd occupied earlier, the one where they had dumped him after depositing him in that cellar, he had just seated himself on the floor again when he heard the cellar door open. Quickly, he looped the ropes about his wrists, tucking the loose ends between his legs to camouflage the fact that he was no longer bound.

It wasn't Lady Marchebanks this time. Luckily for him, it also wasn't Bechard. Not yet, at any rate. But he would be coming. No, this time it was one of Margaret Hazelton's lackeys. The man carried a tray of food. It was the first sustenance he'd been offered since he'd arrived there.

"Bechard will be 'ere in three days' time," the man explained. "The lady of the 'ouse says we're to keep you strong and fit for 'im."

"Naturally," Highcliff replied drolly. "I would hate to disappoint him by not being in top form to withstand his torture."

"I can leave you to starve till then," the man said. "Makes no difference to me."

"No. I'll gladly take the food. Thank you," he said. If he could keep the man talking, he might find more information about who was in the house. "Did you prepare it yourself?"

The man laughed. "Do I look like a cook? No. Ain't slaving in no kitchen for you nor anyone else. The missus done it. Does all the cooking and cleaning while her brother and I do the heavy work."

Two men. One woman. It would be a mistake to discount her just for being female. He'd learned long ago that they could be just as deadly as their male counterparts, if not more so. And then there was Lady Marchebanks. If she was in the house. "I see. Have you been married long, then?"

"Too long," the man scoffed. "What's wiv' all the questions?"

"It gets a bit lonely down here," Highcliff answered smoothly. "A bit of conversation to pass the time is all. I've spoken to no one but Lady Marchebanks in what is it now . . . two days? Three?"

"Three," the man answered very helpfully. "She kept you insensible for the first day. Said it would make everyone's life easier till we could get word to the Frenchman."

The door at the top of the stairs opened. "Kenner, get up here! Quit talking to him, you daft bastard!"

"Now look what you've done," the man groused accusingly. "You've got me in trouble with me brother-in-law."

Highcliff gave every appearance of contrition as he murmured, "My apologies. It was not at all my intent. I will not keep you further."

The man, Kenner, grumbled under his breath as he made his way back up the steps to what he could only assume would be the kitchens. When he was gone, Highcliff shed his useless bonds once more and then began prowling the cellar. He needed something that would suffice as a makeshift weapon at the very least.

In the far corner, in the most shadowed recesses, he found it. The remnants of a wine bottle that had been dropped, by the thickness of the dust covering it, many years earlier. The upper portion of the bottle, still corked, had rolled beneath a shelf. Retrieving it carefully, he concealed it within his coat pocket. There was also a heavy stone, no doubt fallen from one of the many columns that supported the floor above him.

It would be another long day in the darkness, a long day of waiting. But when night fell, when the house was asleep, then he'd find his way out. And he'd be back for Lady Marchebanks and her compatriots.

THE HOUND WAS in his carriage parked outside the Bow Street office. It was just after dawn—the time he was normally seeking his bed. He waited, somewhat impatiently, for his trusted ally to emerge. The doors burst open in a flurry of activity and several Runners hit the streets in a jovial fashion. They'd been given their day's tasks, it seemed. After a moment or two, Ettinger appeared. More subdued than his compatriots, he stopped and looked around, observing the street for any signs of danger. When his gaze landed upon the carriage, the man sighed heavily before heading in his direction.

There was no hesitation as Ettinger climbed into the carriage. "I've told you I'm done," he said. "I can't do this job serving two masters. And our interests have diverged."

The Hound smiled but it was a grim expression. "They have realigned. Highcliff is missing."

Ettinger shrugged. "Toff is always missing. A man in his line of work has to."

"This is different. Miss Darrow has asked me to locate him. He was gravely injured and lacks his usual ability to defend himself . . . I fear he may have gotten himself into a very sticky situation," the Hound explained.

"And Miss Darrow asked, and you've never said no to a pretty face in your life," Ettinger replied. "Though normally they're more inclined to lift their skirts than Miss Darrow would be."

"I have no desire to get under Miss Darrow's skirts."

Ettinger cocked one eyebrow at that.

"I have no desire to get under Miss Darrow's skirts that I ever intend to act upon," he corrected.

"Now *that* I will believe," Ettinger agreed.

"Also, she's more than a pretty face . . . and well you know it!"

Ettinger sighed wearily. "Aye. I do know it. And not the sort to go into hysterics without reason. If she's worried, there is likely cause."

"Find out what you can—where he was seen last, who has spoken to him. It was a gaming hell, but which one remains to be seen. I'll be heading back to Mayfair and asking his servants what they have seen. Stavers will be looking as well. We all know he has his own talents in that arena," the Hound replied.

"Where did you acquire Stavers? I've always meant to ask," Ettinger murmured.

"He acquired me," the Hound replied. "When I was but a green lad."

"You've never been a green lad."

The Hound laughed. "You'd be surprised, Ettinger. You'd be surprised. Now, find out what you can. I'll do the same. You'll come to the club this evening just before opening."

"I have a job, you know. Cases that the Crown expects me to solve. And I can't do that if I'm spending all my time working on cases for you."

"I strongly suspect, given Highcliff's activities, that the Crown would be very forgiving of your shirking assigned responsibilities in favor of this particular quest."

"Bloody 'ell," Ettinger muttered under his breath, his accent slipping back into the cockney cant of his youth. "Fine. I'll do it. But not for you. For 'er."

"I don't much care why you do it," the Hound replied. "So long as it gets done."

From the Diary of Miss Euphemia Darrow, May 19th, 1809

The carriage was set upon by thieves. It is not an unexpected occurrence given these very dark and trying times. Poverty begets crime, and crime, unfortunately, begets more poverty when fathers and mothers are taken away to the gaol. But the thieves were routed. I am young, yes, and female. But that hardly means I must be a helpless victim. My mother, my father, and my very forward-thinking governesses taught me to defend myself, and I did so with all the ferocity I could muster.

Still, there was a hero in this tale. A young man on his way home from University. The second son of a duke. Tall, handsome, charming—and utterly perplexed when I did not need his assistance. Though his attempt at heroic intervention was a bit late and entirely unnecessary, I must confess that I found him intriguing. Very intriguing. Though I suppose I should simply admit it here. After all, no one else will ever read this. He was impossibly handsome. With his dark hair and well-hewn features, he was surely the most attractive man I have ever seen. And yet, I sensed a sadness in him. A loneliness, I think, that may match my own.

I know why I am lonely. I know that I am being banished here by my father, hidden away as a dirty secret. What is the source of his melancholy?

Chapter Seventeen

EFFIE WAITED UNTIL she saw the butler leave Highcliff's residence. It was terrible to be skulking about in the mews. Draped from head to toe in a black wool cloak, she had been lurking there for hours, waiting on the butler to depart on some errand or other. Unlike most upper servants in a household, because Highcliff kept such sparse staff, he often had to go to the market or butcher himself. And like all good servants, he never exited the front door. He always came out through the kitchen garden.

When he'd passed her, Effie gave him just enough time to get out of earshot before going directly to the garden gate. There, she let herself in, sticking close to the garden walls as she made her way around to the terrace door that led to Highcliff's study. She knew that he often came and went through that door, just as she knew that, by his own admission, he kept a key hidden behind a loose brick. Feeling her way around the door frame very carefully until she found it, she pried the brick loose, sacrificing a fingernail or two in the process.

With key in hand, she unlocked the door and slipped inside. Each step was cautious—quiet and careful. Not an easy task in a room that was dimly lit at best. Shadowed by the trees in the garden, very little light penetrated beyond the doorway. The fireplace was dark and cold, and none of the candles had been lit. It was quite clear to her that the butler had no expectation of Highcliff returning any time soon . . . if at all.

Ignoring the frisson of fear that snaked through her at that thought, Effie made her way to the desk and, with hands that shook, lit the single lamp that had been placed there. It was disappointingly neat and tidy. No helpful notes, no telltale scribbles in the leatherbound journal that rested on the blotter. In fact, the journal was curiously cryptic. The only notations in it were abbreviated to the point of being indecipherable. Or was it a code known only to Highcliff? Finding the latter to be more likely and knowing she hadn't the time to break the code before the butler returned, Effie slipped it inside the satchel she wore draped across her body beneath the cloak.

Systematically, she searched each desk drawer. Anything of note, of interest, or that she simply couldn't make sense of went into that satchel. She'd sort it all out once she was at home and the threat of discovery wasn't looming over her. The butler had never cared for her, she knew. He thought her impertinent and fast. Given the number of times she'd shown up unannounced and unexpected on Highcliff's doorstep, it was little wonder. As it was, she very much feared that if he caught her in Highcliff's study, with the temporarily purloined items in her possession, he would summon the Watch and have her carted away. She was facing enough scandal already without adding more to it.

In the first drawer, she found nothing of note. Extra quills and nibs, bottles of ink, Highcliff's seal and wax—typical items a man would have available at his desk. The second drawer was locked. Using a hairpin, she worked patiently to pick the lock—a skill one of her streetwise students had imparted to her. When the lock snicked softly, she opened the drawer and found weapons. A wide variety of them was laid out on a bed of felt. There were several pistols in various sizes, along with an assortment of blades. Dangerous, though not unexpected.

But it was the third drawer which gave her both answers and more questions. The first thing locked away in that treasure trove was a packet of letters. Letters, more specifically, that she had written to him many years ago. He'd never answered them, yet he'd kept each one. Based on the shabby state of the paper he had read them many times.

It embarrassed her to think of what was in those letters. The painful hopes and wounded feelings of her youth had been poured out onto those pages as she'd implored him to at least let her know if he was well. He never had. She'd spent the entirety of his time in the war praying for word of him, hoping against hope that he yet lived. And when he'd returned after his imprisonment—impossibly thin and pale with haunted eyes—she'd written once more. It was the last letter she'd written to him, as it too had gone unanswered.

Every one of them was there. Every last letter, read to the point of falling apart. The ink was faded, the paper creased and crinkled. There was dried blood on some of the pages, mud and dirt on others. Tied up in a length of black ribbon, they hinted at something more than just sentimentality. He'd kept them for a reason.

Digging further, she found the miniature he'd once begged her for. She'd commissioned it to be painted as a gift for her father, but after he'd banished her to the country, she'd chosen not to give it to him. Instead, it had been gifted to Highcliff for his birthday. The ornately carved trim around it was bent. One of the hinges was broken. A single fingerprint in either mud or blood smudged over the velvet backing. It had the look of an item that had been well loved, well carried, and travel worn.

"What are you doing, Highcliff?" she whispered softly. "How am I to ever know what you mean when everything you say and do is contradictory?"

There were other items in the drawer. Pressed flowers that she recognized as having come from Strathmore. Stones they had collected along their many walks through the grounds and parklands during that one magical summer. A small snuffbox held a lock of her hair that she had given him once. That small, locked drawer seemed to have served as a shrine to their shared and painful past.

It was impulse, but Effie grabbed those items too, as well as a small leatherbound journal tucked into the very back corner. Perhaps they would offer enlightenment about something other than Highcliff's whereabouts. Perhaps they might tell her what was in his heart and what was in his mind.

The front door of the house opened. She heard it squeak. In a house with so few servants, it was terribly quiet. Even the slightest noise sounded like a cacophony. Dousing the lamp, Effie then closed the desk drawer as quickly as she dared. Her breath caught at even the slightest noise.

When there were no longer outward signs of her pilfering, she darted toward the terrace doors. The study door opened just as she ducked behind the heavy drapes.

"Mice," the butler muttered.

From between the drapes, she could see him glancing about the room suspiciously. After a moment, he simply stepped out, the door closing softly behind him.

A relieved breath rushed from her with such force it left her feeling quite lightheaded. Leaning against the door frame for just a moment to regain her equilibrium, she then opened the terrace door once more and slipped out.

It was growing dark already, the blue of the afternoon sky fading into the gray of twilight. Keeping to the shadows near the garden walls, Effie made her way slowly and steadily to the gate. With one glance behind her to make certain no one was watching, she slipped out into the mews once more and headed back to her school.

※

IT WAS DUSK. His dinner had been delivered by the same man who'd brought him a meal that morning. There was no sound above him. The kitchens had grown quiet, a sure indication that the man's wife had finished her duties as cook. The last light would soon disappear, and the cellar would once more be nothing more than a black pit. It was now or never.

With his makeshift weapons, Highcliff made his way to that window. It still wouldn't open, but with the kitchen quiet, he could risk the sound of breaking glass. Shrugging out of his coat once more, he placed it against the grimy glass. With the stone he'd found earlier, he carefully knocked out one pane of glass at a time. He used just enough force to shatter each pane, one by one, until the crisp night air surrounded him, tamping out the fetid stench of that cellar.

Carefully, he wrapped his coat around the rough, glass studded wood to protect his hands as he began to force it upward. Slowly, with patience and far more care than he truly wished to employ, the window began to inch open. Every noise made him pause, every creak of the old house halted his progress as he listened intently for any sign that his actions had been discovered. But none came.

At long last, after applying a bit of leverage and ingenuity, the sash raised enough for him to make good on his escape. Hoisting himself up, he crawled through that narrow opening. Ignoring the broken glass that dug into his elbows and knees, along with the pain in his still injured ribs, he managed to get himself fully outside.

For a moment, he lay there on his back in the patchy grass, savoring the feeling of the cool, damp air as it settled over him. Staring up at the ever-darkening sky, not a star was in sight through the coal smoke that enshrouded the city. But there were no cloying smells, no dampness, no dank air to fill his lungs. It was all blessedly clean. Or relatively clean. It was London, after all.

Getting to his feet, he retrieved his coat from the broken window, but it was shredded beyond use. Still, he didn't wish to leave it behind. Tucking it beneath his arm, he went straight to the garden wall and hoisted himself over it. His feet had just touched the ground when he heard the hue and cry. His escape had been discovered. Crossing the patchy lawns and fallow gardens of several more houses, he came to one that appeared to be in greater disrepair. That meant fewer servants and less chance of discovery.

Winded from his exertions, he cursed under his breath as he made his way to the kitchen door of the house and found it unlocked. He ducked inside. There were only a few servants bustling about so he ducked behind a cupboard until they passed. He would conceal himself somewhere in the house until everyone was abed, and then he'd make his way home. He'd have a bath, a shave, clean clothes. Then he would get Effie the hell out of London. He'd send her somewhere safe. *Because Bechard knew about her. Bechard knew just what she meant to him.*

Easing his way across the corridor, he ducked into a storeroom and created a burrow for himself behind barrels of root vegetables.

"How the mighty have fallen," he whispered on a soft chuckle. "Saved by a bunch of turnips."

Chapter Eighteen

ETTINGER HAD FOUND what he needed. Servants at the gaming hell were keen to talk for a bit of coin. And he'd yet to meet a working girl in a bawdy house who couldn't be persuaded to part with her secrets for a guinea or two. It didn't hurt that they found him handsome. And most of them thought that a man in his position, a Runner, might be persuaded to make an honest woman of them for the right reasons. The gents and peers who were their customers might be above them, but a man in his profession was attainable.

If he'd been inclined to marry at all, he wouldn't have minded so much. But he had too many masters in his life already. Between Bow Street and the Hound, he didn't have time for anything else. There were barely enough hours in the day to eat and sleep, much less to please or appease a woman.

Settling back against the hard driver's seat of the carriage, he cursed Highcliff. He cursed the Hound. He cursed Miss Euphemia Darrow. Draped in a three-caped redingote with a worn beaver hat perched atop his head, he looked like any other servant in livery. And since the street was dotted with houses that the rich and powerful provided to their mistresses, a coachman waiting on the road for his employer was not an unusual sight, after all. It was, in that regard, the perfect disguise.

Shouting drew his attention. At a house midway down the street, the front door flew open, and a man came running out. It was obvious from the way the man was dressed that he was of the serving class, though likely not a servant in the true sense of the word. He was too rough around the edges, his clothing too coarse and, even from a distance, Ettinger could see that the man was far from clean. Even in such a middling neighborhood, any employee showing up in such a manner would be frowned upon. No, that was no servant, he thought.

Curious, Ettinger watched the man. His head swiveled side to side. He was clearly looking for something. *Or someone.* Then the man began to run. Down the street, pausing to look in gardens or between houses—his movements weren't furtive, at all. But they were panicked.

Highcliff, Ettinger thought. The man had clearly escaped, and his captors were now in pursuit. But he was smart and had likely gone to ground, which would only make Ettinger's task of getting him home even more difficult. Because now he had no idea where the bastard had gone off to.

"Bloody everlasting hell," Ettinger cursed softly.

Climbing down from the box, Ettinger traded the tall hat for something more nondescript and discarded the heavy, caped cloak. It would be easier to blend if he looked like someone who simply lived there rather than like a coachman far from his coach.

Keeping his steps leisurely, he traversed the street in the same direction as the other man. Perhaps the man had some inkling of where Highcliff had gone. Ettinger certainly hoped so. A wild goose chase was not how he wanted to spend his evening.

Rather than follow the man down the street, Ettinger did something a bit smarter. He ducked down a narrow alley between the houses to reach the mews. From there, he began peering over gates and fences, looking for any sign that Highcliff might be lurking there.

Peering over one back gate, he noted how derelict it appeared. Shutters were loose and hanging haphazardly. The garden had been left fallow for more than one season by its appearance. Opening the gate cautiously, he stepped inside, his boots crunching on the dry, dead grass.

Cautiously approaching the door, he knocked loudly. Only moments later, a portly housekeeper or cook appeared. "Yes?"

"Ettinger, ma'am, from Bow Street. I'm searching for a fugitive," he lied.

"Well, there are no fugitives here, sir!"

"The man is a slippery one. He eases into houses during the bright light of day while servants are busy with their work, conceals himself, then robs the place blind after dark when everyone is abed."

The housekeeper laughed, though it was a bitter sound. "What's left to rob? Ain't even been paid in months. Woulda left already, had I a place to go!"

Ettinger offered his most charming smile, "I'd feel better about your safety and the safety of everyone else in the house, madam, if you'd allow me to do a quick search."

The servant's eyes widened, and she brought her hand up to her throat, clutching it in that age-old gesture of self-protection. "Is he dangerous?"

Biting the inside of his cheek to keep from laughing, Ettinger answered solemnly. "Yes, ma'am. He can be very dangerous. Let me do my job, and then you may be certain everyone inside is safe."

She stepped back, opening the door wide. "You're not in a Bow Street uniform," she noted, suddenly suspicious.

"I'm a thief-taker, ma'am. We don't wear the uniform. Easier to catch the criminals if they do not see you coming," he explained with a wink.

The woman might have been old enough to be his mother, but she wasn't dead. That was made glaringly apparent when she blushed and giggled as she let him walk past her into the house. "It might be best if you make yourself scarce, madam. If there is a struggle, I would hate for you to be injured."

"Of course," she said. "I'll be in my room . . . just there. And I'll lock the door."

When she had gone, Ettinger began making his way through space, one room and one cupboard at a time. When he came to a storeroom, he opened the door and stood there for just a moment. He didn't have to look for Highcliff. He knew the man was there. Immediately.

"Are you coming out or must we keep up this farce?"

A second later, a barrel of some sort of unidentifiable vegetable shifted slightly. Highcliff's head appeared above the rim of that receptacle. "That all depends on who sent you here."

"The Hound, of course. Courtesy of Miss Darrow. Why she'd bother being worried about your worthless hide is a question no one can answer," Ettinger groused. "Are you coming out or do I have to haul you out?"

There was a bit of shuffling and then Highcliff rose to his full height. Dirty, disheveled, bloodied and battered—the man looked like he'd been through hell.

"Christ, where the hell have you been?"

"In a cellar," Highcliff answered. "A dank and dirty cellar. But there's much more to discuss than simply where I've been. More pertinent is who put me there. Margaret Hazelton lives."

Ettinger's eyebrows shot up. "Then who the hell is buried in her stead?"

"Apparently a loyal family retainer whose loyalty was not at all rewarded." Highcliff was brushing as much of the dust and dirt from him as possible. "And there's worse news still. She's been in contact with one of my oldest enemies, someone who will make anyone dear to me suffer as a means of making me suffer. And he knows about Miss Darrow. He knows how to find her. Her death would be nothing but sport to him, but he'd make her suffer terribly first."

"Do you have a plan?"

"I do. I mean to take Effie far from London, to take her somewhere that I can protect her. I will take her to Highview. The duke be damned."

"WHAT DO YOU mean he's gone?" Margaret Hazelton, Lady Marchebanks, all but shrieked at the men she'd hired to guard Lord Highcliff.

"There was a window in the cellar, my lady," one of the men admitted. "We never noticed it when we was down there because it was so dirty. 'Tis a wonder 'ow 'e found it in the dark. That was 'is escape route. Went over the garden walls and disappeared into one of the 'ouses on this street."

"Then search them," she snapped. "Search every last one until you find him!"

The man, hat in hand, shook his head. "We can't, m'lady. That would draw too much attention. You're supposed to be dead, after all."

She screeched. Her hand shot out, snagging a vase from a nearby table which she immediately threw with remarkable aim toward the man's head. Had he not ducked, she'd likely have killed him with it. Taking this job, working for her, had been a mistake from the start. But he was realizing now more than ever just how terrible that mistake had been. Vicious, stark-raving mad, and hell bent on vengeance was a dangerous combination.

"Find him," she hissed out through clenched teeth. "Find him and bring him back here. If he isn't here when Bechard arrives, we will all pay for it with our lives."

"Then maybe you should 'ave thought of that before you wrote to 'im."

Her eyebrows shot up and she turned the full power of her icy stare on him. "Do you know what Bechard means in French?"

"Never saw no need to learn the Frog tongue," he replied.

"It means Butcher. It isn't a name at all," she said warningly. "It's a title that he earned. He likes to slice up his victims . . . while they live. Small cuts, slivers here and there. At least that's how it starts. You see, he wants to know how much pain a person can tolerate before they break and beg for death. And I will be the first to let him know that you were the one who allowed Highcliff to escape."

"Now, see 'ere . . . it weren't like that. I didn't let 'im go!"

"It doesn't matter, does it?" she asked with a challenge in her voice. "I'll say whatever I must in order to save my own skin. If that means letting the lot of you pay the price for it, then I will. You have only one option—find Highcliff and bring him back before Bechard arrives. Or face the consequences."

He should have known better than to work for toffs.

From the Diary of Miss Euphemia Darrow, December 26th, 1816

It's Boxing Day. The girls, all eight of them now, have been given their gifts, small though they were. Bits of ribbon for their hair, mostly, and a doll for the smallest amongst them. They've all become very close, almost sisters in a way. They look after one another and it gladdens my heart to see it.

This was certainly never the direction I thought my life would take, but I am thankful that it has happened. It started as a whim—an impulse, really. But they give me far more than I give them. My days are not wasted pining for a disingenuous man. Instead, they are filled with purpose. I do not have a husband. And I do not have children of my own. But these girls are mine as surely as if I had given birth to them myself. I love them all so dearly, and that has been my salvation. As it has for Mrs. Wheaton, I think.

For this whole day we have feasted on the glorious treats that Mrs. Wheaton has made for us all. She spoils them but would deny it with her dying breath. We've never spoken much about her past, but I know her husband died many years ago and that she had one daughter, who is now also passed. Despite her often brusque manner, she has a heart of gold. I've seen it with every sad, broken child that winds up at our door. She showers them with food and love in equal measure, making them feel safe and cared for when most of them have never known such a thing.

In her own way, she does the same for me. Every time I speak to my father, or encounter his wife and my half-sisters, I come home in a black mood. She'll bring me tea and the special scones she always makes when someone is sick or hurt.

It was a blessing when she knocked on the door and announced that she'd heard of my school and that I needed a housekeeper. If it weren't for the Hound's generosity, I would not be able to pay her. As it is, I am still certain that I do not pay her what she is worth. May the Lord bless her for staying on for so little and giving so much of herself.

Chapter Nineteen

EFFIE HAD CALLED in countless favors. She had a total of ten students in her charge now, and, for their safety, they would all have to depart London. She'd sent round notes to all of her former students who were now married and established in households of their own. They would each be welcoming one or two of the girls into their homes until she was certain London was safe for them again.

For herself, she wouldn't risk going to Strathmore. Being in the same house as Alexandra would make them easier and more convenient targets. The last thing she intended to do for the monster who had murdered Miss Clark in cold blood was to make his goal more easily attainable.

As she tidied her desk, putting away the last of her stationery, she simply stopped, holding the paper in her hands. She couldn't say what it was that alerted her to the fact that she wasn't alone. He made not a sound as he entered the room behind her. And yet, Effie felt his presence. Instantly and with complete certainty, she knew that it was Highcliff. Whirling abruptly, she found herself face to face with him. His condition was positively shocking. It took her a moment to even formulate a response to his arrival. Relief, hope, agony at seeing the sort of pain that had been inflicted on him yet again—there were so many things. In the end, she elected to simply address the one fact that could not be denied or ignored.

"Well, you look just awful," she stated simply. It was true. He had fresh bruises on his face, a nasty cut on his hand, and he was streaked with dirt from head to toe.

"It's lovely to see you, too."

The caustically uttered phrase was nearly her undoing. She wanted to weep with relief and joy. She wanted to rail at him for putting himself in danger. She wanted to grab hold of him and never let go so that she would always know he was safe. In the end, she folded her hands neatly in her lap and spoke to him as if he were a misbehaving pupil. "Where have you been?"

"That is a very long story, and one that will be best told on the road. Pack. Whatever you need. I cannot say how long we will be gone. At least until I know you will be safe here in the city."

"I had already planned to go," she said. And then, with much more hesitation, she continued, "I made a mistake, Nicholas. A terrible mistake."

He stiffened, tension filling his body and making him appear larger, menacing even. Then he went still. "What sort of mistake did you make, Effie?"

"I went to Garraway's . . . and now Henrietta Clark is dead." Just uttering those words aloud, making that statement, left her feeling hollowed out from grief and guilt.

"She would have died anyway," he said. "The people who want Alexandra's origins concealed—the same people who want me dead—would leave no stone unturned, Effie. I found her initially by following them. They led me to her. If her death is on anyone's conscience, it should be on mine."

She shook her head as she turned to place one more item into her bag. After all, leaving the school did not necessarily mean leaving all her work behind. "No. You have enough on your conscience already. You told me to leave it alone—to stay away from her and let you handle things. As always, I presumed to know better. I failed to heed your warnings, once more refusing to accept any boundaries set by a man, even if they were set for all the right reasons. I—well, when I hadn't heard from you, I decided to take matters into my own hands. It was pride that sent me after her when I had been told not to interfere, Nicholas. And she paid the price for it."

"I cannot offer you solace," he said. "I am too filthy to touch you. But I can tell you that it is absolutely not your fault. Of course, I could tell you that from now until eternity and it would make no difference. You, Effie, have always had an overly active sense of responsibility." He paused. "It's one of the things I have always loved about you."

Her heart thundered, beating so fast that it made her feel faint for just a moment. By the time she had settled her nerves and could turn back to face him, he was gone. He'd left as silently as he'd entered. His words had rocked her to her very core. Did he mean them? But then, he hadn't said he was in love with her. He had said he loved her. There was a difference and well she knew it, because she had been in love with him for most of her life.

The room felt so empty when he was not in it, so Effie exited her study and made her way upstairs to her chamber. There was still much to be done.

Moments later Mrs. Wheaton came in. "He'll be back shortly. I don't like you going off with him. But I'd like it even less if you stayed here and something horrible happened to you."

"I'm not going alone, Mrs. Wheaton. You are coming with me. I will not leave you here to face these murderers alone!" Effie protested.

"I'll have the Hound across the way to help . . . and Mr. Stavers."

There was something in the way the housekeeper had said Stavers' name that alerted Effie. "Mrs. Wheaton? Are you . . . are you involved with Mr. Stavers?"

"What Mr. Stavers and I are, Miss Euphemia Darrow, is none of your concern. You might pay my salary, but we both know that you are not now, nor have you ever been, the boss of me," the housekeeper snapped.

"You mistake me, Mrs. Wheaton. It is not censure, at all. I like Mr. Stavers. I always have. He looks rough, certainly. But he's always been kind to me. I've yet to see him when he passes one of the girls on the street that he doesn't offer them a sweet or a coin. That man may have spent most of his life battling with nothing but his bare hands, but he's a kind heart and a generous nature."

Immediately, Mrs. Wheaton relaxed. "Well, then... we are friends. I've never agreed to be more than that with him though he has certainly asked. Though at my age, there's very little risk," she said. "You'll be going off with *him*, and there'll be no hiding the truth about your condition. He'll know soon enough. And if doesn't, he's more of a dullard than ever I took him for."

Effie sighed wearily. "I know all of that, Mrs. Wheaton. I will worry about it when it happens. Right now, we have enough to worry about without adding more problems to the situation. I'll deal with that later."

Mrs. Wheaton shrugged. "He has a right to know. Whatever else I may have to say about the man, he has a right to know."

"He will, Mrs. Wheaton—when I am ready," Effie snapped. "Can you not leave this be?"

"No, I cannot. You're like my own daughter. I've taken care of you and looked after you as I wish I had done for her," Mrs. Wheaton stated. The words were infused with the woman's own brand of affection. Never effusive but always sincere. "He's hurt you. And I daresay you've hurt him just the same. But it's not about the two of you now, is it?"

With that final parting shot, Mrs. Wheaton turned and left the room, leaving Effie alone with her tumultuous thoughts.

They'd never been at odds so much. In all of her life, Mrs. Wheaton had been a bastion of safety and security—always there with a warm hug and some sugary treat from the kitchen. But now, it seemed that any time they spoke more than a word to one another, they were in a disagreement.

"Why can't life ever be simple?" she asked, sinking onto the edge of her bed.

There was no answer, of course. Only more questions and an endless amount of turmoil.

―――

HIGHCLIFF BATHED QUICKLY and dressed in clean clothes. Even as he did so, his butler, and sometimes valet, was packing a bag for him. Normally, he would have seen to the task himself, but time was of the essence. It was a full moon. That would allow them to travel through the night. It would take three days to reach Highview, and there would be a battle once he got there.

The last time he had spoken to his father had been the day he left to join the army. *The day he had left Effie and all his hopes and dreams behind.* He'd been told never to darken that door again, and he had not. But the situation had changed since then. He was no longer the younger son who would not inherit. He was, despite his suspect paternity, the heir to the dukedom. No one would bar him entry as the future duke when the current duke was a bedridden invalid. If they tried, they'd soon enough find themselves seeking a new position, and sooner rather than later if the gossip about the duke's health was to be believed.

"My lord, your things are ready," the butler intoned. "Are you certain this is the best course? It is very unlike you to run from a battle."

"This is not a battle. It is an ambush. They will be hiding around every street corner, lurking in every alley, and I am not their only target. They will come after anyone who is close to me. To that end, you and the other servants need to depart. There are funds in the study—the normal hiding spot—to get the lot of you to wherever you wish to go."

"For how long, my lord?"

"For as long as it takes. Use those funds as you see fit. I know you'll take care of the others," Highcliff said. His life as he knew it, his life in London, was over. He doubted very much that he'd ever come back to that house. If his presence at Highview didn't kill the duke, then nothing would. The son of a bitch would live forever out of nothing but spite.

Another of his few servants knocked on the bedchamber door. "The carriage is ready, my lord. And Mr. Ettinger has sent several guards over to ride with you out of the city."

"Excellent," Highcliff said with a nod, "I'll be down momentarily."

Alone with Highcliff once more, the elderly butler looked at him. "I have been with you since you returned from your imprisonment my lord. I have kept every secret. As you have devoted your life to the Crown, I have devoted mine to you—I know that I owe you my life. I implore you to let me accompany you."

"I cannot do that. Because if the worst happens, I need you to inform the Crown about all that I have discovered and cannot yet prove," Highcliff insisted. "Tell them about Margaret Hazleton's ruse, tell them about Bechard. And tell them about Alexandra . . . that if her mother and father can be identified, they will know the name of their traitor."

The butler nodded solemnly. "I will, my lord."

Highcliff nodded, more to himself than to the servant. Then he picked up his bags and made for the stairs and the waiting carriage. As promised, there were several armed outriders—enough that anyone intending to waylay the carriage would have second thoughts about the matter. He would fetch Effie and then be off to Highview and their very uncertain welcome.

Chapter Twenty

EFFIE WAS SILENT as the carriage rumbled along. There were too many jumbled thoughts clouding her mind for her to give voice to any of them. He'd left her all those years ago, without a backward glance—or so she'd thought at the time. Now, with his admission that he loved her and her discovery of the letters and other mementos of their past, she was beyond confused about him.

"You're thinking very loudly," he noted.

"Why did you tell me that you loved me?" Instantly, she longed to call those words back and her evaporating pride with them! It galled her to sound so desperate and needy, even if that accurately reflected her feelings for him. But more than ever, it was imperative that she know the truth of his heart—before she shared with him her own damning truths.

For the longest time, he remained silent, not saying anything at all. When he did speak, the words were uttered softly. So softly that she had to strain to hear them.

"Because I do love you. Because, despite every effort to the contrary, I have always loved you."

"What does that mean precisely?"

He shook his head in a gesture of frustration. "What the bloody hell does it ever mean when a man says that he loves a woman?"

"It could mean any number of things," Effie snapped. "It could mean that you care for me. It could mean that you hold me in the same affection one would a sister or a cousin. It could mean that you value my friendship. Loving someone and being in love with someone are dramatically different things and you owe me some sort of clarification regarding which camp you fall into."

Effie had no warning. He simply grabbed her and hauled her across the expanse of the carriage until she was completely wrapped in his arms. Had anything ever felt so right? No, she thought, it hadn't. After all they had been through, the anger and resentments, the fear . . . to be held by him again was simply miraculous. The heat and strength of him that flowed into her, shoring her up when she'd felt so desperately uncertain before, was a thing of beauty. "You have been my friend . . . but so much more. And I have never considered you a sister."

Effie graced him with an arch look, her brows rising imperiously. "You're taking liberties."

"You're giving them," he shot back. And then there was no more talking. His lips touched hers, moving over them in a masterful way that left her breathless and flushed.

How could he do that to her with only a kiss? How could he have her desperate and wanting, ready to throw away everything she knew to be right and proper for a chance to once more feel the pleasure he could give her? It was that recklessness he inspired in her, that willingness to throw caution and commonsense to the wind, that had put her in her current delicate condition.

"No," she finally said, pushing away from him. That little bit of distance was just enough to provide a reprieve.

"No?"

"No," she repeated. "Things between us are far from settled. Giving in to our baser urges would only complicate matters. We need to talk, Nicholas. Not compound our mistakes."

"Eighteen years without you were the only mistake I made, Effie. I was a child when I left . . . a child desperate to protect you the only way I knew how. I had to give in to my father's demands that I join the army. And I didn't want you to be hurt. I didn't want you to sit there waiting for me when I knew that I would likely never return."

"Your father's demands?"

Nicholas sighed. "You had to know that I would not have left you that way by choice. At the very least you must have suspected that it bore the mark of his hand. If I hadn't left, if I had not entered the army as he demanded, Effie, I cannot say what he would have done to you."

"So you caused me pain in order to spare me pain," she surmised. "How daft are you?"

He laughed at that, as she would have expected him to. But there were clearly things he had not told her. Things he would not tell her.

"It sounds foolish to you, I know. But I had reasons for what I did, Effie. Reasons that I cannot explain to you. But everything I have ever done, I have done to keep you safe. Can you trust that?"

"No. I cannot. You ask for blind trust, Nicholas, when you are unwilling to give me the same."

"You're wrong. I trust you. I trust you more than any other person in the world. I know you would never betray me . . . but you are my greatest weakness. If any person truly wished to destroy me, they only need to come after you."

Effie heard the fear in his voice. It was a fear that she understood. On the cusp of all they'd ever wanted, the fear of losing it became all the more profound. "Nothing will happen to me, Nicholas. I will be fine."

"I know you will. I have my own emissaries and network of people who will aid me in keeping you safe," he said. "And I'm tired of running, Effie. Tired of hiding behind this bloody mask and pretending to be something I am not while everything I want slips through my fingers."

"Aren't we running now?"

"No," he answered with a cold resoluteness to his voice that was positively terrifying. "What we are doing now is choosing the location of our battle. London offers too many hiding places. At Highview, anyone who does not belong will be immediately noted and dealt with. There is no anonymity for our would-be attackers there."

It was a sound strategy, one that made perfect sense. She should have known that he would have a good reason for his choices. "Then we will not run," she said. "We will not hide. Whatever comes at us—whoever comes at us—we will face them head on."

"And will we face our very complicated history head on, as well, Effie?"

That was a question Effie did not wish to answer. Indeed, it was one she could not even begin to consider in that moment. There were too many things still unknown and far too many things outside of their control to make plans for their future. Instead, she disclosed the other pertinent information that she had gained from her meeting with the poor, unfortunate Miss. Clark.

"I have to tell you about Miss Clark," she said, the horror of that sight washing over her again. "About what she told me... about Colonel Silas Winchell."

"I know about Winchell's involvement with the traitors. He and Lady Marchebanks were lovers for years and he's long been on my list of suspects. Rather I had suspected him. It was confirmed when I was abducted from the gaming hell with the aid of Lord Heathcote. But I don't know what his involvement is with Alexandra," Highcliff mused, clearly puzzled by the man's keen interest in a young girl of low birth and little consequence.

Effie reached for her reticule. She'd found a copy of a portrait of the Colonel in a political pamphlet and handed it across to Highcliff. Though the similarity between Highcliff and Alexandra was stronger, it was clear that there was a familial connection between all of them. "Do you not see it?"

"What?"

Effie shook her head. "He is Alexandra's father, though not quite old enough to be yours. She and Louisa are at Strathmore now. I sent them there after my meeting with Miss Clark. But the question remains, Nicholas, who is Winchell to you and what threat does Alexandra's existence hold for him?"

"I don't know," Highcliff answered "But I will find out. Whatever it takes."

⁂

SILAS WINCHELL STARED at the woman before him, his temper rising rapidly. "You had one task, Margaret. Just one. Keep Highcliff locked up. How could you have failed at it?"

"I did not fail. It was those idiots you hired! They missed a window in the cellar, Silas. It was apparently so dirty they never noticed it when they searched it. And yet, with his hands bound and sitting entirely in the dark, Highcliff managed to locate it and utilize it for his escape," she snapped the last words with a very distinct bite. "I'm not any happier about it than you are! He ruined my life and I want him to pay for it."

"We can't afford petty revenge. He and the girl need to be eliminated."

"Bechard—"

"Bechard be damned! His need to best Highcliff is less important than my need to secure my position in Parliament. If anyone finds out about Alexandra—or about her mother—then everything I have worked for will be lost!"

Margaret, as if seeing that she might have finally pushed him too far, leaned in and trailed her fingers lightly over his shoulders, then down to his hand. When she lifted his hand, she placed it on the swell of her breast. "Let's not fight about all of this, darling. I want you to win your seat in the Commons. You will have the power and position you have always desired, and I will begin my new life on the Continent. This plan can still be salvaged!"

He jerked his hand away. "For that to happen, Margaret, I need to be presented with Highcliff's body, the whore's, and her whelp's. That's the only way. If they are all dead, there is no one to say that I left my company in France and returned to England. Given their resemblance, everyone will assume the child was Highcliff's... and based on the date of her birth, there will be no other conclusion to be drawn than that *he* was both a deserter and a traitor."

"Where do you think he's gone?" she asked, her tone petulant. It was clear that her pride, if not her feelings, were hurt by his rebuff.

"He will have gone to the Darrow woman. His obsession with her has grown quite apparent. But they will not stay in London. He will take her somewhere that he will feel safe. I just have to figure out where that is."

"He had a falling out with his father. They haven't spoken in decades," Margaret replied thoughtfully.

"I need to know where he is, Margaret. Not where he isn't!"

She smiled coldly, her eyes gleaming with wicked delight. "If he goes to his father's estate, given that the duke is even now on his deathbed, no one would dare turn him away. After all, in very short order, the title and all of the holdings will be his. Where else would he go but to a place where everyone will be loyal to him out of fear of losing their positions?"

"Are you certain?"

She laughed. "Of course not. It's a guess. An educated one, but still a guess. However, at present, it's the only one we have."

"Where is Highview?"

Margaret grinned. "North of Coventry, along the road to Leicester."

"We'll leave in the morning," he said. "But if you are wrong—"

"He will go someplace familiar... someplace isolated and easily defendable. Not only that, but as I understand it, the estate that Miss Darrow's father essentially gifted to her borders Highview."

That sparked a bit of hope in him, a tiny glimmer of it in an otherwise bleak outlook. "Then let's go get them."

"No," she said. "We'll let Bechard get them. You can keep your hands clean and we can appease our French friend all at the same time."

He leaned forward and took her chin between his thumb and forefinger. "What a devious little minx you are, Margaret! But if you're wrong, we will both pay with our lives. Bechard will kill us or we'll swing for treason. Either way, we'll be rotting in boxes."

"I'm already rotting in a box," she replied, a note of censure in her voice. "Well, someone is, and her stone bears my name, doesn't it? I've already given you my life. I lost everything for this scheme you started. Name, position—all of it. Anything that mattered has been sacrificed for your greed."

"And yours. You certainly never complained about the source of the coins in your pocket," he snapped.

"No. Coin is necessary, after all. Its origins are of no importance. I will never live in the kind of penury that I endured my first year of marriage while my husband squandered my marriage portion at the gaming tables. Poisoning him was the best decision I ever made." Her expression shifted into something shrewd and even threatening as her gaze roamed over him. "Pity it only left him an invalid and did not leave me a widow... at least not immediately. I'll not make that mistake again."

"Is that some kind of threat? That your slow murder of your husband could now happen to me?"

"It's a warning," she said. "I won't be spoken to in that manner. Not by you or anyone else." She stepped away from him then, moving toward the door. When she reached it, she looked back at him over her shoulder, "I'm not capable of love. That's something we have in common. Both of us will do whatever is necessary to survive and to do so in relative luxury. I'd sell my own mother if it meant not being poor and having to wear drab, ugly clothes. And I have something to bargain with when it comes to Bechard that you do not."

He scoffed at that. "Do you really believe that, as appealing as they are, your charms will keep him from slitting your throat?"

"Any man can be led around by his cock," she stated. "You certainly were." Then she simply walked out, the door closing behind her.

She'd betray him to Bechard. That was apparent. Unless he killed her first. It was a pity. He had enjoyed her—not despite her avaricious nature but because of it. Alas, it would be the very thing that brought about her end.

Chapter Twenty-One

THEY HAD TRAVELED as far as they could the previous night. But even with a full moon overhead, it had been slow going. It had been just a few hours before dawn when they finally stopped at a coaching inn and procured a room for the night. Effie had balked when he said they would be sharing a room but, when he pointed out that one woman was already dead, she'd relented. He hated to see her frightened, but he also needed to keep her safe. That could only happen if she allowed him to remain close enough to her to guard her, at least until they reached Highview.

Turning over on the hard floor, where Effie had put him the night before rather than allow him to share her bed, Highcliff winced at the pain in his side. The wound was healing, but the muscles underneath were still tight and sore. He wasn't at his best and he knew it. Unfortunately, so did the people responsible for his injuries. They'd know how vulnerable he was and how vulnerable that left Effie.

There was a commotion in the inn yard below their window. From the clatter, he could only assume it was the mail coach coming through. They'd change horses and be off. But the noise had roused Effie. She rolled over in the bed with a groan. Before he could even say a word, she was flying out of the bed, her hand over her mouth as she dashed behind the screen.

"You're ill," he said.

"I'm not ill," she answered, after she'd finished retching.

"You are! You are positively green with it, and I know damned well it isn't from too much brandy," he snapped.

She emerged from behind the screen, clad only in her nightrail with her long, auburn hair falling over her shoulder in a fat braid. "I'm not ill, Nicholas. I hadn't wanted to say anything. Not yet."

"Say anything about what, dammit? Effie, if you're sick—"

"I'm with child."

The words reverberated inside his head. He knew what they meant, but they still made no sense to him. It was a concept so far beyond his capability to comprehend that all he could do was shake his head.

"I've no expectation of you," she continued. "I knew the risks, after all, when I—well, when I behaved so improperly. And I'm prepared to live with the consequences on my own. I know it will change things. I know that it will be difficult, but there is no one better equipped to teach a child born out of wedlock how to navigate this world than I am."

"Stop," he said.

"Stop what? Worrying? Thinking? Planning for my future and the future of my child? I can't do that, Highcliff."

"Effie, I need a moment . . . a moment just to think," he said. "Give me that and then we will discuss it."

"There's nothing to think about. You are not responsible for this. I did it."

He snapped then. "You didn't bloody well do it alone, now did you? You've clearly had time to adjust to this knowledge whereas I have been taken completely off guard. Sixty seconds, Effie, of quiet, so I can think. That's all I ask."

The moment he said it, he knew that it had been the wrong thing to do. No one knew better than he did why there was no greater sin in Effie's mind than abandonment. After all, every person she had ever depended upon in her life had abandoned her in the past, himself included. From the way her face paled to the rigidity that suddenly infused her spine, he knew she had not seen his request as being for a moment's reprieve. She expected him to bolt and leave her behind once more.

"Effie," he reached for her, but she pushed his hands away.

Instantly, she whirled on her heels and began marching toward her valise. There, she began yanking out a clean traveling dress and her stays. "Take all the time you require. I will procure other transportation today and join Alexandra and Louisa at Strathmore. I am not so foolish as to think I can protect us entirely on my own, but you can certainly coordinate protection efforts from the neighboring estate."

Highcliff scrubbed his hands over his face. He no longer felt like he'd taken a punch to the gut. The shock had subsided just enough for him to really look at her. He could see the proud jut of her chin, the stiffness in her spine and the rigid set of her shoulders that told him she was waiting for him to disappoint her. She was waiting for him to leave her—because he had a history of doing just that. Yes, he'd had his reasons, but she didn't know what they were. And he realized that for her to ever forgive him for walking away, she needed to know why he had.

"When I left you that day, all those years ago, I was cold and cruel. Callous, even . . . as if your feelings didn't matter. It gutted me to hurt you that way, but I felt that I had no choice in the matter. If I hadn't walked away from you when I did, my father would have had you killed. He told me so plainly. I had no money, no skills really with which to protect you. I was a younger son then, with no prospects and no power."

"He was that adamant that you not shame the family by marrying a bastard?"

"No," he admitted. "He hated me so much that he would have done anything to deny me a moment's happiness. It was never about you. It was about having a way to hurt and control me. I told you that you were my greatest weakness. I know that without question because I know what it's like to be faced with the knowledge that I have no way to protect you."

"Did it ever occur to you that I can protect myself?"

"Not against him. Not against the hundreds of men he threatened to hire to see you dead—there was no way to protect you from that threat then. But now... now I have the means to do so. And he doesn't control me anymore. He doesn't deserve the satisfaction of keeping us apart. I had already decided that I wasn't going to let you go again, because I've spent my life loving you from a distance and that has never been enough. But now, knowing that you are carrying a child—*my child*—Effie, there is no power on earth that will ever take you from me. I will follow you to hell if I must."

<hr>

EFFIE HAD NO response for that. Not because it didn't warrant one and not because she didn't wish to give him one. But when he uttered the things she'd longed to hear for so many years, the things she'd wanted—that she had craved—it simply left her speechless. It terrified her. The first time he'd left, she'd ached for him every day. Her heart had broken a thousand times over. What if he left again? What if the reality of being together never matched the romantic fantasies that she'd built in her mind? There were so many things to fear. And that was all laboring under the assumption that they would survive what was to come.

"Please do not say things like that," she whispered. "Do not offer me things that you cannot give me."

"I can. I will," Highcliff stated emphatically. "You trust me to keep you safe. Why can't you trust me to love you?"

"Because some things are worse than death. And having you break my heart all over again is one of them," she admitted, ashamed by the quivering of her voice as she did so. "I didn't scream or cry. I didn't fall down wailing as I tore at my hair. But inside, I felt so cold and so alone. My father had abandoned me and so had you. I was empty. Hollowed out and just broken by it... until I found Lilly and Willa. The need to protect them, to raise them with the kind of love and support that I had not been given—or that had been given and taken away—gave me a reason to get out of bed every morning. They brought joy back into my life. Those girls gave me purpose when I had none left."

Effie turned away abruptly. The tears she'd held at bay for so long were threatening to swamp her. She didn't want to cry but more specifically she did not want to cry in front of him. And there was so very much to cry about. Wasted time. Wasted years. The fear that, if she allowed herself to love him fully once more, fate would intervene and take him away again.

Then she felt his warmth behind her, and the weight of his presence surrounded her. It felt so tempting to give in, to simply lean against him and forget about the risks.

"Effie, I can't make the past go away. I cannot, as much as I may wish, wipe away the years and the loneliness we have both endured. You were never far from my mind. I ached for you. Every single day. I believed I was doing what was best for you—I believed that I was keeping you safe by keeping my distance. And then Devil came to me for help. When I saw you at their wedding, I knew then that it couldn't continue."

"You barely spoke to me. Even when we were alone in the carriage," she said accusingly. "Getting a word out of you was like squeezing blood from a stone."

"Because I was trying to hold the flood gates. If I'd said anything, I would have said too much. This mess with Margaret Hazelton and Silas Winchell... it's been building for some time. I cannot leave the service of the Crown and Whitehall until it is done, but they are all aware that this is the last mission I will undertake for them." He stopped then, his gaze locked on her fiercely and his expression hard. When he spoke again, his voice rang with conviction, "Before Bath, before Alexandra, and long before I knew about the child you carried, I had already taken the steps to free myself from this wretched half-life I have been trapped in for years."

"Why?"

Highcliff's answer was little more than a whisper. But that did not rob it of any of its power. "Because I want to be with you. Because I want a life and a home... I want to love you in full light instead of from the shadows."

It was so strange to dream of a thing for so long and then have it suddenly right before her. The words he'd just said to her were both everything she wanted and everything she feared all at once. For most of her life, she'd managed to convince herself that she had misread his intentions, that she'd seen more in his words to her than truly existed. But now, faced with such a confession, if things fell apart once more, she knew she would not be able to put the pieces together again. It would be her ruin, her destruction. "You are offering me now what I needed you to offer me all those years ago. I have a life, Nicholas, and obligations. I cannot meet the obligations of headmistress and wife at once. Though, to be fair, if I give birth to an illegitimate child, my position as a headmistress might be forever altered."

"I have no wish to take anything from you. I will do whatever it takes... no matter how unconventional our marriage might seem to others."

"Marriage?"

"What did you think I was talking about?" he asked. "The stakes have changed now. It's no longer just the two of us to consider. The world is a very unkind place for those born on the wrong side of the blanket. No one knows that better than we do. You've borne that stigma publicly while I had the luxury of bearing it in private."

Effie shook her head. "I would hardly call it a luxury. Your fath—the duke was cold to you at best and impossibly cruel at other times. You said yourself that he has dedicated his life to making yours as unhappy as he can."

"Don't change the subject. This isn't about the duke, Effie. It's about being a father, something he surely knew nothing about. You accused me of abandoning Alexandra, of walking away from her without a backward glance. Now you're asking me to do that very thing for which you have reviled me."

She could not deny it. She had been doing just that. "I don't mean to make things more difficult. Things are all so confused. I should never have accused you of doing something so terrible. I know you better than that."

"No, you don't. I've been keeping secrets from you for years... and I honestly couldn't say that I was innocent. I've not been perfect. In fact, I've been anything but."

Effie realized that it was time to admit something to herself, and to him. "I think I knew all along. I was pushing you away because I was afraid to need you again—afraid because I have no walls with you. I have no way to protect myself. You have the power that no one else has, Nicholas. You can hurt me. No—you can break me."

He reached out, his hand cupping her face gently. "You have that power too, Effie. With a word, you could destroy me. Don't. Don't do that. Please."

"Let us get to Highview. It would be foolish of us to make promises to one another when we cannot even be certain we will see another day," Effie said, stepping back from him. She needed the space. Being close to him made it hard to breathe and even harder to think.

Highcliff's lips firmed, his jaw going taut. Then he nodded and stepped back. "You know where I stand, Euphemia Darrow, and you know what I want from you."

"I do."

"I will not grovel. I will not beg you . . . I do have some small amount of pride," he admitted ruefully.

"You have more than a small amount. We both do. I daresay that is why we have reached this very difficult juncture." Effie's lips quirked in a smile that more than conveyed the bittersweet feelings he'd stirred in her. It was all that she wanted, and she was afraid to reach out for it. Her words to Minerva came back to her. She could apparently give advice with the best of them, but she was a poor hand at implementing her own words of wisdom.

Chapter Twenty-Two

BECHARD HAD COME. Seated on a hard chair in the sitting room of the small house just outside of Mayfair, Colonel Silas Winchell waited for the Frenchman to arrive at the home that had been Margaret's hiding place. Margaret was gone, of course. She'd fled in the night, and he had no notion of where she'd gone. Wherever it was, he knew that trouble would soon follow.

Bechard's ship had docked just after dawn. There was no escaping the fact that Bechard would be furious when he arrived. Summoning a man of his standing, a man who struck terror in the hearts of anyone who dealt with him, and then informing him that the vengeance he had been promised was just out of reach—that was a recipe for disaster. It was also a way to get himself killed. Margaret had done that. But then everything that had ever gone wrong in his life could be laid at Margaret's door. Had it not been for her influence all those years ago, he would have served out his military career in an honorable way—honorable enough, anyway. And he wouldn't now be a man approaching middle age trying to tidy up past mistakes that could destroy him.

Bitterly, he thought that even his bastard daughter was her fault. After all, he'd been in London because she had summoned him. She had insisted that he must come at once to offer assurance to their partners because they didn't want to deal with a woman. And when he'd wanted to relieve his most pressing needs, needs that had long been ignored while on the front, she'd denied him in favor of her nephew. For years she'd been playing them all against one another, using her charms and favors as both reward when granted and punishment when withheld.

So she'd put him off while welcoming the late Lord Marchebanks into her bed, and he'd sought solace in the arms of a common whore—a woman who should have known how to prevent conception. Now he had a bastard daughter running about who apparently shared enough similarities with him and enough similarities with his bastard nephew to see him hanged if anyone put the facts of it together.

It was bad enough the whore had gone missing. She'd departed the last bawdy house she was working in and had seemingly vanished off the face of the Earth. All three of them would need to be eliminated—Highcliff, the whore, and the child—before he took his position in the House of Commons. But if he didn't deal with the Bechard situation and get Margaret under control, that would never happen. She could destroy him with her recklessness. And that meant she would have to be stopped at any cost.

The clang of the door knocker striking the plate had him sitting up higher in his chair, fear rendering his spine completely rigid. After all, military bearing was a weapon in itself. He'd used it to intimidate men before and, assuming he survived Bechard, would do so again. But first, he had to get through the initial meeting with the man.

One of the hirelings had opened the door, letting the Frenchman inside. When he entered the room, it felt immediately colder. It was as if the man radiated a physical chill.

"Bonjour, Colonel," the man said cordially, but with a coolness to his tone that might have been missed by someone who wasn't in fear for their life. Only the barest hint of an accent tinged his words.

"Hello, Monsieur Bechard," Silas replied. "It was very good of you to come."

The Frenchman's eyes glittered with cold amusement. "How could I stay away? You have something I want very badly. You do still have it, don't you?"

It? What had Margaret told him? "You mean him. You are aware of why she summoned you here, aren't you?"

"Oh, yes, Colonel. I know. And I said precisely what I meant. *It.* He is not human to me. He is a thing to be reviled, to be disposed of after I have inflicted a suitable amount of pain on him." Then the Frenchman turned his head very slightly. It was enough to reveal the vicious scar that ran from the man's temple, in front of his ear, and down all the way to his neck. It pulled the skin taut, stretching one corner of his mouth in a grim fashion. "I have a debt to collect. Margaret, Lady Marchebanks, understands that. Do you?"

Silas felt a shiver of unease snake through him. As a child, he'd once encountered a dog that had gone mad. It had stood before him, blocking his path—silent, still, and no less threatening for it. Bechard reminded him of that dog, of the fear that had consumed him on that day. It was self-preservation which prompted him to offer her up in his stead. "I do. But Lady Marchebanks has a history of promising things she is incapable of delivering. This is one of those instances, Monsieur Bechard. You have been summoned here for naught as she has allowed Highcliff to escape"

"Then she will pay for it with her life," Bechard said. "I do not like being toyed with, Colonel. And if you cannot tell me where to find either Highcliff or Lady Marchebanks, you will pay for it as well."

Swallowing convulsively, feeling compelled to appease the man, he eagerly offered, "I can tell you where I think they have gone. To Highview Manor. No doubt, Margaret is in pursuit of him to his family estate. She hates Highcliff as much as you do. But she doesn't need to come back. In fact, her presence only complicates matters. And if she dies, there is no one to naysay me when I lay the entire treason scheme at her feet. If all the fault is placed upon her posthumously, both of us will be free to carry on as we wish. I'm only sorry that recent events will prevent us from continuing this partnership. But in my new position, when I am in the House of Commons, I could be of great use to you. This could continue to be a very lucrative arrangement."

Bechard raised one eyebrow as he casually picked up a small porcelain shepherdess that had been placed on the table. "I am not your henchman, Colonel." The shepherdess crashed to the floor, dropped as carelessly and with as much notice as one might drop a handkerchief. It smashed against the marble base of the fireplace, shattering into pieces that scattered over the carpet.

"When I am in the House of Commons, I will be a powerful man, Monsieur Bechard—a powerful ally for you to have. And she cannot be trusted," Silas insisted. But he didn't sound powerful as he uttered those words. They were pleading, frightened. Desperate. He was well aware that his life depended on his ability to persuade Bechard to his cause over hers. "If it comes down to it, she will betray us both to save herself... and she knows enough of my secrets and yours to make things very difficult for both of us."

"I have no fear of her or of your English courts. I am far beyond their reach," Bechard said. "However, for a price, I would be willing to make her go away."

"A mercenary now?" Silas asked.

Bechard stared at him for a moment, his gaze considering. Weighing. Measuring. "I do nothing for free unless it is for my own pleasure. I have other uses for Lady Marchebanks. If I am to dispose of her, I will require some degree of compensation."

"You'll have it. Name your price," Silas stated.

Bechard smiled coolly. "Be wary you do not offer more than you want to give."

Silas rose from his seat. Crossing the room, he stopped only a few feet from Bechard and pulled a small pouch of coins from inside his coat. "There's more where that comes from."

Bechard accepted the pouch. But even as he did so, he whipped out a blade that had been tucked inside his coat. The cold steel sank into Silas' gut, leaving a trail of fire in its wake.

"I'm not so easily bought and sold," Bechard said. "If you have so few qualms about throwing her to the wolves, then what is to stop you from then trading my life for your own? You are not the only man with ambitions, Colonel. You and Margaret Hazelton are both a threat to my future plans. Never fear, she'll be eliminated too . . . once I am finished with her."

Silas didn't respond. His hands were clutching at his gut, blood seeping through his fingers around the blade. Then Bechard vanished. One moment he was there, and then he heard only the snick of the front door closing as Bechard once more disappeared into the encroaching fog.

Slowly, he sank to the floor, his body growing weaker with each passing moment. His life had been nothing more than a series of deals with the Devil and he would now have to settle those accounts. The balance would not be in his favor.

EFFIE COULDN'T STOP thinking about what Highcliff had said, about the fact that he'd offered her the one thing she'd always wanted. Being his wife had been the basis of her every dream—from girlhood to womanhood, those dreams and disappointments had been at the heart of every choice she made. But she was so afraid to take that step. Afraid to reach out and fully grasp what she wanted most and afraid to let go of the small portion of it she still held onto. Even as the carriage eased onto the lane that led from the main road to Highview Manor, she was still wrestling with those questions. Could she trust him? Could she trust herself? What would become of her girls? There was no way to manage it all.

"It will not be terrible," Highcliff stated. "The duke is entirely bedridden now. He will not get up from his sick bed and toss us out. Neither will the servants. They all know that it is only a matter of time until the title is mine, whether I want it or not."

"It isn't your father who concerns me, Nicholas. It's us. And I'm not certain how to get beyond that," she admitted reluctantly.

"I cannot bully you into forgiving me for all that has passed between us. And I cannot simply wish it away. Even if it were possible, Effie, I'm not certain I would," he paused, taking a deep breath. When he continued, his tone was introspective, thoughtful. His lips quirked upward, half amused but still tinged with sadness. Bittersweet, like so much of their story had been. "I loved you when you were a girl . . . but I am in awe of the woman you have become. Had we married as I envisioned when I was little more than a boy myself, you would not be who you are today. And that, Effie, would be a terrible shame."

"How do you do that to me? How do you say exactly the right thing?"

"I'm only telling you what I feel, what I know to be true."

The carriage rolled to a stop and Effie looked out the window. It was easier than looking at him. The ostentatious luxury of Highview Manor spread out before them. Footmen were rushing out to meet the carriage and gather their bags. The butler and housekeeper were there, as well. Noticeably absent, as Nicholas had suggested, was the duke.

He climbed down from the carriage first and then offered her his hand. That contact sent a jolt through her, as it always did. Trying desperately to maintain her composure, she stepped down, her boots crunching on the gravel drive.

"Welcome home, my lord," the butler said, bowing. It was cordial, appropriate, and yet oddly stilted. They were uncomfortable with his presence, Effie realized.

"Please do not do that, Milton. It's unnecessary," Highcliff insisted.

The butler stood up, but his back was still slightly stooped, though more from age than from deference. "Certainly, my lord. It is good to have you home." The words were impossibly warm and the sincerity in them was without question. It seemed their reticence was not reluctance or even ambivalence, but shock. These people who had watched him grow from boy to man had not been permitted to see him for decades after Highcliff had been banished by his father, and now he had returned so suddenly with her in tow and in unknown circumstances.

"It is good indeed!" the housekeeper gushed. Her reaction was much more effusive than the butler's. She was clearly pleased to see Highcliff. "I couldn't be happier that you're here. Mr. Milton will see to refreshments, and I'll have rooms readied for you both immediately. Are there servants coming in another carriage?"

"No, Mrs. Stephens," Nicholas answered. "We had to leave London in a bit of a hurry. I have unfortunately created a dangerous situation for Miss Darrow and it necessitated getting out of the city very quickly. To that end, we'll need men patrolling the grounds. I need to be certain that if any strangers appear, I will be immediately apprised of it."

Effie didn't have a chance to see how the servants responded to that. Highcliff was whisking her inside. He took her immediately to the drawing room, a room she had never seen before. While the two of them might have run tame across the properties of Strathmore and Highview, they'd never really been in one another's homes. She hadn't brought him in to hers—it would have been improper since she hadn't been properly chaperoned. And it went without saying that she would never have been welcomed into his home. The duke would have died of apoplexy had she ever crossed the threshold then. Instead, they'd always met outdoors, at different places on their estates or in the surrounding countryside—always in secret, but apparently not secret enough. Not secret enough to keep the duke from knowing, to keep Sutton from knowing.

Only moments later, a maid came in bearing a tray of tea and cakes. "My lord," she said, bobbing a curtsy after she'd deposited the tea tray on the table. "Mrs. Stephens said for me to tell you sandwiches will be served shortly. Cook is preparing them now."

"Thank you," he said.

"And your bags have been taken up to your old room. Miss Darrow has been put in the Green Room, sir."

"No. You will put her in the Gold Room. Next to mine," he said. "Under the circumstances, and with her safety at such risk, I want to be close in the event of any danger."

If the maid thought the request odd, she wisely kept it to herself. She simply nodded, bobbed another curtsy, and replied quietly, "I will inform Mrs. Stephens, my lord."

When they were alone, Effie turned on Highcliff, her cheeks pink with embarrassment. "Now the entire household will presume that I am your lover."

He shrugged. "You are my lover."

"I have *been* your lover," she stated, her emphasis making it clear that it could very well remain permanently in the past tense. His presumptuousness was insulting, primarily because she knew he was right. That didn't mean she had to let him know it, of course. "That has a very different meaning!"

"You will be again. We are inevitable, Effie. We've been on this course for too long to diverge now. When we are married, it will not matter."

There was no time to respond. No time to protest that she wasn't certain. The door opened and that very same maid reappeared. But her face was pale, and it was obvious the girl was terrified. "My lord, His Grace has requested that you attend him in his chambers."

Highcliff turned back to Effie. "The Devil calls . . . we will continue this conversation later."

Effie watched him walk out as she sank down onto the settee. With nothing else to do but wait, she poured herself a cup of tea and tried desperately to calm her nerves and muster her courage. Countless bits of wisdom came back to her from Mrs. Wheaton, from Highcliff, from her own conversations with her girls when faced with such life altering decisions. But all they did was leave her more confused than ever.

Chapter Twenty-Three

HIGHCLIFF PAUSED OUTSIDE the door to the duke's chambers. It had been eighteen years since he had seen him, since a single word had been exchanged between them. Even the tragedy of Sutton's death had not prompted communication. He'd been informed of it by the duke's solicitor. Now, poised to face the man who had made it his one mission in life to destroy his every chance at happiness, he found himself reluctant to cross the threshold. But, as per usual, a helpful servant took the matter out of his hands. A footman simply opened the door for him and stood there, waiting expectantly.

With no option for escape, he entered that room. Despite the meticulous cleaning provided by the housekeeper and the maids, the room smelled of sickness, of the rot that was slowly eating the duke alive. Steeling himself against it, Highcliff passed through the sitting room and into the bedchamber.

The pale figure in that bed bore little similarity to the robust figure he'd last seen. Thin and frail, his skin a sickly gray, only his eyes were familiar. That gaze was as filled with hatred and contempt as it had ever been. It burned through him, the only sign of life in the old man.

"Your Grace," Highcliff said, his tone completely neutral. He hated him. He would always hate him, but he would not be baited by him ever again.

"I told you never to come back here," the duke said, his voice thin and weak.

"I swore I would never return," Highcliff admitted. "It seems we are both having to eat our words on that score. The servants know your days are numbered and that I will soon be paying their wages. They will not toss me out, even if you order it."

"And you brought her," the duke said accusingly. "I'm not so frail that I do not remember the promise I made to you about her. I will see her destroyed!"

"The hell you will." The words were not heated. They were spoken calmly and matter-of-factly. "You haven't the strength to summon your minions, and I have more than the means necessary to see her protected even if you did."

"You think you've won." The words were drenched with bitterness.

"No. I don't think I've won. I think I let you rob us of eighteen years. I simply will not allow you to rob us of any more. But there is one thing I want from you. I want to know the name of the man who fathered me."

"I'll take it to my grave," he said, before succumbing to a coughing fit. When it had passed, blood speckled his lips and the pillow.

"Sooner rather than later."

The duke smiled grimly, showing teeth stained with the blood he had just coughed up. "Even my death will deny you something you want."

"There are other ways of finding out. Your death will finally set me free," Highcliff stated. A hint of bitterness crept in as he continued, "But you'll die knowing that you will never rob me of another moment's happiness. I will have everything you tried so hard to deny me. And I'll do it bearing your title and sharing not a drop of your blood."

Highcliff turned and made for the door. The duke shouted from behind him only to fall into a fit of coughing and gasping. Highcliff ignored it. To the footman posted outside, he said, "He is to have no visitors. And no correspondence from him is to leave this house. If it does, there will be hell to pay."

"Yes, my lord," the footman replied, not questioning either of those commands. The balance of power in the house had shifted to him. Even if the duke continued to draw breath, he was no longer in command of his own home.

Highcliff walked away, heading toward the chamber he'd occupied for most of his young life. He'd never been happy in it, never been happy there. His mother had been a shell of a woman by the time he was old enough to have memory of her, confined to her rooms and barely able to utter a word. The duke had always told him that she'd been broken by the events that resulted in his conception. But the man was a proven liar. He'd say anything to wound. Somewhere in this house, someone knew the truth. And he would find it no matter what. Their very lives might depend on it.

⸻

EFFIE WAS IN her bedchamber, the one Highcliff had demanded she be given. Her things had been unpacked by one of the maids. It had been a very long time since she'd had someone else to attend to such tasks for her. Household chores in her home were divided between the girls, Mrs. Wheaton, and herself of course. Not since she'd left Strathmore had she been waited on so deferentially.

She would be lying to herself if she denied that it stirred old dreams within her. If they had married as she had hoped, if he hadn't left her all those years ago, it would not be a strange house to her. It would be the place that she called home. She would have been managing that house and those servants, no doubt, because surely their marriage would have sent the duke to a much earlier grave. *It still can be your home.*

He'd made the offer. He'd asked her the question. She could have what she desired—to be his wife. All she had to do was say yes. In so doing, she would be given everything she had ever wanted . . . and she would give him the power to break her entirely. She'd survived losing him once. If they married and things soured between them, as they did in so many marriages, could she bear it? As the idealistic and innocent girl she had been all those years ago, such thoughts had never crossed her mind. Now that was all she could think of. She was driving herself mad with it.

The knock on the door halted her ruminations. "Come in," she called out.

When the door opened to reveal Highcliff, she couldn't have been more surprised. "What are you doing here? You cannot be in my room! What will the servants think?"

"Effie, we are private enough here, isolated enough, that it should not matter," he said. "Are you comfortable in this room? It is to your satisfaction?"

"You know that every room in this house is appointed to the highest standards of luxury. I cannot believe that you came here simply to inquire after my comfort."

He stepped inside fully, closing the door behind him. "Of course not. It was a flimsy excuse, one that I knew you'd see through immediately. But I needed to erase the unpleasantness of my confrontation with the duke from my mind. And you have always had the ability to soothe me, to offer me a kind of solace no one else ever could."

Those words softened her. No doubt, just as he planned. "Oh, you are ridiculously charming when you choose to be."

He moved closer, his long stride eating up the space between them. The nearness of him made her shiver. She drew in a deep, steadying breath, but that only made it worse. She could smell the scent of his soap and something else that was just him. It was as intoxicating as it ever was. The urge to lean into him, to feel connected to him in that way, was positively overwhelming. And for just a moment, she wanted to be selfish. She wanted to not think about the future or the past. She wanted nothing more than a moment's pleasure.

Effie reached for him. His arms closed around her instantly, pulling her closer. It was perfection. It was everything she wanted and needed... but only a taste of it. And with him, that would never be enough.

Then his lips touched hers. The sensation flooded her, and she was suffused with heat, need, that familiar ache and yearning. And it simply wiped away all the fears and doubts. All-consuming as it was, it left no room for them.

The kiss, gentle at first, became deeper, more demanding. He was no longer just holding her close. Instead, his hands roamed over her body, awakening every desire she'd attempted to tamp down for months. It didn't matter that she was likely making a mistake. It didn't matter what the future might bring for them. Nothing mattered in that moment but holding onto him in that storm of passion. She wanted to forget about the potential dangers they faced, about the unfortunate death of Miss Clark, and about the momentous decisions she would have to make very soon. Decisions that would impact all of their futures.

Then his mouth left hers, trailing along her neck to that sensitive spot where it joined with her shoulder. When his teeth nipped there in a fashion that was both thrilling and alarming, she couldn't hold back a moan of pleasure.

"You do not need to seduce me," she said. "Just make me forget everything else for a while. Please."

He didn't take her to the bed. Instead, he pulled her with him to the chaise longue placed at the end of it. No clothes were removed. He left them both fully dressed as he bunched her skirts and slid one hand beneath them and unerringly found the place where she ached for him. He touched her so intimately, stoking her body to a fevered pitch. She moved against him desperately, seeking more, seeking that release which she knew he could give her.

When he withdrew his hand, Effie whimpered in protest. But her disappointment was short lived as he moved between her parted thighs. She could feel the buttons of his breeches pressing into the soft flesh of her thighs as he entered her. It was such an exquisite composition of sensations. The heat and fullness, the slight abrasion of his clothes against her skin, and then his lips once more covering hers, this time to swallow her cries of pleasure. With each thrust of his hips, with every surge and withdrawal, she felt herself growing closer and closer to that pinnacle.

His lips left hers. "Look at me, Effie. Open your eyes and look at me."

She did, helpless to resist the command in his voice. His face was beautiful and brutal all at once—hard angles and a fierce gaze, a possessive one. "You're mine," he vowed. "Whatever else happens between us and whatever the future brings—you are now and always will be mine."

Yes.

It was only the flare of satisfaction in his gaze that told her she'd spoken the word aloud. But there was no denying that truth. She was his. She always had been. And as the pleasure swept through her, she realized that he had been right all along. They were inevitable. Tied together by the past, by their treacherous present, and by their very tenuous future.

Chapter Twenty-Four

MARGARET HAZELTON WORE a dark, heavy veil as she exited her carriage and entered the posting inn. A maid trailed behind her. Even in disgrace, she would maintain at least the appearance of propriety. She would not be a heathen—a *hellion*—like Miss Darrow. For herself, she had chosen not to go in direct pursuit of the couple. What she had done was hire an inquiry agent, who had quickly picked up Highcliff's trail. He had indeed gone first to Miss Darrow, and from there the agent had followed them at a reasonable distance, leaving missives for her at predetermined locations depending on which direction they traveled. They had not even tried to disguise their destination. Highcliff, at long last, was going home.

She approached the innkeeper behind the pocked and worn bar. "I believe my brother may have left a missive for me here, innkeeper. I am Mrs. March."

"Ah, yes madam," the man said, all deference and good cheer. "I have it right here for you. Will you be requiring a room for the night?"

"I will, thank you. My maid shall share my chamber and the coachman can bed down in the stables."

"Certainly, ma'am," the innkeeper said. "And how many horses do you have?"

"Two," she replied.

"That'll be three shillings, ma'am."

Looking around at the dilapidated inn that was none too clean, Margaret had to bite her tongue. It was robbery. He might as well have been on the coach road brandishing a pistol. Still, she smiled behind her veil. "Very well, sir." She removed the appropriate coins from the very meager supply in her reticule. She placed the coins very deliberately on the bar, then an extra shilling beside the three. "I am a widow, sir, and my late husband has left me very wealthy. Alas, an unscrupulous man is trying to force me to marry him. I beg you, if anyone should ask after me, tell no one of my presence here."

The man pocketed the coins very quickly. "I will be the soul of discretion, madam." He placed a key where the coins had been. "Top of the stairs, at the end of the hall to the left."

"Thank you, sir. You are most kind." Turning back to her maid, she said, "Come along, Roberta." That was not the maid's name, but she could be trusted to answer to it and keep her mouth shut. They would get a good night's sleep, then they would make their way the following day to the village near Highview Manor. From there, she would summon those she needed to see an end to Highcliff and his governess. It had been a mistake to summon Bechard. She knew that now. But if she could present the man with Highcliff's corpse and tell him how Highcliff suffered as he watched Miss Darrow die, she might just get out of it alive. Regardless, she had known she couldn't simply sit at that horrid little house in London and wait for Silas to trade her life for his own with the Butcher. There was no honor amongst thieves, not even when they were lovers.

No man could ever be trusted, she thought bitterly. Everyone she had ever known had been a disappointment to her. If she managed to survive, she'd never trust another one. She'd certainly never allow herself to become entangled in their schemes to such a degree. It was time to head to greener pastures. Perhaps she'd take herself off to America and get herself a very rich, very sickly husband. The idea of being a wealthy widow in actuality rather than just as a ruse was becoming more and more appealing to her. Yes, it was past time to cut and run and get herself far from England's shores.

HIGHCLIFF STARED AT Effie's sleeping form. After making love to her on the chaise longue, they'd sought her bed and locked out the world for a bit longer. It wouldn't last forever. The dinner hour was looming ahead. He was tempted to ask that they both be served trays in their rooms. Given that there was a secret door that opened between their chambers, they could share their evening meal, and if he was very lucky, her bed for the night.

Careful not to wake her, he reached out, touching a strand of her hair. As gently as possible, he wound the dark auburn lock about his finger, marveling at the silken texture. Everything about her was simply magical to him. In all things, she was perfection—even her fiery temper and sometimes unbending spirit. She held firmly to her beliefs, even when they made her life more difficult than it had to be.

Many times over the years, he'd wondered that she hadn't been married off to someone else. He knew that her father had often lamented her continued and very determined spinsterhood. That was on his head, too. He'd wasted so much of both of their lives, paralyzed by fear of the man who'd bullied and badgered him throughout his childhood. But those days were over. The duke had no power over him anymore. And, as he'd informed his superiors, he was leaving the service of Whitehall. The life of a spy was hardly conducive to having a wife or family. He'd earned his freedom. He'd earned the right to have a little happiness.

"I can feel you staring at me," she said sleepily, not bothering to open her eyes.

"I cannot help myself. I'm afraid if I look away, you'll vanish. I've certainly conjured a phantom version of you in my mind often enough over the years."

Her eyes did open then, and she looked up at him with a strange combination of hope and confusion. "What will happen next?"

"We will get married, presuming you agree," he said. "And we will retire to a quiet life in the countryside. Not here, of course. I despise this place and all the memories it holds. I would happily live with you at Strathmore, or we could go to one of the many other estates that will come to me upon the duke's death."

She frowned. "What did happen to Sutton, Nicholas? I never knew, and I always felt terrible that the last words I spoke to him were so hateful."

Highcliff sighed and then laid back on the pillow, staring up into the ornate canopy of the bed. "They labeled it an accident. He was cleaning a pistol and it went off . . . or so they said. But Sutton had tried at other times to take his life. Many times when we were younger. I do not know that it was suicide, but I strongly suspect it. He might have been the duke's natural son, but the duke had no love for him either. He has no love for anyone—not even the barest hint of affection." He paused, drawing in a deep breath before continuing, "I think Sutton felt that lack more acutely than I did and every slight, every callous insult, every humiliation he endured at the duke's hands weighed on him, until he chose not to endure it any longer."

"I hated you for going away, for leaving me," Effie whispered softly. "But I would rather you had left than continue to suffer his cruelty. I know that Sutton suffered in staying. Now knowing that his suffering may have led to his death—if that had happened to you . . . I can't bear to think of it."

There were things he had to say to her, that he had to explain. "I was cruel to you that day. Cold and unfeeling. You must know that it was all an act. I didn't want you to waste your life waiting for me when the odds of my returning from that war were so slim. The duke had intentionally asked that I be given the most dangerous of assignments. It wasn't murder, so much as arranging for my death to occur. And I knew all that was coming the day I talked to you. So, I wanted to destroy what you felt for me because I wanted you to be free of it... to not be bound by what I could only believe was futile hope."

She propped herself on one elbow and stared at him until he turned to meet her gaze. "If we are going to make this work, there is something we both have to do. We have to let go of what was and focus only on what is and what we want to be. We have both been prisoners to past events for long enough. It is time we moved forward. In light of my *condition* and the rather volatile situation we currently find ourselves in, I believe we should get married as quietly as possible. And as quickly."

Highcliff grinned as he rolled away from her and rose from the bed. They'd long ago shed their clothing and he walked toward that discarded pile heedless of his nudity. Retrieving his coat, he slipped his hand into one of the inside pockets and produced a document. "In my eternal optimism, before I even came to get you at your school, I imposed upon the Archbishop's generosity once more and begged him for a special license... which he granted. We can marry tomorrow morning if you like."

He'd stopped to get a special license before he'd even come to see her, before he'd known. "Before? But you didn't know then about the child."

"Effie I am not marrying you because you are carrying my child. I am marrying you *expeditiously* because you are carrying my child.

⇶⇷

EFFIE BLINKED IN surprise. "I said soon, Nicholas, but I hardly meant within the next twelve hours! I have nothing appropriate to wear for a wedding, certainly not for my own wedding!"

"They might be a bit dated, but I'm certain Mrs. Stephens could find one of my mother's gowns and do something with it. She was her maid for years before taking over as housekeeper," he said.

"The duke would be furious."

"I don't care," he said. "She was his wife, but she was my mother. And as much as he hates the very idea of my happiness, I would like to believe that my mother would have rejoiced in it... and that, wherever she may be now, that she is pleased at the notion of being involved in our nuptials in some small way."

Effie settled back against the pillows. She pulled the sheet up practically to her chin. Nudity was not nearly so commonplace for her. For him, he seemed to be as confident in the nude as in clothes—perhaps more so. Of course, he had reason to be confident. It was all golden skin—and more than a few nasty bruises and partially healed wounds—over hard muscles, lightly dusted with dark hair on his chest and legs. Despite her temptation to do otherwise, she kept her gaze from lingering on any other part of him. It wasn't in her nature to be missish, but being so unbearably bold was something she did rarely—and usually with great regret.

"You are a romantic," she mused. "I'd forgotten that about you. Or perhaps I chose not to remember."

"I will remind you of it," he vowed. "Daily. Now, if I'm not mistaken, we have approximately ten minutes before one of the maids knocks upon your chamber door to help you dress for dinner. What can we do in ten minutes, Effie?"

"Ten minutes? That hardly seems like enough time," she replied coyly.

"I like a challenge," he fired back.

Those were the last words spoken. The only sounds that filled the room after that were pleasured moans and desperate sighs. It was glorious.

From the Diary of Miss Euphemia Darrow, August 7th, 1828

I have taught them to be governesses, to be companions. I have taught them everything they would need to know to guide and teach the children of their employers. I worry that I have not adequately prepared them for other aspects of their lives. So many of the girls have found love in the most unlikely and sometimes most scandalous of places. Several of them have married peers—men possessed of wealth and exalted titles.

Society will not be kind to them. The circumstances of their births, the fact that they were in the employ of these gentlemen, will mark them as social climbers according to the rules of the ton. *That is the most unpardonable sin in many eyes.*

While it may not be easy for them, while they will certainly feel the censure of others, I hope that I have given all of them the confidence in themselves to face it with their heads high. These girls—no, these women, for indeed they are all grown now—are not simply accomplished. They are forces to be reckoned with. And I take great pride in having played even a small part in that.

Whether they are now to be addressed as my lady or your grace, they are still my girls. Always.

As for the rumor circulating that this is not just a school but a matchmaking scheme, that is patently ridiculous. Just as ridiculous as the lady who approached me in a shop about enrolling her daughter as a student to improve her marital prospects. I am not in the business of finding husbands. I'm in the business of shaping and molding extraordinary young ladies, despite their difficult circumstances. Matchmaking, indeed. It's beneath my dignity.

Chapter Twenty-Five

OVER DINNER, EFFIE had persuaded Highcliff to give her another day to prepare for their wedding. And that was how she found herself sorting through trunks in the attic with Mrs. Stephens the following morning.

"Her Grace had some truly lovely gowns. She liked to keep things simple, she did," the housekeeper explained. "Never cared for all the frills like some did. Beautiful as she was, they were hardly needed."

"I wish I could have known her," Effie said. And it was true. She would have liked to have known that someone who shared Highcliff's blood had loved him. It was such a lonely existence that he had lived to that point.

"Oh, aye, miss. And I think she would have liked you very much. You are good for him," Mrs. Stephens said. "He needs a bit of happiness in his life. Heaven knows it's been hard-earned."

Effie said nothing, but she blushed at the compliment. It pleased her inordinately. There was no escaping the fact that a few days in his company and she was once more the awe-struck girl she had been when she'd first seen him eighteen years earlier. Her carriage had been halted on the road with a broken wheel, and the driver had gone to get help. Two men had happened upon her, their intentions far from honorable. But she had never been a helpless female. Her own governess, much to her father's chagrin, had been a woman who believed in a true education for her sex. Effie had rousted them leaving the young Highcliff, then only Lord Nicholas Montford, quite put out at not getting to play the hero to her damsel in distress. Still, even without heroics, the sight of him had robbed her of the ability to speak.

"Try that trunk, miss—the one under the window there. I remember when it was ordered and that was not too long before Her Grace left us, God rest her soul," Mrs. Stephens instructed. "I'll check over here. You'll be needing slippers and the like, as well, if there are any to be had that might fit you."

Effie did as she'd been bidden. There was some trepidation as she opened the trunk lid. After all, it was not unheard of to find vermin taking up residence in such locations. She shuddered at the thought.

But raising the lid, she found no mice. There were no insects or moths. Everything inside had been neatly wrapped in cloth, each item carefully preserved. No doubt that had been Mrs. Stephens' doing, Effie thought. It seemed that the former duchess had been well loved by her longtime maid and housekeeper.

Lifting out the first bundle, Effie unwrapped it carefully. Nestled inside was a gown of pale pink silk. Even after being locked in that trunk for years, there was a luster to the fabric that simply defied reason. She didn't need to look any further. It was the gown she wanted to wear when she married Highcliff, at long last.

She peered inside the trunk again in the hope that there might be slippers or some other item that would complete the ensemble. But the thing which caught her eye was a simple leatherbound book tucked into the corner. Effie lifted it and turned it over in her hand, the front cover falling open as she did so.

The Diary of Elizabeth Montford, Duchess of Clarenden

Effie opened the book, scanning the entries. It appeared that the former duchess had not been a faithful documentarian in her journal. There were large gaps in the dates. Months in some instances. The first entry was dated 1786 and the last in 1793. It was a slim volume to hold so many years' worth of memories.

Nicholas would have been only a small boy during that time. She knew that he had few memories of his mother before she was too ill to actually be a mother to him. Perhaps there was something in her journal that would help him better understand who his mother had been. Tucking the book into the deep pockets inside her skirt, she rose with pink silk.

"I found the perfect dress, Mrs. Stephens."

The housekeeper looked up. Her eyes settled on the swaths of pink silk and immediately tears came to her eyes. "Indeed you did, miss. Indeed you did. You'll look as pretty in it as she did. I'll take it downstairs and get the maids to working on it. A bit of fresh air and lavender, along with a good, gentle press, and it'll be right as rain. I fear the slippers aren't in here, though."

"I have a pair of my own that will suffice. They aren't pink, but they'll be well hidden under the skirt since the former duchess was apparently quite a bit taller than I am," Effie offered in a bright tone, not feeling even an iota of guilt that she'd purloined the private journal of Nicholas' mother. After all, they needed answers about his parentage, and if that book contained them, it simply had to be done.

HIGHCLIFF WAS IN the study, reviewing the account ledger, as it had been revealed to him that the duke had not been able to do so in months. Nothing was amiss, at least at first glance, but it was a tedious task.

A knock upon the door sounded and called out, "Enter."

Milton stood there, ashen-faced and clearly upset. "Your Grace," he said, softly. Those two words told the tale in its entirety even before the man continued, "The former duke has passed."

He waited to feel something, to feel anything in the wake of such news. But if he felt anything at all it could only be classified as relief. That was one threat to Effie eliminated, at least. There would always be more simply because he loved her. He had for as long as he had known her. And he was too selfish to stay away from her, even though, for her sake, he should.

Every effort had been taken to protect her now, to protect all of them. He had men patrolling a permitter around the house. Traps had been laid in the woods for any unwary would-be assassin. There were weapons stashed throughout the house so they would always be convenient. Only Milton knew the truth. It had been necessary to tell him before taking such measures. After all, nothing happened in a house without the butler's approval.

"Summon the undertaker, Milton, and have everything prepared as soon as possible and with as little fuss as can be managed. No one will actually mourn the old sot, and I have no tolerance for such hypocrisy."

Milton, looking slightly scandalized by his apparent lack of feeling on the subject, nonetheless nodded. "Certainly, Your Grace. As you wish."

When the butler left, he leaned back in his chair and scrubbed his hands over his face. He had known it was coming, had known that the duke's days were numbered. And yet, the weight of the burden was suddenly intolerable. It wasn't a title or even lands that he'd inherited but the responsibility. Endless responsibility. It pressed down on him. Had it not been for everything else—their impending nuptials, the safety of Effie and their child, the very thought of Bechard stepping foot on English soil—it might have been bearable.

Tossing his quill down onto the desk, ink splattered the page. Unerringly, his eyes sought out the dark stain on the carpet from where he'd spilled ink all those years ago. The last time he'd been in that room had been the day the duke had banished him, the day he'd walked away from Effie. That wretched day would be forever etched in his memory, and he would never be able to forgive the man who now lay dead upstairs.

Cursing softly, he rose and stalked toward the window. Parting the curtains, he peered out across the acres of parkland. He heard the door open behind him. It was Effie, of course. No one else would dream of entering without knocking.

"Mrs. Stephens informed me of his passing," she said softly. "What can I do?"

He turned toward her. "I am not suddenly struck down with grief, Euphemia. The man was a monster, and the world will be a better place now that he no longer occupies space in it."

"You shouldn't say such things," she admonished softly. "Even if they are true."

"What would you have me say? That I am sorry to see him gone? That I regret we could not make some sort of peace before he shuffled off the mortal coil?" The questions were biting, hard—and she didn't deserve that from him.

"No. I would have you simply say nothing. We will see him buried with enough fanfare to stave off gossip but not so much you'd be required to feign an affection that he was determined to never let thrive," she replied softly, her gaze conveying a wealth of compassion. "But it is certainly permissible to regret what never was... to regret what was never allowed to be. You cannot love a person who refuses to be loved."

He frowned. "Are you speaking of the duke or are you talking about the two of us?"

"Both," she said. "I know we said the past should be forgotten, but the past has made us who we are, hasn't it? I never stopped loving you, no matter how much I may have tried."

"I loved you, Effie. Always. Even when I was not free to tell you so."

"And when you were risking your life dozens of times over in the name of the Crown—did you love me then? Or was it that you hated yourself so much?"

That was a question he could not answer. "Whatever I did then, it is over now. Isn't it? I'm walking away from it, quite happily, to be with you."

"Are you? You see, Nicholas, I wonder if it isn't something else altogether. I think you like the danger. I think you crave it."

"Effie, the life I lead at present does not allow for a family—"

"No. Nor should it. But I need to be certain that in six months . . . in a year . . . that you will not look at me and this child and wish that you were anywhere else. I would rather raise a bastard than an unwanted burden."

He shook his head. "Never that. I'm not giving something up, Effie. This is me finally getting what I have always wanted . . . you. You are not taking me away from anything. And while I never considered fatherhood, it's because it was something beyond my comprehension. To be perfectly frank, it still is. But I can tell you right now, that all I want is to protect you both—to keep you safe and to give you both the life you deserve."

"I'm frightened. I love you so much, but I am so very afraid that—" She broke off abruptly, turning away from him and walking to the window.

He didn't simply let her walk away from him. Instead, he followed close behind her, wrapping his arms around her. "What do you fear?"

She took a deep shuddering breath as she prepared to tell him something she'd never uttered to another soul. "No one, Nicholas, in all of my life, has ever loved me enough to simply stay. My father's absence from my life is a testament to the shame I bring him and his legitimate children. My mother—I know she couldn't help it, but even her dying was a kind of abandonment. And my girls. After all, that is my purpose in their lives—to raise them up, to teach them, and to watch them go off on their own."

"And I left you . . . no matter the reason, it doesn't change that," he surmised.

"That is part of it," she admitted, "I do fear that you will leave me again, but it's more than simply fearing abandonment. I'm more afraid of what I'll become in the aftermath. You see, I survived it once, and likely, I could survive it again. But I'm not certain I'd like who I would become on the other side of it. I found the strength to rise above it and do something meaningful with my life the first time. I don't know that I'd have that strength again. And every day, I become more dependent on you and further from that girl who, at barely twenty, decided she had the skill and experience to operate her own school!"

He pulled her close again, his arms tightening around her in a way that offered the comfort she needed. And in her own perverse and contrary manner, she resented him for it. That he could be the source of her worry and the source of her solace was maddening.

"I've been waiting, Effie. I've been waiting for that wretched old bastard to die so I would finally be free to make you mine," he whispered against her ear. "All I've ever wanted is to be with you. Everything in between was simply a way to pass the time until my life could truly begin. You are my life, Effie. You always have been. We cannot be ruled by our fears—never again."

Effie forced herself to relax, to allow herself to lean into the heat and strength of his embrace. And she allowed herself, in that moment, to feel a glimmer of hopefulness.

Chapter Twenty-Six

IT HAD BEEN late evening when Margaret had finally reached the inn in the neighboring village to Highview—close enough to do what needed to be done but far enough away to avoid detection. Though she had gone to sleep not from exhaustion but boredom. She'd had no wish to endure the company of the coarse and impoverished patrons who occupied the inn and, beyond the company of her maid, there was no entertainment. Even the few male servants were beneath her notice. A handsome and well-endowed footman would have been a welcome sight to be certain.

There was no sound in the room. No floorboards had creaked. No door had opened or closed. And yet, when her eyes flew open in that darkened room, she knew instantly that she was not alone. Sitting up in the bed, she let the coverlet drop to reveal her diaphanous nightrail. "Who's there?"

"You should not have summoned me and then allowed your little bird to fly his coop."

The words were uttered softly, menacingly. The faint French accent that shaped them was all she needed to identify the speaker. *Bechard.* Then he stepped forward into the faint light that filtered through the narrow window. He stood half turned away from her, allowing the faint light from the window to fall on his face. He was not an unattractive man. His profile was aristocratic, with a strong nose, squared chin, and sharp cheekbones. The high forehead and neatly coiffed hair only underscored that. But it was his bearing, the poker straight spine and pulled back shoulders that were truly the hallmark of his upbringing. Whatever state the French government was currently in, the man had been born as a member of the nobility.

Taking a steadying breath, she smiled as she offered, "But I have tracked him down for you again. And as for what will happen now . . . well, if you want him to suffer, I can think of no greater pain than allowing him to finally have the thing he wants most only to rip it away from him."

Bechard's mouth twisted, his lips taking on a cruel appearance. "And what is it that you think he wants more than anything else?"

Margaret knew that answer immediately. Just as she knew that he did. Silas had told her of Highcliff's captivity, of the miniature portrait he'd carried of Miss Darrow all through the battles and his imprisonment. She also knew that the scar on Bechard's face, which he kept concealed from her now, had been a parting gift from Highcliff when he had reclaimed that portrait. "Miss Euphemia Darrow, of course."

Bechard moved closer to the window, staring out into the night. "Ah, yes. *His Effie*." He traced an intricate pattern in the frost that formed inside the window. "He spoke of her often. Called her name when he was unconscious. When I found her portrait and took it from him, he swore to see me dead for it."

Margaret watched as he idly stroked the side of his face, the side he kept hidden, the side that bore the mark Highcliff had left him with. "She is his obsession . . . and his weakness."

"I should think so. More than a decade later and still she occupies his mind! How very strange."

"I have it on good authority from a servant in their household that they mean to marry tomorrow morning," Margaret said helpfully.

"Why would I ever permit him to enjoy a moment of happiness?" Bechard asked, quiet menace filling the question with a kind of threat that she would have to be a fool to miss.

Brazening it out, Margaret smiled. "There is no greater agony he could suffer than to have the promise of happiness ripped from his grasp." She paused for a moment, letting the weight of that sentiment settle between them. Then she smiled coolly, "Let them think they have what they want. And then, when he is least expecting it, take her. Take her and kill her and leave him, briefly at least, in the hell of his grief and guilt—because he brought you to her door. He will beg you for death then."

Bechard remained quiet, standing there in the shadowy darkness, weighing and measuring not just Highcliff's fate but her own.

Having been an avowed and unapologetic opportunist throughout her life, Margaret did what she had to do in order to shift things in her favor. Pushing back the bedclothes, revealing the entirety of her figure to him, she slowly reached up and pushed one strap of her nightrail from her shoulder. The lace at the neckline caught on one pert nipple, pebbled from the chill in the room. She saw his eyes flicker, saw the brief flare of interest. Trailing her fingers from her upper arm, over the top of her breast, lingering there for just long enough to warm his gaze, she then tugged at the silk ribbon which held the garment closed. It parted almost to her navel, barely concealing her breasts. One shrug and it would fall from her completely.

"I am awfully glad you came," Margaret said. "I have been so terribly bored with Silas. But I'd never be bored with you, would I?"

"I am not some callow youth to be so easily led by you," he remarked. "I can see a pair of breasts, even a pair as lovely as yours, and not lose all sense of reason and purpose. Let us be honest with one another at least. You are bargaining your sex for your life . . . and I'm considering it."

Margaret felt a shiver race through her, but it had little to do with excitement. It was a new experience for her, but she feared him. "And what can I do to sway you?"

"Take it off. Entirely. Let me see what I am bargaining for."

Rising onto her knees, Margaret shrugged out of the nightrail, letting it fall to her hips before shimmying out of it entirely. Refusal was no longer an option. "Let me convince you. You are a man of skill . . . and I am a woman of skills, as well."

Bechard shrugged out of his coat. Margaret knew he was either going to bed her or murder her. She had no notion of which. He was a man she could not read. A man she could not manipulate. It would require careful navigation on her part and the sort of humility and subservience that had never truly been in her repertoire. Could she play the part convincingly enough, *cunningly enough*, to survive?

When he approached her, she had to struggle not to flinch from his touch. It was a natural instinct, after all. The man was a predator, and she was his prey, regardless of his intent. But when his hand fisted in her hair, tugging her toward him, she knew she'd won. As his mouth covered hers, kissing her with a kind of brutal possession, she wasn't certain that it was for the better. But if she protested, then her fate was sealed for certain.

IT WAS THE middle of the night, and Effie found herself unable to sleep. Both excited for the day of her marriage to Highcliff and terrified of what their future might hold, she'd tossed and turned until finally giving up altogether.

She'd retrieved the journal she'd found in the attic and was hunched over it with several candles lit as she struggled to read the faded words written there. It was riveting. Within those pages, she had seen Highcliff's mother turn from a young and hopeful bride to a hollow shell of a woman. The duke's cruelty and coldness was described in horrifying detail within those pages. And then the strangest thing occurred. Suddenly, there was a spark of excitement buried within that delicate scrawl, a hint of hopefulness. And as the pages continued, the former duchess finally disclosed the reason for it—she'd fallen in love with a young man, a soldier by the name of Christopher Winchell.

Their affair was well documented in the duchess' diary. There were passages that waxed poetic about him and his gallantry. There were other passages that were so intimately detailed they made her blush. Yet, Effie was happy that the woman who had been so miserable had found some joy in life. Then it all changed again. Christopher Winchell was dead. Shot in some sort of horrible accident on the eve of a battle . . . and discovered bleeding in the dirt by his own younger brother, Silas Winchell.

It had been ruled an accident—the fault, they'd said, of a defective weapon. But the former duchess had not believed that. Her doubts had been recorded in her journal even if she hadn't possessed a clear understanding of what might have motivated such an act.

Given what Effie now knew about Silas Winchell, she could only conclude those suspicions had been well founded and Silas had a hand in his brother's death. The question, of course, was why? What had he had to gain from his brother's death? Could it be the same reason that Alexandra was in danger? Had Silas Winchell been involved in treasonous activity even then? If so, and if Christopher Winchell had discovered his brother's perfidy and threatened to expose him, his death would make sense. And no doubt the duke's boast of having personally killed the man who had truly been Nicholas' father was just that—an empty boast. Something uttered with the intent to cause pain regardless of its truth.

Flipping ahead, her own exhaustion catching up with her, Effie paused when she encountered the first blank page. Then she carefully backtracked. In the middle of October 1793, the duchess had made her last entry. Her words were different, her writing less precise. She rambled needlessly, her normally elegant penmanship sloppy and uneven. In truth, it was rather like the written equivalent of a person in their cups. What had happened? What strange events had occurred in the former duchess' life that had prompted such a decline in her mental state? It was quite clear that she was entirely out of touch with reality at times. Yet at others, she'd been despairing and melancholy—ravaged by her grief over the death of her lover.

A glance at the window showed it to be just after daylight. The household staff would be up and lighting the fires on the lower floors. Effie rose from her present position and immediately winced. Her neck and back ached from having sat hunched forward over the journal. Donning her wrapper, she tucked the volume into her pocket and then left her chamber, making for the kitchens. There was only one person who might be able to answer her questions about the fate of Nicholas' mother, and that was Mrs. Stephens. She had the answers, of a certain. It was simply a question of whether or not she would be willing to share them.

It wasn't difficult to locate the kitchens at Highview Manor. Though she did not know the layout of the house well, at that time of day, one simply had to follow the noise. And the aromas, of course. In her current condition, those odors were hardly her friend. The closer she drew to them, the more ill she felt.

She struggled to breathe only through her mouth to avoid smelling the cooking kippers and eggs, along with all the other sundry breakfast dishes that were being prepared. Entering the room, she caught sight of one of the kitchen girls preparing a duck for the evening meal. The blood and feathers left Effie feeling so queasy she had to look away. But in every direction, her gaze was met with some other horror. Fish. Pheasant. Quail eggs. Sausages and rashers of bacon. Dear heavens.

"Mrs. Stephens," she gasped. "May I speak with you privately?"

The housekeeper, who had been doing inventory of the crockery, glanced back at her. One look at Effie's positively green face and the housekeeper's eyes widened. "Miss Darrow, are you ill?"

"I'm quite all right," Effie lied. "Might we step outside into the garden?"

"Certainly, miss," the housekeeper said and stepped away from her task to head out into the small herb garden that was located just beyond the kitchen door. The summer herbs were giving way to the winter ones, but everything was shrouded in fog. "Is aught amiss?"

Effie reached into her pocket and pulled out the journal. "I found this yesterday. I should have told you. It was in the trunks we were searching and—well, I was curious. I hoped that it might provide some insight into why Highcliff and the duke were always at odds."

The housekeeper frowned disapprovingly, her lips drawing into a thin hard line. "Those were not your secrets to read, miss."

"No. No they were not," Effie conceded. "But I did not read them just to gossip or be nosy. I only want to help him. He needs the truth about where he came from. And I believe, Mrs. Stephens, that you only want to help him, as well. I know the duke was not his father. I also know that the duke lied to Highcliff—to Nicholas—about his mother and the man who fathered him. What lie that was, I cannot say, but I know it has haunted him every day since. Please, Mrs. Stephens . . . there are other things that must be known that are not in this journal!"

Mrs. Stephens stared at her for a moment. "What is it that you wish to know, Miss Darrow?"

"What happened to alter her so?" Effie asked softly. "It seems such a sudden change."

The housekeeper remained stiff, her back rigid and her lips compressed. Then, after a moment that seemed to stretch on forever, she simply deflated on a heavy sigh. "Laudanum, miss. When she would have left him, when she would have taken the young master and fled this place to protect them both, he locked her in her chamber for weeks claiming that she was ill. He forced laudanum down her until she was too weak to fight them. Then he told her that if she did not consent to it, if she did not take it when it was offered, he would poison her bastard son and let her watch him die. So she gave in to his demands... until she came to need it so much she would never leave him, as he was the source of her poison. If she disobeyed him then, he would withhold it, you see? Then she would become so terribly ill. He used it to control her, and eventually it killed her. He let the young master believe that his mother chose to stay here, that she chose to let him suffer at the duke's hands. But there was no choice. None at all."

The horror of what Mrs. Stephens described was simply beyond Effie's comprehension. She'd known him to be cold and cruel. But that was monstrous. "Did he kill Nicholas' actual father?"

"I couldn't say for certain, miss. I would not be surprised if that were the case, though it is just as likely that the young man was killed by his own brother." She paused a moment in reverie. "I was her maid then, you know. I'd never seen her happier than when she had him. The brother was another matter, though... Silas was his name. Cold. Calculating. There was something about him that always struck me as dishonest. He'd not be the sort to turn your back on, that's for certain. But her lover, he was a man that was too good for this world—kind and gentle. Being a soldier was not for him. Who is to say that, had he survived, the war would not have ruined him?"

Effie nodded, sensing the older woman's sadness. She'd loved her mistress, loved her just as surely as Mrs. Wheaton cherished Effie herself. It was a strange relationship that developed between two women who shared no blood but were bonded by tragedy. "Thank you, Mrs. Stephens, for telling me."

"You must think me an awful coward—to know what he did to her and to not try to help her. But he was a powerful man, and we couldn't have stopped him. Not when the law was on his side. Wives are just property, aren't they? Something to be used up and tossed out with the refuse. I held my tongue because that was the best way I knew to be able to stay close and look after her much as anyone could."

Effie did not hold Mrs. Stephens to blame. The world was a very unkind place to women in general, and unkinder still to those in service. "I think, Mrs. Stephens, it was a terrible situation and you did all that you could. The duke wasn't simply powerful. He was petty and spiteful with it. You should give yourself more grace on that point. He'd have turned you out without a reference and then no one would have cared for her."

Mrs. Stephens let out a terrible sound, a gasping sob that sounded raw and wounded. But she quickly composed herself, dashing away a stray tear. "Thank you, miss. You're kind to say so."

Effie nodded. "I will share what I know with Nicholas."

"It will hurt him," she warned.

Effie shook her head. "No, Mrs. Stephens. He is already hurting. This will at least give him a sense of peace, of absolution, if you will. Sometimes that is the best we can offer someone."

The housekeeper was quiet for a moment, then gave a curt nod. She walked away, heading toward the kitchen door. She'd almost reached it when she stopped and turned toward Effie, "I'd rather not have you tossing up your breakfast in the kitchen. It makes a mess to be sure, but it also raises questions that would best be avoided. If you walk around the side of the house, the terrace doors that lead to the morning room have been left open to air out the room."

Relief washed through her. "Thank you, Mrs. Stephens. I will make my way now."

HE WAS IN the library. It was just past daylight, but he'd been up for ages. There were no ledgers or account books spread out before him. There would be no pretense of work on that day. Instead, there was a rosewood box inlaid with mother of pearl. It held his mother's jewels—not the ostentatious pieces the duke had insisted she wear, but the pieces she'd loved and treasured, those she'd been given by her own family as a young woman. A triple strand of pearls that had belonged to her mother, a sapphire and diamond broach that he suspected had been a gift from a lover, and the betrothal ring that had been passed down through her family for generations, and other pieces all rested inside on a bed of velvet. He could have chosen something from the Clarenden coffers. But he imagined that Effie would be very much like his mother in that regard—she would prefer pieces that held sentimental value over monetary value.

A noise caught his attention and he stiffened. Someone was sneaking about on the terrace. Given the danger that they were in, no warning sign could be ignored. It might well be nothing, but it would be better to be cautious than sorry. Reaching into the drawer of the desk, he retrieved the small pistol he'd stashed there, already primed and ready. Between it, one blade in his belt and another in his boot, he felt sufficiently well-armed to deal with whomever was out there.

Easing from his chair so that it made not a single creak, he slipped silently to the doors and eased the latch open. With slow, controlled movements, he inched the door open just enough that he could get through.

Stepping onto the fog-shrouded terrace, he caught sight of movement just ahead, slipping around the corner. The morning room opened on that side of the house. Those doors were opened almost daily. The duke had spent a great deal of time in that room, smoking and drinking brandy. The aromas had saturated the carpets and upholstery. It was one final insult as that room had been his mother's favorite before she was confined to her room. Now even the faint trace of her perfume had been long since eradicated.

Cautiously, he crept around the corner, pistol in hand. But then he simply stopped short. It was not a housebreaker. It was not Bechard nor anyone there on his behalf. It was Effie, slipping about in the wee hours of the morning.

"Shouldn't you be seeing to your morning ablutions? I was given to understand that extra care on one's wedding day was something of a standard," he said drolly, pleased with his own joke.

She gasped and whirled on him. "You frightened me half to death! Do not sneak about that way!"

His eyebrow cocked upward. "Who is sneaking here?"

"I wasn't sneaking. I was entering the house quietly," Effie protested, though her tone lacked conviction. "I needed to speak with Mrs. Stephens, and I couldn't go back through the kitchen because the smell of food makes me impossibly ill right now."

Because of the babe. Every mention of it filled him with a strange mixture of fear and joy and swamped him with a wave of tenderness for her. "What was so important that you felt the need to seek the housekeeper rather than summoning her to you?"

Effie stared at him for a moment, her gaze weighing and measuring. Then she simply reached into her pocket and retrieved a book which she held out to him. "I found your mother's journal... and I read it. There were questions that needed to be answered."

He accepted the book, the weight of it in his hand far more substantial than it should have been—as if the significance of what it held might be a tangible thing. He'd known she kept a journal, but he had assumed that her father would have destroyed them all. "What sort of questions, Effie?"

"About your father... your real father."

"He's a monster. That is all I need to know," Nicholas replied sharply. "He raped my mother. He was responsible for her fragile nature."

Effie reached out to him, taking his hand. "That was just another of the duke's lies, another of his many cruel manipulations. The truth was your mother loved him. And he loved her. And he was murdered, quite likely by his own brother... Colonel Silas Winchell."

Nicholas flinched. "Winchell is my uncle?"

"And almost certainly Alexandra's father. According to Henrietta Clark, it isn't the fact that he fathered a child with a prostitute that he sees as a danger to him. It has more to do with when Alexandra was born. Why would that be?"

Highcliff did some quick subtraction. "Because when she was conceived, he was supposed to be on the Iberian Peninsula. If he was not, if he had deserted his regiment—even temporarily—that would be the death knell for his political aims. It's all coming together now," he said.

"We do not have to get married just now. We can postpone everything until the danger has passed—"

"No," he snapped firmly. "We cannot. We will not. If the worst should occur and I do not survive Bechard and Winchell, I will not have our child born out of wedlock. I will not burden an innocent child with the sort of derision you and I have both suffered in this world. Not only that, to ensure the child's future, we must be wed. It is the only way."

After a moment, she nodded. "Of course. I know you are correct."

"I'm sorry that it isn't what you want," he said.

"I want to be your wife!"

"But not this way," he surmised. "You'd like to be certain we would still be on this path with or without the child. You'd like to be married in a way that does not feel clandestine and hurried—where your father could walk you down an aisle draped with orange blossoms and your girls could be all around you. I wish I could give you that." He did wish it. The last thing he ever wanted was for her to regret tying herself to him.

Effie shook her head as she moved closer to him. Her arms wrapped about his waist, and she leaned into him. "True, I would like those things. But I do not need those things. I only need you."

He sighed again, this time with contentment. Being close to her, holding her, feeling the gentle and tempting weight of her touch, it soothed all the jagged parts of him. "And I need you. Every minute of every day. So go upstairs, get dressed in your found finery and let us get to the church."

Effie settled against him. "In a moment. For now, I simply want to enjoy being close to you. It's been far too many years, Nicholas, since we simply had the pleasure of one another's company with no need for secrecy."

Chapter Twenty-Seven

MARGARET SAT IN the hired carriage, the curtains over the windows parted only slightly. Just enough that she might see out with a direct view of the church. On the seat across from her, Bechard waited patiently, not bothering to stare outside, to examine. It was almost as if he expected that he would simply know when they arrived, as if he were somehow mystically attuned to the man. After so many years of hatred, she supposed he might well be.

She'd bargained with the Devil the night before, trading the use of her body for the continuation of her life. She'd certainly traded it for less in the past. But Bechard was not now her lover. He was not the sort who would ever be gentle and see to her pleasure. No. To him, she was only a thing to be used, and that, more than anything else, prompted her growing fury at him.

"Where is Silas?" It was a question she hadn't dared ask the night before.

"I left him in London, just where I found him," Bechard replied.

"Alive?"

Bechard's smile was answer enough. The unscarred side of his face twisted upward, but the scarred said remained downturned, creating a macabre theater of expression. "He lived when I left, though I can't imagine he survived for very long after. Not with a blade protruding from his gut. I daresay, one would hope for a quick death in that instance."

Margaret schooled her face into impassivity. If he knew that it hurt her, it would only make her appear weak. A part of her had wanted Silas dead—she'd known that he would have had no qualms ending her life. But another part of her was pained by the loss. She hadn't lied when she'd told him she was incapable of love, but she'd cared for him in her own way. And from what she knew of the man across from her, what she had heard and what she had experienced with him last night, he enjoyed inflicting pain on others. Beyond any sexual release she had provided for him, it had been the pain he'd caused that had aroused him. *That had satisfied him.* He was the kind of evil that she'd been warned about her entire life, the scary things whispered of to terrify children into behaving. He was the monster people feared in the darkness. It had been her own shortsightedness, her certainty that she could manage anything, control anything—any man, at least—that had brought him to her and culminated in the misery which she currently suffered.

"Do not think to betray me, Margaret," he warned, almost as if he had the ability to read her thoughts. "I'll slit your throat and leave you bleeding out before you can utter the first word against me."

"I will not speak against you. I know better," she stated. "But do not expect me to stand between you and Highcliff—forgive me, the Duke of Clarenden—when the time comes. I hope he kills you."

Bechard laughed softly, the terrifying sound echoing in the confines of the carriage. "That is the difference between us, Margaret. Revenge was a lark for you . . . you did not devote yourself to it. True hatred, the true desire for vengeance, must be nurtured—fed on a daily basis, and allowed to grow into full bloom."

There was no point, she realized, in trying to hide her feelings about him. He wanted her hate. He wanted her anger and pain. He thrived on them. "My hatred for him does not match my hatred for you at present. I will not throw you to the wolves, nor will I be bitten in defense of you should they attack."

Bechard's smile remained firmly in place. "Every man—and woman—for themselves, it would seem. That's fine. You've served your purpose. And since you were such a good little pet last night, I'm inclined to be forgiving... to a point. Do not get in my way or you will find that testing the limits of my mercy is an unwise course of action."

"I have not been laboring under the misapprehension that you possessed such a quality or that I might ever benefit from it," Margaret snapped. "Let us not spar with words and instead focus on the matter at hand—watching for the runaway lovers to make their way into the church."

Bechard nodded, even as he slipped a thin blade from inside his coat. He tested its sharpness against the pad of his thumb, a thin trickle of blood rolling down toward the palm of his hand. His gaze was locked on the rivulet, focused on it to the exclusion of all else. "Indeed. I want to see the smile on his face... I want to see him happy before I destroy him entirely. You were right in that. It will only make it sweeter. When I am finished with his bride, they will both beg for death."

THE CARRIAGE SLOWED to a halt before the church. Across the expanse of the vehicle, Effie sat poised and perfect. Anyone else looking at her would see only a woman who was entirely at ease, no sign of nerves or doubts. But he was not just anyone. He had known her for more than half her life, even if those years of knowledge had required a safe distance be kept between them. Still, he'd watched her—watching over her protectively but also, if he were honest, somewhat obsessively.

It pained him to think how many nights he had wandered into her garden, staring up at the window he knew was hers. He wasn't too proud to acknowledge it for what it truly had been—pining. He'd pined for her. Day in, day out, during waking and sleeping hours, she'd occupied his mind and his heart too thoroughly to ever allow another to take up residence.

Perhaps it was those years of very acute observation that allowed him to now see past her guise of calmness and quietude. Effie was terrified.

"It won't change us," he said. "It won't change how we feel about one another... or if it does, it certainly will not change it for the worse. I'll never love anyone else the way I love you. I'll never want anyone as much as I want you. Don't anticipate disaster. Not when we are finally on the verge of having what we've both wanted for so long."

She looked away from him, her gaze focused on some point beyond the window, indistinct and distant. Unseeing. Her focus was on something other than just their impending marriage. It was on the whole of their future, and she appeared less than hopeful. "I'm not anticipating disaster. Really. I am nervous, of course. Why wouldn't I be? We are neither of us young and carefree. We are older, Nicholas. Set in our ways. I am very used to being independent. to being in charge of my own life, just as you are. I worry about how we will both adjust to these changes. After all, our temperaments are somewhat fiery. It is not in either of our natures to simply capitulate for the sake of keeping peace and that, in my understanding, is what marriage is all about."

He laughed, but the sound was bitter even to his own ears. It was selfish on his part, he supposed, to want her giddy at the prospect of being his wife. Instead, she seemed resolute—braced for the inevitable failure of the dream he'd nurtured for so long. "If I wanted peace, Euphemia, I would have married some biddable young miss fresh from the schoolroom. I would not have spent half my life waiting for you. Do not look at how we might end before we even begin. If you do, you are damning us to that conclusion."

She looked away. "I haven't been hopeful—not truly—in a very long time. I couldn't let myself be when . . . nothing hurts so badly as disappointment. I don't mean to be difficult. I certainly don't mean to make you unhappy as I seem to be doing at present."

"You could never make me unhappy, Effie. But it hurts me to see you making yourself unhappy . . . or worse, refusing to allow even the possibility of happiness. I'm asking for your trust. Can you give it to me?"

"I want to . . . I think I can. And then the doubts seem to swamp me all over again. It's like being in the sea when the current is too strong," she admitted softly.

"Then I shall just have to distract you," he stated. "I shall have to drown out the doubts that keep assailing you."

"How?"

Nicholas reached forward and grasped her hands, hauling her across the expanse of the carriage until they were both sprawled inelegantly on the seat he'd occupied singly only a second earlier. He didn't explain his methods. Instead, he demonstrated them. Kissing her soundly, claiming her lips with all the pent-up desperation of a man who had been denied his greatest desire for nearly two decades. It was hunger and longing mingled with the accumulated need from years of loneliness and misery, and all of that perfectly balanced with the promise of fulfillment—the promise of true happiness.

He kissed her until they were both gasping for breath, until their hearts were racing and the blood was singing in their veins. "Every time your doubts threaten to consume you, you only need to say 'kiss me', and I shall. I will banish those shadows for you until eventually they will simply admit defeat and never return."

She smiled up at him, her lips kiss-swollen and trembling slightly. "Sometimes, like now, you make me feel like that girl . . . the one who waited for you that day at the border of our estates, so full of hope for a blissful future."

"You are her. But you are also a woman of the world—wiser, more knowledgeable, and yes, more cynical. But we are all a product of our past and present . . . and our future hopes. I never gave up on you, on us, whatever I told myself or others. I simply bided my time until I could have what I wanted with the least risk to you," he admitted. "And if I'd had the strength to be honest with you about everything that day, perhaps your doubts wouldn't be such a plague on you now."

"I would never have accepted it," she said. "I would have insisted that we do what we wanted and damn the consequences. We both know that. And then my school would never have been founded, my girls would never have the lives and the futures that are now laid out before them."

"The silver lining?"

"No," Effie said. "I cannot think of what I've achieved as simply the best outcome of a bad situation. I think, if we are to be free of the pain of our past and accept the beauty of the future that lies ahead, then we have to accept that perhaps fate had other ideas for us both. Perhaps being denied this for so long, we should simply appreciate it all the more for having had to wait for it, rather than anticipating failure. Maybe this is how we were always meant to be?"

"We are . . . we are meant to be. Now, we have a vicar waiting for us. Are you certain?"

"Of course I am not certain. But I mean to do it anyway," she said with an impish grin. "You need to make an honest woman of Nicholas Montford . . . make me a duchess!"

Chapter Twenty-Eight

NICHOLAS HAD ENTERED the church before her. Though they had traveled alone in the carriage save for the driver, it was obvious to her that there were people standing guard all about the church's entrance. There were also men present who were surely in the employ of the Hound. They had the look of London toughs rather than country folk. It made her feel strangely safe. She also recognized several of the footmen and stable hands roaming the streets. It reminded her of all the many reasons why she loved Highcliff. Even when they hadn't been speaking to one another with regularity, she knew he'd been looking out for her. He would always take care of her. It was simply his nature.

After a moment, the vicar's wife appeared in the church's massive door, "It's time, my dear," she said.

Effie nodded, clutching the small posey that Mrs. Stephens had placed in her hand before she'd departed the house that morning. But as she entered the church, a frisson of fear snaked down her spine. It had nothing to do with the man who waited at the altar. Instead, it was a curious sensation—of being observed, stalked even.

Glancing over her shoulder, she saw nothing of concern. There were carriages in an inn yard across the way with people bustling about them. Focused on their own tasks and destinations, the bystanders appeared to be oblivious to her and her inner turmoil as she wrestled with that mysterious feeling of dread. Shaking off the sensation, Effie entered the darkened interior of the church. Dim light filtered in through the stained-glass windows, and several candelabras glowed warmly near the altar.

In the front pew, she could see familiar faces. Louisa was there with Alexandra. And her father. Somehow, Nicholas had reached her father. The Duke of Treymore had left London, left his wife and legitimate daughters, and was in attendance for her wedding. How Nicholas had done it she could not fathom, but it served to further eradicate those doubts they'd discussed only moments earlier. Nicholas would have had to summon her father even before he had secured her agreement. He'd risked complete humiliation just so she could have her father present. With a husband who would go to such lengths to see to her every whim, how could she not find happiness?

A slight sound to her left caught her attention and she glanced over to see two men lurking in the shadows. The Hound of Whitehall and Ettinger, the Bow Street Runner, were also in attendance. It was such a representation of her life as a whole—caught between the upper reaches of society with her ducal father and the rookeries where her mother had grown up—that she could not help but smile. And in truth, so long as the Darrow School continued, she would always be bound to those dark, winding streets through the poorest and most desperate areas of London. She wouldn't change it for the world. *And he would never ask her to.*

It was that thought, that knowledge of who he was, that offered her the final bit of clarity she required. Each step grew progressively more decisive and certain. By the time she reached him standing so proud and tall before the slight form of the country vicar, she was beaming at him—convinced that, at long last, all would be right in their world.

And then the ceremony began. Simple and direct, it was incredibly short. Bookended by prayers that felt somewhat hypocritical given the circumstances of their marriage and the fact that their relationship had already proven to be a fruitful union, she wisely kept such observations to herself. The only words that escaped her lips were those the vicar prompted her to repeat and two very simple words which changed her life forever. "I will."

She wouldn't say that it was anticlimactic. But rather, the simple ceremony did not reflect at all the significance of what had just taken place. She felt entirely transformed by it. As they signed the church's register, the enormity of it was simply beyond measure.

And then it was done. Complete. One chapter of their lives was over and the next was set to begin. It felt right. It felt as if she were finally where she should have been all along. All the various segments of her life had intersected in one place, at long last.

Nicholas announced to the small group of gathered guests, "There will be a wedding breakfast at Highview. We would be very pleased if everyone could join us to celebrate."

And then it was well wishes with enthusiastic hugs from Louisa, slightly less effusive congratulations from Alexandra and then her father was standing before her. He kissed her cheek. "Euphemia . . . Effie," he said, defaulting to the diminutive which was so much more natural for everyone when speaking to her. "I'm so very happy for you."

Effie kissed his cheek in return. "I'm happy, too. And happier still that you are here with me."

"Your stepmother and your sisters—"

She shook her head. "You need not explain. They are entitled to feel as they do." In truth, she didn't want to think of them on what should be a happy day.

Her father's jaw firmed. "No, Effie. They are not. It will change. I will not have it any other way. It's gone on long enough. I'll not see my family, all those whom I love, split apart by jealousy and foolish resentments. You are my daughter. And I have let them rule us for far too long."

It was too much. To hear him say the very things she had longed for, the things that would have eased the heartache and loneliness she'd felt as a young woman banished from her family—it was more than Effie could take in. She felt so overwhelmed by it all that she elected to simply put it away for the moment. There were too many emotions, too many different directions. She needed a reprieve from some of it at least.

"Later," she said. "There will be time enough to sort it out later. But for now, today is only for happy thoughts. I've certainly waited long enough for it, don't you think?"

He nodded, smiling. "Yes, you certainly have. I always knew it would come down to this. You are his destiny just as he is yours. It's been that way from the time you first met. I should have intervened—I should have stopped Clarenden from keeping you apart."

Effie shook her head. "It's how it was all meant to be. And now it's time to return to Highview, celebrate with our wedding breakfast."

"And the former duke? When is he to be buried?"

Effie sighed. "He already has been. Highcliff saw to it at dawn this morning. It was simple, with no fanfare, no false mourning. Quiet and with as little fuss as possible. It will likely be a bit of a scandal. But I suspect that everything we do from this point going forward will be a scandal. And I find I do not care. It is worth it. To be with him is worth any cost."

<hr>

NICHOLAS WATCHED HER talking to her father. He saw the peace it brought her. Whatever efforts it had taken to bring it all together, it had been well worth it. When they all exited the church, a peculiar feeling overtook him. It was one he'd encountered many times in his life. Danger. But it had a very different effect on him now. Because it was no longer just him. There was Effie to think of, their child to think of.

As he walked toward her, ready to escort her to the carriage, he could not shake the feeling that danger surrounded them. Guards had been placed all around the perimeter of the church. There were teams of guards in two coaches that would follow them back to Highview. Ettinger and the Hound were both present and, though he did not care for the Hound's interest in Effie, neither would ever permit anything to happen to her. Even as he tried to convince himself they were safe, his skin prickled. His hair stood on end and his pulse beat at a frantic thrum. Still, he offered Effie a reassuring smile as he held out his arm for her. As they walked, he scanned the surrounding area for any danger.

Then the world erupted into flames and smoke. The force of the blast sent the pair of them hurtling backwards to the ground. He wrapped his arms about her, trying to break her fall and shield her from the impact.

Chaos ensued. The structure that exploded was a small linen draper's shop. A newer and primarily wooden structure, it would burn quickly. But it was the building's proximity to the church and to another building on the opposite side that prompted such great urgency. The danger of letting a fire get out of control in such close quarters was well known to all of them.

Struggling to sit up, he ran his hands over Effie's arms and legs. "You are unhurt?"

"Only shaken, I think! Alexandra? Louisa?"

Nicholas turned and saw the young women being bundled into a waiting carriage by Ettinger. "They are well and whole. Our Bow Street friend is seeing to their safety."

"Thank heavens," Effie breathed.

Though it went against every instinct he possessed, he had to get Effie to safety, and he had to stay behind to deal with the blast and ensuing blaze. "I have to get you back to Highview. This fire is more dangerous than you know. The armory, where crates of gunpowder are stored, is only a few doors down. The structure is stone and will hold against the flames, but the heat... Effie it could destroy the entire village if it goes."

"I will go with Alexandra and Louisa," she said.

"Ettinger will go with you. I know that Bechard has a hand in this... and Margaret Hazelton is no doubt close by. Explosions are rather her stock in trade," Nicholas noted, thinking back to the explosion that had very nearly ended his life.

"They're here, aren't they?" Effie asked. "I could feel it before I walked into the church. I could feel them watching us."

"Go with Ettinger," Nicholas said sharply. "He can keep you safe."

Even as he uttered the command, he was waving Ettinger over. "Get her back to Highview. I assume you are well armed?"

"I've got a brace of pistols," Ettinger replied.

Nicholas nodded. "You'll need more. Check under the seat in my carriage. You'll find what you need. Stop for no one. Shoot first and question later."

Ettinger nodded, then helped Effie to stand. The pink gown was covered in dust and debris. Her hair was mussed and there was a faint tremor in her as she looked up at him. "Be careful, Nicholas. I couldn't bear it if you were hurt again."

Nicholas knew that he wasn't the target. If he had been, that explosion would have been more powerful. They weren't trying to kill him. At least not yet. First, they wanted to make him suffer, and he possessed no greater weakness than his bride.

"Keep her safe," he commanded Ettinger, then whirled away, disappearing into the chaos.

Chapter Twenty-Nine

THEY WERE HALFWAY to Highview Manor. Mr. Ettinger was riding up top with the coachmen and there was a wagon of guards before them and another one bringing up the rear. Inside the carriage, they were all very quiet. No one dared speak lest something should be happening outside that they needed to hear.

The carriage wheels hit a particularly large rut, and the vehicle bounced alarmingly. Immediately, it was apparent that something was wrong. The driver called out in alarm as Louisa grabbed for Alexandra when the child nearly fell from the seat. Effie was hanging onto her own seat with a fierce grip. The carriage began to list drunkenly to one side before rolling to a stop.

"Are you unharmed?" Mr. Ettinger called out.

"Yes," Effie replied, all but shouting to be heard. "We are well. What has happened?"

The door to the carriage opened and Mr. Ettinger climbed inside as he explained, "Ambush, Your Grace. A trench was dug in the road and concealed with leaves. It looks like the wheel has been tampered with so that a hard jolt would snap it. And we've lost our guards behind. I've no notion what's become of them."

Your Grace. Even in the midst of their current terrifying situation, that caught her off guard. "Mr. Ettinger—"

Effie never finished that statement. A loud crack rent the air. Pulling back the curtains, Effie looked at the road before them and saw that an ancient and hollowed out tree at the bend in the road had suddenly exploded in flames. Weakened from blight and now rocked by the blast, the massive thing tumbled, crashing to the road with a force that rattled the earth beneath them. The terrified horses reared, and the already battered carriage began to break apart, bits of wood snapping as the horses bolted, dragging part of the equipage with them. The coachman tumbled to the ground, his arm tangled in the reins as the runaway horses dragged him away.

Now, already listing to one side, the carriage abruptly tipped forward. There was no hope of retaining their seats. Louisa and Alexandra tumbled to the floor as Effie was thrown backward against the seat. Her head smacked against the carriage wall with enough force that she saw stars. Mr. Ettinger caught her before she too fell to the floor.

Addled from the force of the blow, it took her a moment to fully comprehend what had happened. *Ambush.* The word he'd used to describe their current predicament took on ominous significance. They were now completely stranded. No horses. The carriage broken beyond repair. Any attempt to flee on foot would make them highly visible targets.

The muffled sound of voices outside had Effie bracing for the next disaster. But when the door to the carriage was wrenched open, Mr. Ettinger was prepared. With his pistol drawn, he faced down the person, but he hesitated. From her vantage point, Effie knew why. He would have expected a man, not a beautiful and refined blonde, a woman she recognized as Margaret Hazelton, Lady Marchebanks.

His split-second hesitation cost them all dearly. The woman raised her arm and fired the small muff pistol she held, the pistol ball striking Mr. Ettinger in the shoulder. The gun fell from his hand clattering to the floor and sliding beneath the girls' feet.

He slumped to the floor, his hand covering the wound that was already bleeding profusely. Louisa screamed, Alexandra had gone pale and quiet... and Effie reached a terrible decision, but it was the only way any of them had a chance at survival. "I will go with you if you leave the girls unharmed," she offered quietly.

The woman smirked in satisfaction. "I had an inkling you would say that. I've no interest in these children. And with Silas dead, this one," she waved a hand at Alexandra, "is no longer a threat."

"If Winchell is dead, why are you doing this?" Effie asked.

"For vengeance. Highcliff—forgive me, the Duke of Clarenden—ruined my life," Margaret said. "Had he simply minded his own business, I would still be the toast of society!"

She had never actually been the toast of society, Effie thought. In fact, Lady Marchebanks had been barely respectable. Between the rumors of the family's impoverishment and her scandalous affair with her husband's nephew, a man who was actually a year or two older than the lady herself, most people in society snubbed them entirely. But it seemed that Lady Marchebanks had rewritten her history to serve her own narrative, and something as inconvenient as the truth would not be tolerated. Her own accountability for her predicament would never be accepted.

Lady Marchebanks continued, blithely and willfully ignorant of the skepticism of those around her, "And now I will ruin his life by taking the one thing he treasures most—you, Your Grace. You are his greatest weakness. It will destroy him. Now get out of this coach."

Effie made no move to follow the woman's directive, but Mr. Ettinger, injured as he was, lunged forward. It sent Effie sprawling backward against the seat even as Margaret Hazelton screamed. The Runner had been armed with more than a pistol. He lunged at the woman with a knife that had been concealed in his sleeve. Margaret jerked away from him, but her feet tangled in her skirts and she stumbled. The knife blade caught her cheek, slicing the perfect skin. Mr. Ettinger slumped onto the floor once more, his energy sapped by the effort to defend them.

The screeches that erupted from the woman were deafening, but the man who appeared behind her quieted her. He said nothing. His presence alone was enough to hush the hysterical woman, not because it calmed her, but because it absolutely terrified her. That much was evident from the way she trembled and shrank from him. Then he raised his pistol and leveled it directly at Mr. Ettinger, who lay on the carriage floor, breathing heavily and bleeding freely.

"Can you do nothing correctly, Lady Marchebanks?" He uttered with a sneer, but it seemed to Effie that he enjoyed deriding the other woman. Then he turned his attention solidly on her. "Your Grace, you will come with us now or I will put a hole in his head. I promise you that it will end his ill-considered heroics . . . permanently."

Effie considered her options, weighing them heavily. There was danger in attempting to evade him, but to go with him was certain death. And she had little doubt, even if she did manage to flee successfully, he would make those who remained behind pay for the insult. He was not the sort of man to simply accept defeat. Her gaze moved from Alexandra's frightened face to Louisa's. They were counting on her.

"There was one shot in this pistol, Your Grace, and it is spent on your Runner here. But I have another pistol in my pocket. Which one of these lovely young women are you willing to sacrifice for your rebellion?" he demanded calmly.

"Neither," Effie snapped, her answer quick and decisive. "I will go with you, quietly and cooperatively, but you must allow them to go free. No harm is to come to them."

He stared at her, his gaze searching. After a moment, he nodded. "You have my word."

Effie made to exit the carriage, but suddenly Alexandra launched herself at Effie, wrapping her in a tight, fierce hug as she sobbed. It was so out of character for the child that Effie had no notion what to do with her. But even as she thought it, Louisa was moving forward to pry Alexandra's hands from her and, in the process, deposit Mr. Ettinger's forgotten pistol in the pocket of Effie's dress. It was a testament to Louisa's early years in the rookeries as a pickpocket that it was such a seamless and smooth deposit. Had it not been for the weight of the pistol against her hip, Effie would never have known the girl had done it.

"Enough!" the man shouted, pulling the second pistol from his pocket. "I am out of patience. Come!"

Reluctantly, Effie pried herself away from the weeping girl—who had the audacity to wink at her—and moved toward the carriage door. As she exited, climbing down carefully, she moved toward the terrifying scarred man. When she was clear of the door, the pistol in the man's hand fired. The sound, so close to Effie's ear, left her reeling. Even then she was whirling about to see the terrible result. Mr. Ettinger lay on the floor of the carriage. He was no longer clutching his injury but instead lay terrifyingly still as Louisa began ripping at her petticoats and using the shredded fabric to staunch the flow of blood from his wounds.

There was so much blood, Effie thought with a pang. If the man survived, it would be a miracle. And if he did, would he ever be the same? It pained her to think of it. But she had no chance to question or to offer even a hint of advice to the girls as she was being dragged away toward waiting horses. Without preamble, she was tossed atop the saddle—a sidesaddle, no less! Ropes had been woven through the stirrup and various parts of the saddle and the ends of those ropes were looped around her wrists and pulled taut. Bechard tied them with an expertise that was disheartening. She had enough freedom to grip the saddle to steady herself should the horse stumble, but not enough to raise her wrists to her mouth and work those knots with her teeth. And riding side saddle, bending forward to do so was not an option. It would overbalance her and send her sprawling toward the ground where she would be dragged by the horse or trampled. The man had thought of everything.

"We aren't going far," he said. "Not to worry."

Margaret Hazleton had mounted her own horse sidesaddle and was still muttering under her breath about her ruined face as the macabre trio headed into the woods. Effie had no notion of what had happened to the guards behind them or those ahead of them, but it terrified her to think that so many men might already have been murdered at the hands of a madman and a spoiled, vain woman. And she thought of Mr. Ettinger and could not halt the hot tears that rolled unchecked down her cheeks.

She would escape. How and when, she could not be certain, but she vowed that she would do so. And this man would harm no one else that she cared for. Whatever the cost, she would be certain of that.

"IT WAS GUNPOWDER. Stolen from the armory," the Duke of Treymore said. He'd stayed behind to fight the fire with Highcliff. "Only a small amount . . . enough to create a diversion."

That was precisely what Nicholas had feared. The fire, once contained, gave every appearance of having been artfully staged to burn for only so long. The small shop and the bolts of fabric housed within it were a total loss. But the church and the building on the other side of it were safe. Most of the items in the armory had been moved further down the street, far away from any lingering embers that might bring about more destruction. In short, the situation was contained.

"I have to find Effie," Nicholas said fiercely. "I cannot help but feel that was simply a distraction orchestrated to separate us."

"The Runner is with her. Surely that would be enough," the duke said worriedly.

Highcliff shook his head. "No. Not this time. Ettinger is a good man... and an even better shot. But these people are not just common criminals, Your Grace. They are something else altogether."

"You need not 'your grace' me, Nicholas. You are now my son... my daughter's husband. And I might remind you that we are of equal rank. You may call me Treymore. Or William, if you prefer."

"Very well, William... I must go. I must find Effie and ensure that nothing has happened that would place her in danger. Will you oversee things here?"

"Gladly. Find her, Nicholas. Find her and keep her safe," the man charged him. "I believe in you, son. The two of you deserve a chance at happiness."

Nicholas headed directly for the local livery where he knew several mounts belonging to the former duke would have been stabled. Quickly saddling a large bay gelding, he hoisted himself up, ignoring the pain in his ribs. A glance over his shoulder showed the Hound already mounted and waiting for him. Nicholas' eyebrows arched upward. "You ride?"

"I do occasionally leave London," the Hound replied sardonically, no trace of the cockney accent present. It was not the time or place for artifice.

"So you do."

"You know she's likely been taken," the Hound said stiffly. "That fire was too easy to put out, too easy to contain. It was intended not to destroy but to delay. It was planned to the most minute detail."

Nicholas nodded. "I'm aware."

"And you are aware, then, that he is waiting for you to come for her. It's all a trap."

Nicholas scowled at him. Of course, he knew. And it mattered not at all. "Try to keep up. I'll be riding fast and hard."

Those were the last words uttered as they thundered from the stable yards and onto the road that would lead toward Highview

Manor and Strathmore Hall. They were less than a mile outside of town when they discovered the first wagon of guards. It was overturned into the river, several of the men severely injured, one dead, and those uninjured working to free a man trapped underneath one of the horses which had broken its leg and had had to be put down.

"How bad?" the Hound snapped.

"Just stuck, sir," the man called back. "The riverbed is soft enough that he's not crushed by the weight. But it's a big animal and we're having a time moving it."

"How did it happen?" Again, the Hound barked the question in a tone that brooked no hesitation.

"Shots fired at the horses, sir. Grazed the rump of one, spooked it and sent us all flying," the man answered. "Whoever did it was lying in wait for us."

"There's a farm half a mile cross country, due west," Nicholas informed them. "The man will have a team of oxen that can haul the horse's carcass off of him. It'll be quicker. When it's done, anyone uninjured and able to fight, head toward Highview Manor. If Effie and the others have reached it, they will need to be protected."

"Aye, Your Grace," the man agreed and then took off in the opposite direction, heading for the farm as instructed.

Nicholas and the Hound shared a look of concern. If they'd sabotaged both wagons of guards, that would leave Effie and the girls with only Ettinger to protect them. Skilled and fierce as the man was, he was still only one man. And it appeared that Bechard had hired his own band of henchmen to aid him in his quest for vengeance. He and Lady Marchebanks could not have done all this alone.

"If we find him, we kill him. And Lady Marchebanks," the Hound said. "These are not the sort of people who stop. Ever."

That suited Nicholas perfectly. He was not inclined toward mercy, not when Effie's life was on the line.

Chapter Thirty

WITH THE COACHMAN dead and Mr. Ettinger gravely wounded, Louisa had commanded her to go off in search of help. But Alexandra understood that she could not just go up to any local farmer and ask for assistance. Simple, country people were no match for the sort they were up against. Highcliff—no, the duke, she corrected herself—would know what to do.

To that end, she was running down the country lane as fast as her legs would carry her. Even when her side began to ache, when she was breathless and panting, still she ran. Her feet pounded against the packed earth as she headed toward the village and what she could only hope would be a dashing rescue.

The pounding of her pulse in her ears almost drowned out the sound of approaching hoofbeats. By the time she saw the riders barreling toward her, it was almost too late. Uncertain at such a distance of who they might be, Alexandra halted so quickly she nearly stumbled and fell. Instead, she pitched herself to the side, falling into the thick bushes that lined the side of the road. The briars pulled at her hair, snagging her dress, and the stockings she wore offered little protection for her legs as they scraped her skin. Still, she made not a sound, peering out until they were close enough to determine their identity.

Finally recognizing the duke and the Hound, she lurched forward out of the bushes, further tearing her dress and her skin in several places. Scraped, bleeding and breathless, she waved her arms to get their attention and both men slowed but were still dangerously close to her. One of the horses reared on its hind legs. Those deadly hooves flailed above her for a moment, before settling onto the ground once more, far too close for comfort.

"You could have been killed!" the Hound snapped at her. "Have you no more sense than to run out in the road before a galloping horse?"

Alexandra didn't bother to acknowledge his criticism. There were more pressing matters to attend to than her wounded feelings or bruised pride. "Mr. Ettinger has been shot. Twice. It's bad. Very bad. Louisa is with him now. But the Frenchman took Effie. She went with him to save us. The woman with them is half-crazed because Mr. Ettinger cut her face... she's almost mad from it," Alexandra explained. She'd been succinct in her explanation out of both urgency and exertion. She was still breathless.

The Hound reached down, hauling her up into the saddle before him. Then they were flying down the lane once more, the big horse moving beneath them in a way that made Alexandra close her eyes. She wasn't normally one to be afraid, but the height and the speed of the beast left her shaking. But she never uttered a word of complaint. She understood that speed was necessary. Mr. Ettinger's life was hanging in the balance and so was Miss Darrow's—the duchess.

Would she ever grasp the new titles? Would it even prove necessary?

That last thought only heightened her fear. She prayed she'd have the opportunity to get it wrong and be gently corrected. Unlike every other adult who'd ever tried to teach her anything in her life, Effie did not yell or scream. She never cuffed her or boxed her ears or thrashed her hand with a cane. Instead, she explained calmly what was wrong and how it was to be done correctly. In all of Alexandra's life, Miss

Euphemia Darrow, now the Duchess of Clarenden, was the only person who had ever truly been kind to her. Even her own mother hadn't been so gentle or loving.

And then Alexandra did something she'd hardly ever done in her young life. She prayed. Unlike when she'd bowed her head and stood quietly as others around her in the workhouse offered their pleas to the Lord, she actually prayed. Silently, she pleaded with God, or the Fates, or whomever might be listening, to spare the new duchess, to spare Mr. Ettinger, to see the good people to safety and the wicked people punished. Despite the terrible things she'd witnessed and endured in her life, there was just enough of the innocence of childhood in Alexandra to have the faintest belief that fairness could still exist in the world. In the end, she wasn't certain her prayers would do any good at all, and she wasn't even certain she believed there was a God or that he listened to baseborn girls such as herself. But she hoped he existed, and she hoped he was the sort of God Effie had told her about—one who was merciful and just.

>>><<<

THEY DID NOT ride fast, but as they neared the small wood and stone structure in the forest, Effie realized that speed had not been necessary. They were only two miles or so from the carriage and poor Mr. Ettinger. She prayed that Louisa would have the sense about her to send Alexandra for help and that someone would find them all before it was too late for the Runner. It broke her heart to think that he might die because of his attempt to save her. For herself, she was fairly certain that her fate was sealed.

There was little doubt that the man, whom Lady Marchebanks had called Bechard, meant to see her dead. He'd said very little, but then he did not need to speak. The truth was there in his eyes for anyone to see. He looked at her as if she were a thing to be disposed of, not a person. To him, she was not even human but was simply a tool to be used for his vengeance. As for Lady Marchebanks, she was focused only on the wound to her face—on the idea that her beauty, which she had traded on so frequently, had been taken from her. She wailed near incessantly about it until finally Bechard whirled on her and leveled the pistol directly at her face.

"I will give you more than just a scar. Think carefully before you utter another sound, Margaret," he snapped.

"I'm ruined," she whispered.

"There are worse things in life than being scarred," he said, his own scarred face twisting with wry amusement. "Test me, Margaret, and I will be certain that you live a long life with your scarred face and more daily agony than a person can endure. I could remove your nose... your ears. I could carve a bit of flesh from your cheeks. Indeed, that little scratch that the Runner gave you will be nothing in comparison. Now cease your wailing."

Effie held her breath, waiting for the impetuous woman to say something that would drive the man over the edge. The barely leashed violence within him was terrifying, and she didn't understand how anyone could ever imagine challenging him when at such a disadvantage. She prayed the woman came to her senses, not because she had any great love or even mercy for her, but because she wasn't certain she would be able to stomach what Bechard had planned.

Remaining silent, Effie waited, the heavy feeling of dread pressing down on her. Fear was a terrible burden. Fear for herself, for Nicholas, for the Hound who was undoubtedly at his side, for poor Mr. Ettinger, and for her girls—not just Alexandra and Louisa, but all of them. If she did not return, if the worst happened, she had no notion of what might become of them.

At last, Margaret simply snapped her mouth closed. Her venomous gaze revealed her hatred of him. Bechard, unmoved by the display, turned his horse back onto the path and smiled at Effie as he did so.

But the smile left her so cold that she shivered from it. *Like an icy hand on her skin.*

He spoke softly, so softly that she had to lean forward to hear him. "It's a pity, Your Grace, that Margaret hasn't your ability to retain her composure. I daresay this will not end well for either of you, but at least you might preserve some of your dignity."

"Nicholas will come for me," she said.

Bechard nodded. "Indeed, he will, Effie. I'd rather planned on it. Make no mistake . . . one must first catch the bait in order to catch the fish. And you make excellent bait. Most excellent."

Then he was moving forward again, his horse trudging along the path in front of them that led through the woods as he tugged on the reins of Effie's mount which then plodded along behind him. She struggled in vain against her bonds, twisting her bound hands again and again. The rough fibers of the ropes at her wrists tore at her skin leaving it raw and tender, cut in places and terribly bruised in others, but still she continued. The time they were en route to their destination was her only chance since he could not keep his eyes on her all the time.

Despite the pain, she continued her efforts because the alternative—simply giving in to whatever it was he might have planned for her—was not an option. The weight of the pistol in her pocket was a tangible reminder of what hung in the balance. For the first time in her life, she was truly in a situation where she must kill or be killed. When it came to needing to protect her own life and that of her unborn child, she knew she would not hesitate to end him. She could not afford to be merciful.

Aside from the pistol, there was one other advantage Effie did have. She knew these woods. It might have been years, but these were the same woods where she and Nicholas had met in secret so many times when they were younger. If she could get away from him, even with a momentary head start, there were half a dozen places she still remembered clearly where she might be able to conceal herself until a rescue attempt could be mustered.

Bechard spared a single glance over at his shoulder in her direction. There was something in his gaze, in the knowing smirk that curved his cruel mouth. He knew what she was about and he didn't even care. *Because he believed she would not succeed.* That thought sapped Effie's strength for a moment, dampening her resolve and creating a feeling of helplessness in her that threatened to swamp her. But the things she'd achieved in life had not been attained without being willing to meet adversity head on. In fact, she prided herself on it. If it were one of her girls, she would tell them to never give up, to be vigilant for any opportunity to escape. How, then, could she do less?

With renewed determination, Effie kept working towards freedom. She'd not give him the satisfaction of being cowed and docilely accepting of whatever fate he had in store for her.

Chapter Thirty-One

ETTINGER HAD BEEN taken to a nearby farm to be treated for his wounds. Nicholas had sent two men back to the village to fetch the doctor and any of the local women who were skilled at healing. Between the Runner and the men injured when the wagon had overturned, there was more work than one man alone could ever manage.

The first wagon had also been accounted for. They had been too far ahead and did not realize until it was too late that they had left their objective in the dust behind them. By the time they had doubled back and returned to the scene of the now ruined carriage that had been taking Effie to Highview, it was too late. Effie had been taken and Ettinger was injured.

It had seemed the better option to leave them behind to deal with the wreckage and set out after Bechard with just himself and the Hound. Stealth was their greatest weapon. Louisa had told them that Bechard had led her through the woods after putting her on horseback. As they set out after her, Nicholas could feel the cold fear riding him while a million doubts plagued his mind. *What if they were already too late? What if Effie survived and their baby did not? Would she hate him for that? Did Bechard know about the child? If so, it would only increase the danger.*

It might have been a lifetime since he'd haunted those woods as a boy, a preferable alternative to the manor where the duke's censure was ever present, but Nicholas knew little in the area had changed. That path through the woods led only to one source of shelter—an abandoned grist mill. The stone had cracked after hundreds of years of use and the demand for milling in the area had decreased to the point that repairing it had not been feasible, mostly because the former duke had refused the expenditure. It was a testament to the vastness of the Clarenden holdings that they were still wealthy at all, as he'd been determined to beggar himself rather than leave anything behind for Nicholas.

"The mill is half a mile ahead," Nicholas said, keeping his voice pitched low. It was clear, based on the steps taken thus far, that Bechard was not working alone and that he had significantly more help than just Margaret Hazelton. There had to have been several teams of men in place to carry out the sabotage on the wagon of guards. Those men could even now be lurking in the woods, watching for anyone that would attempt to mount a rescue. If Bechard thought he was cornered, he'd slit Effie's throat before they had any hope of getting to her.

The Hound nodded. They moved deeper into the forest, the trail all but disappearing. Through the trees, there were glimpses of the structure. Nicholas signaled for them to dismount there. With the horses secured, they crept forward, moving soundlessly through the foliage. Nicholas was surprised at the ease with which the Hound navigated the task. For a man born and bred in the cesspits of London, the countryside clearly posed no obstacle for him.

With weapons drawn, they used the concealment offered by the trees to draw closer and closer to the structure. There were no raised voices, no horses, but there was a thin trail of smoke coming from one of the chimneys inside the old stone building.

"They're inside," Nicholas said.

"Perhaps. But if this man is as tricky as you say," the Hound mused, "This could all just be some elaborate ruse. He could have taken her anywhere."

Knowing it was the truth did not make it easier to hear. Still, Nicholas gave a curt nod. "It's a starting point. Time is on our side, however. He wouldn't have been able to get far with her. And if I know Effie, she's already plotting her own escape."

"On that point, we are in complete agreement," the Hound stated. "I'll make my way around the back. I'll need five minutes to get in position before you approach the front."

Nicholas nodded, but his gaze never left that curling trail of smoke that filtered up from the chimney. It was the only sign of life, and that terrified him. Shouting down the rafters would not endear her to Bechard, but it would at least afford him some peace of mind that Effie was still alive. He could only wait and do something he had not done in years—pray.

>>><<<

THERE WAS NO roof on the old mill. The thatch had long since rotted away leaving only timbers. But above them, bare branches swayed in the breeze and the sun shining through them left a dappled pattern on the earthen floor below. It might have been a pretty scene, had it not been for the horrible circumstances which had brought her there.

Effie was on the floor, the once beautiful pink dress—her wedding gown—now dirty and torn. Her hands, bloodied from her efforts to free herself from her bonds, ached terribly. But it wasn't the physical pains that left her trembling. It was the fear, the constant anxiety of not knowing what was to come. So she remained watchful and made not a sound even as Lady Marchebanks was weeping softly in the corner, staring into a small sliver of glass that remained in one of the windows. The small laceration to her cheek no doubt magnified in her mind.

But Effie, tossed unceremoniously to the floor upon their entry, had found her own treasure. A single loose nail had lain on the floor next to a broken board that had been pried from one of the windows. With that nail concealed in her hands, she carefully began plucking at the fibers of the ropes binding her, patient and determined.

Watching the woman, Effie could not quite countenance Lady Marchebanks' degree of desperation over her appearance. But the woman was not in the same immediate danger of losing her life as Effie was. Perhaps a scar was her greatest worry, but it was not Effie's. *Her life. Nicholas' life. The life of their unborn child.* Those were the things that weighed on her mind, not something as inconsequential as such a minor disfigurement.

Yes, the cut would scar. That was without question, but it was a small, neat slice. No more than two inches wide. It was a wound that would heal, if she permitted it to, leaving only a faint line in its wake. With proper care, it was quite possible that no one would ever know it was there unless they were looking for it.

Unlike Bechard. The scar on his face was an angry, jagged thing. He blamed Nicholas for it. That was evident in the fact that he would touch that scar every time Nicholas' name was mentioned. It was the source of his hatred and the cause of his quest for vengeance. But she needed him distracted. She needed him talking so that, if in the process of freeing her hands, she made a sound, he would not hear it. Like any vain person, he would love the sound of his own voice. And if she could keep him talking, it might also allow her to stave off whatever painful torment he had planned for her. At least for a while longer.

"What is it that makes you hate Nicholas so?" Effie asked, the question soft and barely more than a whisper. Though it was purposeful, engaging him in conversation was the last thing she wanted. Listening to more of his obsessive madness and hatred could only further cement in her mind just how insane he was. With no accountability for his own actions, he only seemed to see what had happened to him and not that he had brought about his own ruin. It occurred to

Effie that the commonality between every villainous or wicked person she had ever known in her life was their supremely self-serving nature. They lacked the ability to see another person's wants, needs, or even suffering as being more important than their own.

"This," Bechard said as he perched on the sill before of a now vacant window. It was an excellent vantage point that would allow him, just by the turning of his head, to watch the path that led to the mill and also keep an eye on its unwilling occupants. He raised one hand, his fingers trailing along that scar. "I was once accounted to be the most handsome of men in France. Until he destroyed my face."

He was still handsome. Despite the scar, there was still beauty in his face. But that beauty was eclipsed by the coldness in him, by the cruelty that was so evident in his icy gaze.

"And Nicholas did that to you?" Effie asked.

"Yes... He made quite a nuisance of himself during the war, you see. Conflicts between nations are nothing more than opportunity for men with vision. And it was thanks to my vision, and Marchebanks' lack of fidelity to his country, that we were all amassing a significant fortune. But Highcliff had to interfere. He uncovered a cache of documents that revealed far too much about our little enterprise. It wasn't personal then. I needed to eliminate the threat posed, and I needed to know if he'd revealed our scheme to his superiors."

"So you tortured him," Effie said. "For nothing more than profit."

Bechard shrugged. "Profit is the deciding factor in whether or not I indulge my predilection for inflicting pain. Regardless, the incompetent men working for me had failed to secure his hands, and when I made the mistake of turning my back to him, he reared up, grabbed a bottle of wine that was on my desk and smashed it. We fought... bitterly. And this was my reward. He slashed my face with that broken bottle and left me ruined. I nearly died from the infection that raged afterwards." He stopped, leaning forward and resting his hands on his knees as he peered at her curiously. "Do you know how much this world prizes beauty above all else?"

Effie shook her head. It was a question that had no proper answer. Anything she said to him would be the wrong thing. She shifted slightly, as if trying to find a more comfortable position, but in fact she simply drew her knees up to conceal the fact that the ropes at her wrists were beginning to fray.

"If you are beautiful enough, you can truly get away with murder. People assume that anyone who looks angelic is angelic, often regardless of any evidence to the contrary. No one questioned me. I had the trust and confidence of every person I encountered... and now people look at me differently. They ask questions, they are curious about what I might have done to earn such a mark... and that has affected far more than just my luck with ladies. It's altered my financial situation. You see, when you look like a villain, people assume you are one."

There was no need to point out that he had earned that mark, that Nicholas had almost died as his captive. He'd been starved, beaten, tortured, and when he'd come home, he'd been haunted. She knew that because she had seen him. His pain had seemed to reach out to her. Bechard *was* a villain, regardless of how he might see himself.

Thinking of just how broken Nicholas had been when he'd returned for that short time after his captivity brought Effie only pain. She'd not been allowed to offer him any comfort or to ease his suffering, however she might have longed to. She'd watched from afar, hating him and loving him all at once. But pointing any of that out to Bechard would not help her.

"You are still a handsome man. Just as Lady Marchebanks is still a beautiful woman."

Bechard laughed. "Flattery will not spare you, Your Grace. I wonder, when your own face is so marked, will you feel that such scars are not a defect? Perhaps Highcliff's—forgive me, *His* Grace's—love for you will not bear up under the strain of your disfigurement. Let us put it to the test, shall we?"

He was off of the windowsill and moving toward her so quickly that Effie didn't even have time to struggle to her own feet or scoot back from him. When he grasped her bound arms, the ropes digging into her abused flesh, she let out a sharp scream. But all of her determination had borne fruit at last. With the added pressure of him pulling at her so, the frayed ropes finally snapped. Somehow, she managed to hold them loosely in place and clutch the nail in her hand, concealing it entirely even as she struggled against him.

He leaned in, his breath fanning over her cheek in a manner that made her skin crawl. Then he dipped his head and pressed a hot kiss to her neck, his teeth clamping down on the tender flesh where her neck and shoulder met. Immediately, she stopped moving. It had been obvious from the gleam in his wicked gaze that her pain was his pleasure. This was a man who enjoyed hurting others.

"You are a monster," she whispered hotly. "Not because of the scars on your face but because of the blackness of your character!"

He crouched low before her, gripping her face in a bruising manner, his fingers squeezing painfully along her jawline. "My dear, you have no idea how right you are . . . but you are mistaken if you think I find that to be an insult. I want to be the monster. I have always wanted to be the monster. I simply never wished to look like one."

Effie was hoisted to her feet by that same brutal grip as he rose. When finally he released her, she stumbled backward. Had it not been for the stone wall directly behind her she would have fallen. Her face ached, but nothing compared to the misery created by the knot of fear that had settled in her stomach.

"He will come for me," she said. Her bravado might have been false, but her faith in Nicholas was not. She had no doubt that he was already searching for her. The only question was whether or not he would find her in time.

Bechard held his knife up, inspecting it carefully. "What part of you shall I carve up first?"

Effie had nowhere to go. The wall was at her back and he was in front of her, blocking any potential escape. Thinking only of the best way to protect herself, she lashed out at him with the nail she'd concealed in her hands, the ropes finally falling away.

His other hand shot out, snagging her wrist to pull her forward. Effie screamed, even as she struck out at him. The nail scored his skin, dragging over the soft flesh just below his ear and arcing over his jawline. Blood welled immediately from the cut she'd made and the cold fury that suffused his face then was something from her nightmares. She prayed Nicholas was close by, prayed for any intervention at all. Because it seemed her time had run out.

Chapter Thirty-Two

THAT SHORT, SHARP scream had taken years off his life. Crouched in the overgrown bushes that grew against the side of the mill, it took every shred of self-control he possessed not to simply go charging in. Timing was everything, after all.

With bated breath, Nicholas waited for the signal from the Hound. When it finally came, it was not subtle. The back door to the mill came crashing inward, slammed by the force of the Hound's boot against it. The moment was not wasted. Nicholas dove in through the open window, weapons drawn as he came up in a crouch, facing Bechard.

Instantly, Bechard hauled Effie around in front of him, one arm wrapped about her as he held the knife to her throat with his other hand.

Margaret Hazelton did not even seem to see him or the Hound. She was focused only on the reflection of her bloody face as she rocked back and forth, weeping brokenly. But it would be a mistake to discount her entirely. Just because she was not an immediate threat, that did not mean she was harmless. But all his attention was focused on Bechard who now held Effie before him under his wicked-looking knife.

Bechard eyed him coldly, a smile tugging at the unscarred corner of his mouth as he peered at him just above the top of Effie's head. "I'll slit her ear to ear. She'll be dead before her body hits the floor," the Frenchman warned.

"Let her go," Nicholas said softly. "You wish to fight me? Fine, we will fight. Just the two of us."

"Oh, no. I have no wish to fight you," Bechard replied evenly, almost congenially. "My wish, Your Grace, is to break you. To destroy every reason that you have to want to live . . . and only then will I take your life."

Those words chilled the very blood in his veins. Because he knew that Bechard meant every one. It was not the first time he'd engaged in such a campaign against those he thought had wronged him. After he'd escaped from him in France, Bechard had set a course of vengeance against every man who had been part of the network of intelligence agents that Nicholas had worked for and with. Some had been murdered in cold blood. Others had suffered fates that, if asked, they would say were far worse than death. Their families and loved ones had suffered at Bechard's hands just as Effie did now. And this moment was the culmination of it all. The brutal finale of a years-long vendetta.

"I knew you were a madman," Nicholas said, goading him intentionally. "But I never took you for a coward. Do you think you can only best me if I am shattered with grief first? Surely a man renowned for such skill with a blade must think more of his abilities than that!"

Bechard glanced behind him and gave a warning shake of his head to the Hound. The criminal immediately stilled, glancing up at Nicholas to wait for his signal to attack. Nicholas kept his gaze locked on his old enemy, on the man who had traveled so far to avenge himself for an injury that had never been intended to scar, but to kill. He'd tried to slit Bechard's throat with that broken bottle as he made his escape, but he'd been too weak. The Frenchman had forced his arm upward and the jagged glass had cut his face instead. Given what they were now facing, Nicholas wished fervently that he'd found the strength in those moments to overpower the bastard and spare them all their current ordeal.

"Face me like you actually have a shred of honor," Nicholas challenged once more. "Face me like you deserve to be called a man." Even as he issued the challenge, he could see Effie's hands twisting in front of her. They were bloodied and raw from the ropes that had cut into her delicate skin.

"Why would I do that? This isn't a question of honor, Your Grace. It's a question of vengeance. I do not wish to simply best you, but to make you suffer," Bechard replied, flicking the knife against Effie's throat. A thin trickle of blood flowed from that small prick and Effie gasped in either pain or shock.

Over Bechard's shoulder, Highcliff could see the Hound creeping forward once more, moving with silent menace toward his target. Keeping him distracted, Highcliff continued. "If you wish to make me suffer then make me your prisoner again. You tortured me for months, starved me, deprived me of sleep, beat me. And if you spare her, I will submit. I will not attempt to escape, I will live apart from her for the rest of my days, if I must, if it means she will be safe."

Effie made a sound of protest, but she did not speak. She could not for Bechard's other hand had suddenly covered her mouth. With the tip of the knife, he drew a faint line over the skin of her collarbone, blood welling from the intentionally shallow cut. It spilled onto the pink silk of her wedding gown and the sight of it made him ill.

But Effie was not just a damsel in distress. She was resourceful and strong. And no one had ever possessed the degree of fierce determination that she did. Nicholas knew that as he watched her hand slip into her pocket. All at once, Effie raised her other hand to shove Bechard's knife away from her at the same instant that the loud report of a shot rang out.

Bechard made not a sound, but his expression slackened. He staggered backward, the knife falling from his hand as he clutched at his wounded thigh. Blood pumped from the wicked gash high on the man's leg. From the rapidly spreading stain, it was clear that an artery had been severed. Bechard would be dead in minutes, but until his heart ceased to beat, he could still pose a threat.

Even as Effie moved away from the deranged man, Nicholas was diving forward, grasping for the knife that had clattered to the floor. And when Bechard, with the last of his strength, charged at him, he lifted that knife and plunged it into Bechard's gut. The man fell to the floor, the Hound behind him, his hand covered in blood and a second blade protruding from Bechard's back.

It was impossible to say which of their blows had ended him. It could have been the blood lost from the gunshot. Or it could have been either of the stab wounds. But as Nicholas and the Hound locked eyes, an unspoken agreement formed between them. The responsibility for his actual death would be assumed by one of them. Regardless of the circumstances, that was something he did not want Effie to live with.

"What about her?" the Hound asked, gesturing toward Lady Marchebanks.

Nicholas rose to his feet, already moving toward Effie. "She will face her punishment as she ought to have the first time."

"She will never stand trial," the Hound insisted. "She is clearly mad now, even if she was not before."

"That is neither our choice nor our problem," Nicholas stated coldly. "It is for someone else to decide her fate. We must simply deliver her into their hands."

"No," the Hound replied. "You have done enough. I will see to it. Lady Marchebanks will get the justice she deserves."

⇶⇷

SAFE IN THE circle of Nicholas' arms, Effie finally drew a breath deep enough to dispel the terrible tension that had held her in its grip from the moment Bechard had pulled her from the carriage. But the Hound's words troubled her. He meant to kill her, Effie realized. The Hound intended to eliminate the threat that Lady Marchebanks posed to her or anyone else. But she could not permit him to do that. Not out of any love or even compassion for Lady Marchebanks, but for his own sake. The Hound might strike fear in the hearts of men, but she knew him differently. She knew him to be a lover and protector of all women. From the youngest to the oldest, every female he encountered he looked after in some way. If he took Margaret Hazelton's life, the cost of such an action would be too high.

"Do not harm her," Effie insisted. "She is not worth that stain upon your conscience."

"My conscience is absent, Your Grace, and my heart completely black. Surely you know that by now," the Hound insisted.

"Not it is not. If it were, you would not have risked life and limb to save me. Let us see to Lady Marchebanks. We must make our way back to London right away regardless. I need to summon my girls back to the Darrow School and resume their education. It has been sorely neglected of late, and that is not something I can afford to ignore any longer." She looked up at Nicholas, a question in her eyes. "Alexandra?"

"She and Louisa are well," Nicholas answered. "Louisa was tending to Ettinger, and Alexandra ran for help, meeting us on the road. They are safely ensconced at a farmer's home, and the physician was summoned to tend our injured friend."

Effie was almost afraid to ask the question, but she forced herself to utter the words. "Will he live?"

The Hound's face was etched in hard lines, his dark eyes glittering with a kind of anger that she had never seen in him before. "There is no way to know . . . not yet. He is a contrary sort. Perhaps if I tell him to go on and meet his maker, he will live to spite me."

Effie did not smile at the jest for she could see clearly how distressed the man was at the prospect of his friend's death. The Hound would never have called Mr. Ettinger his friend, and perhaps they should not be classified so. In many regards, she felt they were much like brothers. She knew they had come up together, pulling themselves from the ranks of crime and poverty only to go, for the most part, in different directions. "Go to Mr. Ettinger, Vincent."

He stared at her blankly for a moment. It was a name that he rarely heard. In fact, no one had called him that for years. "I have never told you my given name."

Effie shook her head and explained as kindly as possible, "You are not the only one with a network of spies and informants. You are a good man, Vincent Stafford. I made it a point to find out all I could about you the first time you brought a disheveled little girl to my door."

The Hound ducked his head in a gesture that might have been sheepish on any other man. "Your Grace, you are a marvel and I both envy and pity your husband the merry chase you shall lead him." He paused, considering. "I will not see the woman dead by my own hand or my own orders. I shall deliver her to authorities that will decide her fate. Now, the both of you should go. You will have guests waiting very worriedly for you at Highview Manor."

Effie stepped forward, wrapped her arms lightly about the Hound and pressed a kiss to his cheek. "Thank you . . . for everything you have done today, and everything you have done in the past, both for me and my girls. You have been a true friend."

"No one can ever know that," he said. "It would ruin you to be known as my friend . . . either of you."

Effie shook her head. "I am now a duchess. I do not conform to standards, sir. I set them. Isn't that right, Nicholas?"

Nicholas stepped forward then, extending his hand to the Hound. "I'm not in the habit of denying my friends for the sake of public opinion, especially when they have gone to such measures to prove their loyalty. You will always be welcome in our home."

"You wouldn't say that if you knew the truth about me," the Hound insisted.

"You mean that you are the illegitimate son of the former Duke of Clarenden? That he left you to rot in the rookeries? Though given his lack of paternal inclinations, you were likely better off," Nicholas offered.

"You knew. For how long?"

Nicholas sighed. "I've always known. My older brother, Sutton—half sibling to us both—told me of your existence. I didn't put two and two together until a couple of years ago. You look like him... like Sutton. He was slighter than you, rail thin and rather fragile. In body and spirit. The former duke broke him. He destroyed him little by little every single day until he could stand it no more and—I fear—took his own life."

Silence stretched between the three of them, the heaviness of that subject after the turmoil of the day weighing on all of them. Finally, Effie let out a huffing breath. "There you have it, Vincent. You are not simply our friend, but part of our family. As such, you are required to visit us often."

He hugged her back then, closing his arms about her and lifting her off the ground. "I will consider it. Now go. Go, and I will see to this miserable shrew."

Chapter Thirty-Three

It had been one week since their wedding. Seven days since Effie's abduction by Bechard. They had elected to leave Highview three days prior and had reached London and the familiar comfort of her school only the night before. Despite all the turmoil, or perhaps because of it, Effie was eager to get back to the normal way of things, whatever that would be now that they were wed. Other than a nightmare or two, some scrapes and bruises that were an unfortunately vivid reminder of it all, she was none the worse for wear. As for Nicholas, it seemed that every time he looked at her, every time he noticed some new mark or even the slightest injury, he became furious all over again.

Lying in bed, locked in her husband's embrace in that last hour before dawn, Effie reflected that everything they had endured was worth it to be where they were. Turning her head slightly, she studied him. He truly was terribly handsome. With his chiseled features and dark hair, he had always had the look of a fallen angel to her. And now, with the little bit of silver at his temples, that seraphic beauty was only more pronounced. Her lips curved upward in a satisfied smile as she let her gaze roam over him. She might have had to wait for him, but he was certainly worth it.

"You're thinking very loudly again," he said, without bothering to open his eyes.

"Am I? Does it matter if they are only good thoughts?" she asked.

He cracked one eye open then, looking at her with a wicked gleam in his eyes. "That you can think at all feels very much like a failure on my part. Perhaps I should endeavor to render you incapable of thinking or speaking again . . . so replete and satisfied that you will not even be able to stand long enough for your maid to help you dress."

Effie pursed her lips, as if she were considering it more as an offer than a threat. "Is that supposed to be a punishment?"

"I should certainly hope not," he growled playfully even as he rose above her. His weight rested on his forearms, but the length of his body was pressed intimately against her.

Effie shivered at that touch, as always, rendered nearly senseless by the overwhelming love she felt for him—and the need. He had but to look at her and he could awaken her desire. "Do you not have to be at Whitehall? Are they not deciding the fate of Lady Marchebanks this morning?"

"They will decide it without me," he said. "They have all the evidence I accrued during my initial investigation—before she buried one of her servants in her stead," he said, dipping his head to press soft kisses along the column of her throat.

Each kiss was punctuated with a nip of his teeth or a flick of his tongue. By the time he reached her collarbone, Effie was breathless. Her hands came up, her fingers roaming over the heated skin of his broad back, her nails digging into the flesh there. Her head tipped back, a soft sigh escaping her parted lips as she was poised to give in entirely—and then a harsh knock sounded on the door, effectively ruining the mood.

"You'll be wanting breakfast before you start your day, and I'll not be serving it to you in bed, duchess or no!"

Mrs. Wheaton's northern-tinged accent was harder, owing to her general state of being put out that there was now a man ensconced in the female bastion of the Darrow School.

"Will she ever stop hating me?" Nicholas asked with a pained expression.

"She doesn't hate you," Effie said gently. "She simply doesn't trust you. And no. By virtue of your sex, you shall always be in the category of unknown threat for her. Though I imagine, once I give birth to this child, she will thaw toward you somewhat. Nothing melts Mrs. Wheaton's heart quite like a baby."

"Or Stavers. Did I tell you that he was serenading her over the garden wall last night? Standing out in the mews, bold as brass, crooning a love song!"

Effie blinked in surprise. "Stavers? Was he any good?"

"Good at what?"

"Singing!" she said, smacking his hand away from her hip as she struggled to get up. "She'll only come back if we do not emerge from this chamber within minutes."

"It isn't even sunrise!"

Effie smiled. "The day starts very early when you run a school for girls. But on the upside, the days end early, as well."

"And do headmistresses have time to slip away in the middle of the afternoon?" he asked, emerging from the bed, heedless of his nudity or the chill in the room. It was certainly not having any withering effect on him.

Effie silently cursed Mrs. Wheaton herself—just a little. "I should be able to do so. And where would I be meeting you?"

"I do have a house of my own only a few streets away," he reminded her, gently nipping at her shoulder.

"Two o'clock?" she asked, half-heartedly tying the tapes of her petticoat. It went against every instinct and desire she possessed to be putting clothes on in that moment rather than taking them off.

"Is that the earliest you can be persuaded to meet me?" His lips trailed from her shoulder, up to her ear, his breath fanning hotly over the sensitive skin.

"Well, I could postpone the interviews I have for a new headmistress."

Abruptly, he let go of her and stepped back. "No. Those interviews most certainly cannot be postponed. We need a new headmistress in this school so I will have more of your time, not less."

Effie turned to face him. "And you... will I have more of your time? Or will Whitehall persuade you back into the fold?"

"No. I will never go back to that. I want no more danger. No more enemies. I want long, leisurely mornings in bed with my wife and endlessly passionate nights to prove to her how very brilliant she was in agreeing to marry me."

Effie made a moue of disapproval. "Strutting peacock," she snapped, though it lacked heat.

"If you're interested in a strutting cock—"

"Stop!" she nearly shouted, though laughter bubbled up from her even as she uttered the admonition. Laughing with him, when they'd been little more than children, had been some of the very best moments of her life. And now she'd have those moments again, every day. "I love you, Nicholas. In spite of your vanity and your horrendously ribald wit."

He pulled her into his arms once more, kissing her soundly before drawing back. "I think you love me for my vanity and my ribald wit. I'll make a raucous hellion of you yet."

"Half the world already thinks I am a hellion because I had the audacity to have a job that does not involve being some man's mistress," she pointed out. "Now put on your trousers before a gaggle of impressionable young girls start traipsing about the corridors. There are some things I am not willing to educate them about just yet."

※

HALF AN HOUR later, Nicholas was fully dressed and making his way from Effie's school on Jermyn Street to his own house on Park Lane. An unsigned note had arrived just as he was leaving, requesting his presence at home. He knew it was the Hound. Despite their protestations, he had so far refused to openly associate with either Effie or himself. The man might be the king of London's criminal underworld, but he was a right snob. More so than many of the society matrons who deemed themselves the gatekeepers of the *ton*.

When Nicholas opened the door and stepped inside, he was somewhat taken aback. Effie, in advance of them moving fully into his home once she'd hired a new headmistress, had staffed his house to her specifications. It was no longer dark and dusty. Instead, it was filled with light and the scent of fresh beeswax.

"He is awaiting you in the library, Your Grace."

The butler remained. On that point, Nicholas had drawn a firm line. The man was nearly ready to be pensioned off, after all. And despite what Effie believed, the butler did not dislike her at all. The contrary old man was actually rather fond of her, even if she did behave shockingly at times.

Entering the library, he found the Hound still wearing his evening clothes and drinking a brandy. "A bit early, isn't it?"

"You haven't been married long enough for it to have turned you into such a boring and tedious stickler for propriety yet," the man replied with feigned boredom as he lifted his glass and took a long sip.

"Not at all. I simply prefer not to imbibe until after breakfast… at least," Nicholas replied in the same tone of false ennui.

"Early for you is late for me… I haven't been to bed yet," the Hound said, taking another sip with a challenging stare.

Nicholas didn't take the bait. After all, they might not be friends, but they were far from enemies. "What brings you by?"

"Ettinger is chomping at the bit to return to London, though I think your Mrs. Stephens is reluctant to let him go," the Hound explained.

"She would be. And my money is on her. She'll have her way whether he likes it or not. And given the nature of his injuries, I cannot help but think he is not yet ready for travel."

"I'm in agreement. And I have a bit of work for him that can be done from his sickbed. The man loves a puzzle and I have one that has been plaguing me for some time. But that isn't the only reason I came," the Hound reached into his pocket and pulled out a slip of paper. "Her direction."

"Whose direction?" Nicholas queried sharply. "Did Lady Marchebanks escape?"

"No. Nor will she. They found her dead in her cell this morning. She apparently took her own life."

"So was said the last time," Nicholas snapped.

The Hound swirled the brandy in his glass in a slow, deliberate manner. "I saw her myself. It is true. Someone smuggled poison into her. Who that was remains in question, but it certainly implies that there were more players in the plot than just herself, Winchell and Bechard."

"We always suspected that. Lady Marchebanks wound up involved courtesy of her lover—the nephew of her husband, but the scheme itself had been going for ages. Long before she got into it."

The Hound leaned back, propping his feet on the desk and making himself thoroughly at home. "How did this evolve exactly? I can't imagine that an English lord just wakes up one day and decides to involve themselves in the treasonous sale of arms to his country's greatest enemy."

Nicholas shook his head. "It started out as simple smuggling. The elder Marchebanks always had his hands in that. During the war, those smuggling contacts began moving things other than brandy. By that point, the elder Lord Marchebanks was already quite ill—hovering at death's door. His nephew and heir was apprised of the change in their scheme and, rather than put an end to it, expanded the operation and made a tidy fortune that he never managed to hold on to."

"And Bechard?"

"Family business, as well. He'd been in it since he was a boy, courtesy of his own father," Nicholas answered. "And I, courtesy of my father's direction to my commanding officers to put me in the most dangerous missions possible, found myself directly in the middle of it all."

"Well, if you are correct and there are other players still at large, the game is not over yet."

"It is for me. I've given enough of my years to the service of my country. I mean to be selfish now and spend the rest of my days as I choose rather than as I am directed."

The Hound chuckled. "You really do not understand marriage, at all. You've simply traded one master for another. Whitehall will not let you go so easily. They will come calling, begging for favors here and there. Once a spy, always a spy."

"I no longer care. They can ask all they wish, but I will not endanger Effie, our child, or her students by playing their games," Nicholas said. And it was true. He didn't care. Not anymore. It was time for someone else to give up their home, their comfort, the love of those closest to them in the name of the King. He was done with it.

"Nor should you." The Hound paused. Then he waved the bit of paper again, "The direction is for Pearl. Alexandra's mother. I thought, as a belated wedding present to Her Grace, you might actually claim the child as your own and spare her the indignity of ever being identified as the daughter of a traitor."

Nicholas stared at that slip of paper. "How did you find her?"

The Hound shrugged. "I might have known where she was all along. The perfectly bourgeois merchant who has decided to marry her might have done so at my behest. Just as he might have taken her away from the bawdy house . . . also at my behest. He has a brother, you see—a young man who gambles heavily and loses poorly—

making him particularly amenable to my various requests. And it was better for her to be out of London."

"Winchell."

The Hound nodded. "Winchell, indeed. I had my own reasons for wanting to make his life a misery. Of course, it's a moot point now. As for Alexandra, go see about giving that young girl a respectable name and endearing yourself to your lovely wife in the process. For myself, I have a pair of saucy beauties waiting to warm my bed and send me off to an exhausted slumber."

"You can lie to others, but I know you're only talking about that devoted pair of spaniels that like to play fetch with you for hours."

The Hound narrowed his eyes. "And how would you know about Bess and Bitty?"

"Your lovelorn butler confesses all to Mrs. Wheaton. And I eavesdrop shamelessly," Nicholas replied. "As I no longer need to deal with the mess of tying up the loose ends surrounding Lady Marchebanks, and justice, after a fashion, has already been meted out, I will use my time to see my solicitor and determine what precisely one must do to declare oneself the father of a twelve-year-old girl."

Chapter Thirty-Four

Effie entered the house on Park Lane. The butler nodded to her in greeting. "Your Grace," he intoned formally.

"Is my husband home?"

"Not as yet, Your Grace. He bade you wait for him in the study. He had an appointment and will return shortly."

"Was anything the matter?"

"I do not think so, Your Grace. He simply had to meet with his solicitor. Estate matters, I suppose."

Effie nodded. That would make sense. There had been a great deal of business that required his attention. Apparently, the former duke had been neglecting many of his estates for some time. Setting it all to rights would take time and no small amount of money.

Crossing the wide expanse of the hall to the study, she entered the room and seated herself on the large leather sofa that faced the fireplace. She was beyond tired. To look at her, no one would even guess that she was with child, and yet, she was constantly exhausted from it. Within minutes of sitting down, she had drifted off to sleep.

When she awoke, it was nearly four in the afternoon. She had slept for almost two hours, and she was no longer alone. Nicholas was seated in a chair nearby, staring into the fire. "Goodness... Mrs. Wheaton will be beside herself!"

"I sent a note," he said softly. "I informed her that you have been working entirely too hard and that you would be spending the night at this house so you could be well-rested for tomorrow."

"I am never well-rested when we spend our nights together," she pointed out.

Nicholas looked at her with one brow lifted in censure. "I'd point out that it was not I who initiated last night's rather energetic conjugal exercises, wife. That instance can be laid solely at your feet."

"I didn't say it was your fault. It was an observation, Nicholas, not an accusation," she replied smartly. "I should be upset with you for your highhandedness, but I am so tired, I cannot muster it. I will gladly sleep here for the night and sleep in tomorrow morning. I can afford to do that as the new headmistress for the Darrow School will begin her training tomorrow afternoon."

He smiled then, clearly happy at her announcement. "So you found a worthy candidate, then?"

"More than worthy. I believe that Miss Dargavel will be a remarkable headmistress. She worked as a governess herself for ten years and as a teacher at a school near Brighton for some time. I worry, of course, that Mrs. Wheaton's rough ways will be too much for her. Miss Dargavel strikes me as a much more genteel woman than I have ever been," Effie admitted.

"And what does this genteel woman think of your school for the forgotten by-blows of noblemen?"

Effie grinned. "Miss Dargavel is something of a reformer, in fact. She firmly believes that no child should ever be punished for the sins of their fathers or the exploitation of their mothers."

Nicholas nodded then. "I expect that was all she had to say and the position was hers. Did you even check her references?"

"Of course I did! I have only received a reply from Miss Honoria Blaylock, for whom Miss Dargavel has recently served as a companion. But it was a glowing recommendation. Truly."

"Honoria Blaylock? Do you know how many times she has been

arrested?" Nicholas demanded. "That woman would protest the opening of a tea tin!"

"Yes. And I am quite pleased that she may take an interest in my school now. She and Miss Dargavel are friends, after all. And the school can always do with patrons. She is terribly wealthy."

"So are we," Nicholas pointed out.

"Yes, but you have much to do to set the ducal estates to rights. Wouldn't it be better if the school functioned independently and supported itself rather than being a drain on your finances? I certainly have brought you no dowry at all. Heavens, I long ago spent every shilling my father settled on me and then some!"

"We are fine. And the school will always remain open, Effie. For as long as you wish it to. I don't care if it drains the coffers completely dry. Now, let's talk about something else."

"What would you like to talk about?" she asked.

"How difficult it would be for me to persuade you to come sit on my lap," he teased.

Effie rose and crossed the small distance between them. Lifting her skirts just a bit, she settled herself in his lap, facing him, her thighs straddling his. The very intimate position left her in no doubt of his desire for her. "Like this?" she asked, her expression the very picture of innocence.

"Wanton hussy," he accused, but even as he said it, his fingers were tracing delicate circles over the silk of her stockings, before gliding up her legs and beneath her skirts.

"You've ruined me. Thoroughly."

He leaned forward, pressing his lips to her neck, just below her ear. "And what do you have to say about that?"

Effie smiled as her arms came around him and she shivered at the sensations he stirred within her. "Do it again. And again."

As always, with Effie, the teasing never lasted long. He needed her too much. The desire for her was more intense than ever. The more he had her the more he wanted her. Within minutes, their clothing had been discarded on the floor and he had her rolled beneath him on the rug before the fire.

It was quick, fierce—like a summer storm. There was no finesse or slow seduction. There was only heat and need and frenzy. But she met him, matching his rhythm, clinging to him and urging him on. Every sound she uttered, every scrape of her nails on his skin, heightened his pleasure—and the wilder and more demanding he became, the more she responded in kind. They were gasping, straining toward their release. And when it came, it left them mindless and numb. Like soldiers after a battle, they lay there in the aftermath too stunned to speak or move.

When at last he did move, it was only to dislodge one of her shoes which was digging into his hip. She rolled to her side and snagged a watch fob that had been jabbing her in the ribs.

"We are entirely too old for this," she said. "There is a perfectly good bed just a few yards away. And we are on the floor like heathens."

"We'll get there eventually," he said. "But Christ this floor is hard!"

A giggle escaped Effie, the sound bubbling out of her in a way that reminded him so much of the way she had been as a girl. The more time they spent in one another's company, the more bits and pieces of their former selves were resurrected, brought back to life.

"Let's not have dinner downstairs." Effie made the suggestion as she was struggling to sit up. Her stays and chemise were half on and half off, twisted about her in a way that was terribly restrictive.

Nicholas thought about offering his assistance, but the truth of the matter was that he didn't want to get up and he also very much enjoyed the view. "Shall we starve then?"

"No, Nicholas. Do not be obtuse. We will have a tray brought to our chambers. But in order to get to our chambers, I must get dressed and I think I may have to simply cut this chemise off of me. I will never get it untangled from my stays."

Taking pity on her, Nicholas levered himself up and simply undid the ties of her stays, easing them from her shoulders. Without the restrictive garment atop it, she could manipulate her chemise into a more natural position. "Don't get dressed. I'll call for a maid and have them bring you a robe."

She gaped at him. "And how would we explain why I removed my clothing in the study? Absolutely not!"

Nicholas chuckled. "Effie, you are a duchess. You do not have to explain to anyone why you do anything. But if it will make you feel better, I will spill a bit of brandy on your clothes, and we can say the scent of it was making you ill."

She stopped her twisting and considered him. "Oh, that is very clever."

"I was a spy. I told lies professionally," he pointed out.

"Yes, but anyone who knew you was not fooled by your lies. I always knew that it was all a ploy! And now, everyone else will too. You've already given up your popinjay wardrobe for a more somber palette and people will begin to wonder."

He didn't care. Let them wonder, he thought. He owed no explanations to anyone and neither did Effie. Shrugging into his shirt and setting his breeches to rights, he rose to his feet and padded to the bell pull. Immediately, one of the new maids that Effie had hired for the household appeared in the corridor. "Fetch Her Grace a robe."

The maid's eyes widened in shock, and she blushed riotously. Nonetheless, she bobbed a quick curtsy, and mumbled "Yes, Your Grace," before running off.

Behind him, he could hear Effie sputtering. Turning to face her, he stated very boldly, "You might as well get used to this. And so should they. We've eighteen years to make up for, and I don't intend to confine our amorous pursuits solely to the bedchamber." He put a hand to his back and turned his neck to one side, feeling it creak in protest. "Though, to be fair, that does have its benefits."

Moments later, the maid returned with a heavy velvet robe in a rich, emerald green. She passed it through the door to him and he in turn helped Effie into it. "This isn't mine," she protested.

"It is, actually," he said. "As a surprise gift for you, I contacted your dressmaker and had several items made for you. They were delivered this morning and I had the maids put them away in your wardrobe."

"You know I have sufficient clothing of my own."

"Actually, since every time your father gives you a new gown, you immediately turn around and have it remade for one of your pupils, you do not have sufficient clothing, Effie. You certainly do not have sufficient clothing for a *duchess*," he corrected. "And not to be unkind or overly blunt, but it will not be long, Effie, before your current clothes do not fit you properly."

She gasped in mock outrage. "If you tell me I'm growing too plump—"

He put a hand on the slight rounding of her stomach. "Perfectly plump. Perfectly mine. That is all. Now, let us go upstairs, and perhaps, we can manage to make love in a somewhat civilized fashion rather than falling on one another like ravening beasts."

"I rather like it when you fall on me like a ravening beast."

"Hussy. Wanton, shameless hussy. Thank God!"

Chapter Thirty-Five

H E'D SLIPPED OUT of the house, leaving Effie sleeping peacefully in their bed. So it was getting late when Nicholas found himself in the Cheapside home of a cloth merchant by the name of Henry Bardwell and his wife, Alice—formerly Pearl. Mr. Bardwell was still at his office, and he was having tea with the lady of the house, as it were. The woman had been very popular at the houses where she had entertained clients. But the almost mousy, painfully modest creature before him bore little resemblance to the once flamboyant cyprian who had offered her services to some of the most wealthy and powerful men in all of England.

"While I am certainly honored to host such an exalted person in my home, Your Grace, I cannot imagine what business would bring you to Cheapside," Mrs. Bardwell said. Though she smiled, the expression was tight and false, her words coming out high and sharp. She was clearly afraid that her old life had come to call.

"I came to speak to you, Mrs. Bardwell, about your daughter. About Alexandra," he stated bluntly.

"I have no daughter," she denied quickly. "I have never been married until recently. My husband and I have no children."

"Oh, your husband certainly does not," Nicholas replied smoothly. "But you had quite an interesting life before settling into such respectability. He truly does not know that you were one of the most sought after soiled doves in all of England, does he, Pearl?"

She blanched, her face turning stark white and her spine going completely rigid. "You cannot be here," she hissed. "I'm not part of that world anymore! I have left it all behind."

"I know that. Just as I know you want nothing that links you to your old life to stain your husband's reputation and make him regret giving you this new and respectable existence," Nicholas surmised.

"That's quite right, Your Grace. And anyone coming here asking for Pearl needs to take their leave immediately!"

Part of him understood, but part of him was appalled that she had so little love for her daughter that she could so easily cast her aside. "And Alexandra? What would you have her call you? Pearl? Alice? Mother? Mrs. Bardwell?"

"I'd not have her call me any of those things. I left her in the care of others and that's the best I could do for her," the woman snapped defensively.

"Now you can do better," Nicholas said, producing several documents from inside his coat. After speaking to his solicitor that morning, the man had drawn them up and they had been delivered by courier while Effie slept. "This is a sworn affidavit that I will submit to the parish church where Alexandra was born to alter the register of her birth and list me as her father. The second document gives her fully into my care and names me as her guardian. The third document... well, that's a bit trickier. It's a contract of sorts to ensure that you never approach Alexandra for anything in her life, that you never openly acknowledge her as your child and that you foreswear any right or claim to her, her property, or her person."

"She has a father, and it isn't you!"

"She did have a father. Now she has a dead one," he responded coolly. "Silas Winchell is dead. And you certainly have no intention of opening your home to her and having your new husband raise your illegitimate daughter who was spawned by a man who will soon be exposed as having been a traitor to his country. I offer you the perfect solution, Mrs. Bardwell—for you and for Alexandra."

She rose and walked to a simple mahogany writing desk in the corner. "Bring them here. I will sign them and then you will be gone."

"Yes," he agreed, getting to his feet and following her to the desk. He watched as she scrawled her signature on the documents, sanding each one and then handing it back to him.

"It's done now. She's yours for whatever it is you want her for," she sneered the last in an accusing tone, implying that his motives were deviant in nature.

Nicholas eyed her with contempt. "You may have risen up out of the gutter, Mrs. Bardwell, but the gutter is still very much a part of you. Alexandra will live a good life. She will be acknowledged openly as my daughter—and my wife and I shall treat her as just that. She will want for nothing and will have every advantage in life. I say that only as a defense of myself against your dirty and wicked thoughts, not because I presume you care."

"It makes no difference to me," she said. "All women are victims to a man's whims. Sooner she learns that the better off she will be."

The front door of the house opened, and Mr. Bardwell's booming voice filled the hall. "Alice? Alice, where are you?"

"I'm in here," she said, her gaze almost challenging.

Mr. Bardwell stepped in through the pocket doors and then looked at Nicholas in surprise. "Who are you, sir?"

"I am Nicholas Montford, Duke of Clarenden," Nicholas replied smoothly.

"And what business have you with my wife?" Mr. Bardwell demanded sharply.

"I came to offer my condolences on the loss of her sister, Miss Henrietta Clark."

Bardwell frowned at Alice. "You told me you had no siblings. No family at all."

"I do not," she said. "His Grace was mistaken. It was another Alice Clark who was her sister, not I."

"Yes," Nicholas agreed. "It is a common name, after all. My apologies for bothering you with this matter, madam. I shall not keep you further. Mr. Bardwell," he acknowledged with a slight nod. With that, he spun on his heel and departed. He had what he came for, after all. And Alexandra would always be safe from her. Now he only had to tell Effie that the child she would bear him would not be their first child, after all.

Effie awoke to a dark room and an empty bed. Reaching out, she found Nicholas' pillow cold to the touch. Wherever he had gone, he had left some time ago. Rising slowly, she stretched and reached for the robe. The green velvet felt luxurious against her skin, a decadence she would never have indulged in for herself.

In truth, he had been correct when he had said she'd given away most of her suitable gowns. But she could hardly send her girls out into the world with naught but the clothes on their backs. Most of them were to be working in noble or affluent households and would need at least one dress that would serve them well in social settings. She was aware that she had sacrificed much for her pupils over the years, but she had no regrets on that score. What they had given back to her was priceless, after all. Having those girls in her life had given her direction and purpose when those things had been achingly absent otherwise. They'd offered a distraction from her own unhappiness, a place to put all the love she had to give when she had thought she would never have children of her own.

How strange it was, after reaching an age where she had given up hope of such things, to suddenly find herself a wife and expectant mother. The changes in her figure were subtle, at least under the forgiving silhouette of current fashions. Moving toward the mirror that flanked the dressing table, she stared at her reflection for a moment, smoothing the green velvet over the slight curve of her stomach.

There had been so much happening—with Nicholas' injury at first, then with the death of Miss Clark and the realization that she had placed Alexandra and herself in such danger—that the child she carried had not been her most immediate concern. Now, with those distractions eliminated, she could not help but think of it. Would it be a son who would look like his father and have his penchant for adventure, or misadventure, as it were? Or would it be a defiant and headstrong little girl with Nicholas' black hair and her eyes? The possibilities were endless.

That thought brought tears to her eyes. Possibility. That had been the thing most absent from her life before. Even with her students and all the love she had given and received from them, there had been something missing—the possibility of *more*. Of happiness. Of completion. And now she had those things. Everything she had ever wanted was suddenly there, not just out of reach as it had seemed for the last eighteen years. The future she had envisioned all those years ago had come to fruition, even if it had come about not quite in the way she had initially imagined.

And that was how Nicholas found her. The door opened slowly, quietly so as not to wake her, she suspected. Then for the longest moment he simply stood there staring at her. "I thought you would still be asleep," he murmured.

"I woke up alone," she said. "And the bed was cold so I knew you'd been gone for some time. Why?" There was no accusation in her voice, just curiosity.

"There was something that needed taking care of. Something that we needed to have settled once and for all," he replied, stepping deeper into the room. He closed the door behind him and then pulled several documents from the pocket inside his coat. "I wanted to be certain before I said anything."

Effie accepted the documents once he reached her. Sitting down at the dressing table, she lit the lamp there and began to peruse them. With each line that she read, she began to comprehend more fully the enormity of what he'd done.

"She isn't your child," Effie said.

"She is now," he replied. "Would you have me leave her future hanging in the balance? Left to the whim of a woman who cast her out without a care?"

Effie shook her head. "No. Of course, I would not."

"And, for better or worse, she is my blood. Therefore she is my responsibility. Legally, without these documents and without the alteration of her birth record, I cannot do anything for her."

"The world will know her as your bastard."

He nodded. "Better the bastard of a duke than the bastard of a traitor."

There was no rebuttal for that argument. And, in truth, she didn't want to rebut him. Alexandra had been deeply scarred from all that she had seen and endured, and being her parent would not be an easy thing for either of them. But she loved Alexandra—adored the child. The girl was bright and funny, eager to learn and absorb anything that anyone would show to her. Despite her very rough start in life, there was an innate kindness in the child and a wealth of love. "If I hadn't loved you before, I certainly would now," Effie uttered softly. "Thank you. Thank you for this, for her, for everything."

"Don't thank me," he said. "It is the very least that I should do."

"To take on the care of a young girl as your responsibility? To see her reared, fed, clothed, educated, and eventually married off at your expense? That is an incredible undertaking, Nicholas. It's impossibly generous. You've always given more of yourself and taken far less than was your due—and always in a manner which would never see you lauded for it as you should be. Perhaps the world will never know how brave you are and what you have sacrificed, but I know. And I will not let it go unmarked."

He moved behind her, his hands settling on her shoulders. "I do not need recognition, Effie. I only need you. Now come to bed, and tomorrow we shall speak to Alexandra and see what sort of future she's envisioned for herself and if she's even amenable. In truth, it may all be for naught."

Effie shook her head. He didn't understand, truly, what it was to be unwanted. His gesture, which to him was about obligation and responsibility, would represent so much more to that child. She doubted that he was ready for the emotional response it would bring, but she would be there with him. Through everything yet to come, she would always be with him.

EFFIE'S SMALL STUDY was utterly silent. Effie was seated behind her desk while he perched on the corner of it. Alexandra was seated in front of them in one of the smaller chairs that faced the desk. In her hands, she held the documents that her mother had signed the night before.

"I don't understand," she said. "I read them, but there were lots of words I didn't know."

Effie smiled at her. "It's simple really. Nicholas, who is now the Duke of Clarenden, will be listed on the parish birth register as your father. He will be acknowledging, publicly, that you are his child and will be taking care of you henceforward."

Alexandra frowned, then began to chew her lip nervously. Finally, she looked at Nicholas directly and countered, "But you're not my father. That horrible man who took Miss Darr—the duchess was my father. Why would you say that you are?"

Nicholas met her gaze just as directly and answered her with complete sincerity. "No, I am not your father. And yes, you are correct. Silas Winchell was your actual sire. But Silas Winchell's older brother was my father. That makes us cousins, Alexandra. We are blood, at least. You are the only family I have—you and Effie—and I want to offer you all the protection that I can. This is the easiest way to do that, to make sure that you are always safe and cared for and that you never again have to worry about someone sending you off to unknown relatives or to the workhouse. Those things will never happen to you again."

Effie said nothing, remaining still. But tears threatened. Somehow, against all odds, he'd said exactly the right thing to her.

After a moment, Alexandra carefully folded the documents as if they were something precious. And Effie supposed that they were. When they were placed safely on the desk, the girl suddenly launched herself at Nicholas. She threw her arms about his neck and hugged him fiercely as she sobbed brokenly.

Nicholas blinked in surprise but hugged the child in return. "I didn't mean to make you cry," he murmured in confusion.

"Those are happy tears, Nicholas. I daresay in a household with two females in residence, you shall begin to understand the difference," Effie answered softly. "Now, Alexandra, let him go, dear. I think he needs to breathe."

Reluctantly, Alexandra did release him, pulling back to reveal a red nose and a face streaked with tears. "No one has ever wanted me. Not even my own mother. I feel so lucky that you found me!"

"It wasn't luck, Alexandra," Effie said. "It was fate. We were meant to be a family, and my finding you simply set in motion the events that would allow that to happen. Fate will always find a way."

"Will we live here?"

"No," Nicholas answered her. "You will move into my house on Park Lane, as will Effie. A new headmistress will be running the school, though I daresay that Effie will remain very involved. You may still attend school here if you like, or we can hire a governess to tutor you privately and teach you all you need to know. I will leave that to you and Effie to decide."

"I want to come to school here," Alexandra said. "My friends are here."

"Then you shall," Effie agreed. "But for now, why don't you go upstairs and pack your things? I will go and pack mine. After all, the new headmistress will be needing my room. And tonight, we shall all sleep in our new home."

Alexandra, still sniffing and wiping her eyes, rose and left the room. But her steps were curiously lighter than they had ever been, displaying an exuberance that the child rarely had.

"You're certain those were happy tears?" Nicholas demanded as soon as the door closed.

Effie laughed. "I promise. And one day soon, you will be able to discern the variations."

He shook his head as he levered himself up into the chair recently vacated by Alexandra. "I pray that you give birth to a son because three females in one house is too many for my poor nerves to take. War, intrigue, and espionage were not so perplexing!"

Effie rose and walked around the desk to where he sat, settling herself on his lap as she looped her arms around his neck and kissed him sweetly. "Living in a house full of women will certainly be an adjustment. But as one of those females is your wife, there are certain to be benefits. Are there not, Your Grace?"

He smiled, against her lips, murmuring softly, "Indeed, there are, Your Grace. I love you, Euphemia Montford, Duchess of Clarenden."

"And I love you. I loved you when you were simply Nicholas Montford, and then when you were Lord Highcliff, and now when you are the Duke of Clarenden. Prince, pauper, or master spy . . . I will always love you."

The kiss that followed that statement was not sweet. It was full of heat and sensual promise. It was full of the decades of longing and loneliness that they had both endured. And when it was done, she rested her head on his shoulder, content in his arms in a way that she had never been in her life. Any pangs of regret about stepping back from the day to day running of her school were eased by the promise of a family of her own. Nicholas, Alexandra, and their own children—the one she presently carried as well as any others they might be blessed to have, either by birth or other manner of collection—it was more than enough for her.

"This is all I have ever wanted," he said, murmuring the words against her ear. "Just to be with you. And you are right about one thing, my beautiful wife. Fate will always find a way. We were meant to be."

Effie smiled softly. They would not always agree. Both of them were stubborn, set in their ways and possessed somewhat passionate and fiery natures. They would battle. But there were some things they would never argue about and that was certainly one of them.

Epilogue

From the Diary of Miss Euphemia Darrow, April 21st, 1829

I have served my last day as the acting headmistress of the Darrow School. Miss Dargavel has proven herself to be very capable and efficient and also very warm and giving with the girls. We've added several new students, already. The house is once more at capacity. Alexandra and I have both moved permanently into Nicholas' home now. It has not been without its challenges, I must admit.

We are both quite used to living on our own, to doing things our own way. Marriage, this blending of our lives, has certainly been an adventure. There is no one I would rather share that adventure with. We have so much time to make up for, so many years wasted. I refuse to allow small and petty differences to rob us of any more of it, and I have to believe that he feels the same. When I make changes to the running of this house, like hiring a bevy of servants or redecorating rooms to bring light and life into this house, he simply shakes his head, smiles, and lets me do as I please. In all, it's working out rather well.

"What are you scribbling so furiously about?" Nicholas voiced the question from the doorway of their bedchamber.

Effie looked up from the dressing table where she had sat to record her thoughts in her diary. It was something that she rarely did anymore. She was too busy with other things. But it did help to clear her mind at times.

"It's just my diary. I've been keeping them for years," she admitted. "You feature very prominently in many of the entries."

His brows lifted in curiosity even as a smile curved his lips. "And do they detail how handsome and irresistible you find me? Or that you'd like to throttle me on a regular basis?"

She couldn't halt the throaty laugh that erupted from her at his question. "It's a bit of both, honestly. Though, I have to say that it's more of the former than the latter of late."

"In that case, put your diary away and come to bed, my beautiful wife," he suggested. "I'll do something suitably wicked to warrant inclusion in your journal."

Effie looked down at her now prominent and very round belly. "You cannot possibly find me attractive right now. I can barely stand to look at myself."

"You've never been more beautiful. And I will never not want you . . . never."

Effie sighed happily and got up from her chair, closing the distance between them. When she reached him, she rose on her toes to press her lips to his. It was a sweet kiss, more about affection than passion, but that was there, as well, lurking under the surface and ready to sweep them away at the slightest provocation. Before that could happen, she pulled back from him. "I love you so much. I thought I loved you when I was younger, when I was a girl of eighteen. But the thing I've learned, Nicholas, is that the older I get, the deeper my capacity for love. And as happy as I am with you right now, in ten years or twenty—"

"Let's aim for at least forty, Effie. We deserve it," he corrected her.

"Forty then," she agreed with a laugh. "In forty years, the love I feel for you then will have grown beyond measure."

"As it should," he said simply, even as he swept her up into his arms to carry her to their bed. "Because I will spend every day of my life guaranteeing your happiness. Starting right now."

Clothes were discarded carelessly. Words gave way to sounds of pleasure. And diary entries . . . they would simply have to wait.

THE END . . . *sort of.*

Author's Note

Initially, the Hellion Club was envisioned as a seven-book series, culminating in the Happily Ever After story for Effie and Highcliff. But it grew. Characters like Ettinger and the Hound wormed their way into my heart and, hopefully, into yours.

So the Hellion Club will continue! There will be another seven books coming over the next couple of years. The first two will focus on Ettinger's story and then the Hound's. Then Louisa will get her own story. And eventually, so will Alexandra, Marina, Emily and all the other children who made appearances in these books. They're like my family now and I'm just not willing to let them go. I hope you'll continue to follow along with this wonderful, made-up world of mine and that you'll love them all as much as I do.

About the Author

Chasity Bowlin lives in central Kentucky with her husband and their menagerie of animals. She loves writing, loves traveling and enjoys incorporating tidbits of her actual vacations into her books. She is an avid Anglophile, loving all things British, but specifically all things Regency.

Growing up in Tennessee, spending as much time as possible with her doting grandparents, soap operas were a part of her daily existence, followed by back to back episodes of Scooby Doo. Her path to becoming a romance novelist was set when, rather than simply have her Barbie dolls cruise around in a pink convertible, they time traveled, hosted lavish dinner parties and one even had an evil twin locked in the attic.

Website: www.chasitybowlin.com

Made in the USA
Middletown, DE
19 March 2023